CANDLELIGHT
Ecstasy Supreme

**"ADMIT IT, KATIE. YOU THOUGHT
YOU COULD SEDUCE ME INTO GIVING
YOU, EXACTLY WHAT YOU WANT."**

"You really are an arrogant cad!" she told him angrily.

"Hey—you just said your career was at stake. I'm just trying to find out how important it is to you."

"I was right to hate you when I was twelve," Katie retorted.

"Keep on lying to me and you won't get a thing."

She lifted her chin, her eyes hard as flint. "I never intended to seduce you."

Kent laughed. "No, maybe you didn't. But your editors intended for you to."

CANDLELIGHT ECSTASY SUPREMES

DANTE'S DAUGHTER

Heather Graham

A CANDLELIGHT ECSTASY SUPREME

Published by
Dell Publishing Co., Inc.
1 Dag Hammarskjold Plaza
New York, New York 10017

For my Aunts
Grace Astrella and
Ida Mangiulli
with love

Dell ® TM 681510, Dell Publishing Co., Inc.

Candlelight Ecstasy Supreme is a trademark
of Dell Publishing Co., Inc.

Candlelight Ecstasy Romance®, 1,203,540, is a registered
trademark of Dell Publishing Co., Inc., New York, New York.

ISBN: 0-440-11653-8

Printed in the United States of America
First printing—January 1986

To Our Readers:

We are pleased and excited by your overwhelmingly positive response to our Candlelight Ecstasy Supremes. Unlike all the other series the Supremes are filled with more passion, adventure, and intrigue and are obviously the stories you like best.

In months to come we will continue to publish books by many of your favorite authors as well as the very finest work from new authors of romantic fiction. As always, we are striving to present unique, absorbing love stories —the very best love has to offer.

Breathtaking and unforgettable, Ecstasy Supremes follow in the great romantic tradition you've come to expect *only* from Candlelight Ecstasy.

Your suggestions and comments are always welcome. Please let us hear from you.

Sincerely,

The Editors
Candlelight Romances
1 Dag Hammarskjold Plaza
New York, New York 10017

PROLOGUE

"Fourteen, eighty-three . . ."

Sam Loper, the quarterback, was calling off the numbers, hunched at the scrimmage line. Eighteen sweating, panting, and tautly wired men were listening intently, straining to hear. This was it—the last play of the game as the thirty remaining seconds in the final quarter ticked away.

The Sarasota Saxons from Florida needed a miracle to win. They held the ball, but they were forty-five feet away from a touchdown and they were behind the Grizzlies by three points.

Everyone wanted that ball—everyone except Kent Hart, super receiver and veteran of too many games to count.

His thoughts were running along a different vein as he heard Sam's numbers change in warning. The defense they were facing had just switched their tackle positions, and the Saxons play would change.

Don't throw it to me, Sammy. Please don't throw the damn pigskin to me!

"—ten—"

Inwardly, Kent was groaning; every inch of his body seemed to be groaning. He'd been tackled to the ground at least ten times already, tramped by guys averaging six feet four and two hundred and eighty pounds. Where did they breed these guys? he wondered with a shake of his head. Football players were supposed to be big, yeah, but this was pushing it a bit far.

To make matters worse it was a cold, late November day, and a drizzling rain that felt more like snow flurries or tiny daggers of ice was falling.

"Fifty-four!"

The crowd roared; every person in the stadium seemed to stand in unison like a giant wave as the last number was called and the ball was hiked into the quarterback's hands. Sam started to move backward as massive defensive tackles rushed in to try and sack him.

Kent began to run—instinctively more than anything else—toward the goal line, with his eyes back on Loper. There was a huge heap of tangled men before the quarterback, who was still managing to dance backward.

Then Kent saw that Sam had his eye on him, too. Kent was the only receiver who had a prayer in hell of getting the ball. Tony Cleary, a giant raised in the Nebraska cornfields, was bearing down on him, but he couldn't make it—not before the ball could be thrown and fly the distance through the air.

Kent's arms went up. Instinct or conditioning? he wondered in split seconds of self-directed humor. And in those same split seconds his mind was also asking another question: What the hell am I doing out here? A grown man earning his living by running around with a pigskin ball. I'm too old for this. I'm too—

Thunk!

The ball seemed to spin straight into his hands with a malicious will all its own. Kent automatically tucked it in against his chest. He took a deep breath and started running again—but not without a quick glance down the field.

Hail Mary. It looked like a buffalo stampede! They were charging after him. Oh, man. He'd been hit one time too many already today. The coaches should have pulled him out of the game.

Instinct. His feet moved mechanically. His muscles strained, stretched, tautened . . .

He heard his own breath, like a whistle on the wind. No, it

was more like a damned chugging steam engine. The drizzling rain or snow—whatever the hell it was—pelted against him with greater fury, slicing into his face, and he was perspiring! Sticky sweat was dripping into eyes, blinding him.

All around him, the crowd was screaming, shouting, jumping up and down.

But Kent barely saw the stands because something stood before him that promised safety and reprieve: the goal line. That magical scratch on the earth that would get him off the field and signify the end of the game. He could feel the ground thundering behind him. He ducked his head and glanced back. Tony Cleary was right on his tail, and Bob Hedgekin, all three hundred pounds of him, was probably right behind Cleary.

A burst of adrenaline raced through Kent's blood. He was on fire. Everything hurt; his ankle hurt from the first tackle he'd received during the first quarter; his kneecaps burned; his shoulder was in agony; and his muscles ached . . . every single one of them, individually and then all together in a shrieking harmony of pain.

But that line, that magic line, was just ahead of him.

Please, God, he thought desperately, just let me get over that line—and away from these two-ton maniacs.

He should have been thinking team spirit. He could win this game for the Saxons. A touchdown now would take the game, keep them in the playoffs, maybe even help get them to the Superbowl.

Team spirit—great. He was a team player, but right now he was running in the interest of self-preservation.

Wham!

Kent let out a grunt as someone slammed against his left shoulder. Then long, muscled arms flew around his legs.

Kent saw the ground before him, flying up to meet him. But he also saw that line, the magic line. Furiously, he pitched his shoulders forward, throwing himself as far as he could. The air was alive with howls and shrieks.

All Kent cared about was the ground as it rushed toward him with an ungodly speed.

Slam!

And he was down, twisting his face automatically to save his already twice-broken nose.

He was over the line. He smiled because he had won the game for the Saxons, but the flight hadn't saved him—impetus was still sending the defensive tackles flying.

"Ah, come on, guys," he shouted, "have some heart—I'm over the damn line!"

But the stampede didn't stop. Bodies were still hurtling forward, one by one. Tony Cleary landed on him first, charging into his ribs. Someone else collided hard into his hip. It was a damned pileup! Bodies continued to fall, with Kent on the bottom. An elbow jammed into his gut, a knee into his back . . .

He lay there, trying to breathe, feeling the mud under him and the weight on top of him. Then the bodies started moving. The crowd was still screaming. The game was over. Miraculously, the Saxons were the victors.

"Hell of a catch, Hart," someone said regretfully. It was one of the bodies crawling off him. Kent couldn't even see who.

Vaguely, he heard the crowd's chant taking form. They were shouting his name. "Hart! Hart! Hart! Hart!"

Ah, yes! Hail Caesar! he thought—if they only knew he had been running to save his own skin.

Kent closed his eyes and opened them again. Sam Loper was there, extending a hand to him. "We did it, dammit, Kent! We did it! Thirty seconds remaining, and we pulled it—"

Sam broke off as his jubilant teammates rushed him, tossing him up in the air, catching him to carry him off the field. To his pained horror, Kent realized he was about to receive the same treatment. Harry Kolan, one big s.o.b. out of Alabama, was throwing Kent up. Kent was six feet three and a healthy two hundred pounds himself; Harry Kolan threw him around as if he were a baby. But only to lift him. Kent found himself balanced on the shoulders of two of his teammates. He was cold; his teeth were chattering. But the crowd was still roaring, all the football fans who had followed them to this, a key playoff game—people who had spent their savings on a trip to California just to support the team in their rise to the top . . .

He tried to smile. He tried real hard. Kent thought it was more like twisting his lips into a position, then allowing the rain to freeze them there. He lifted a hand to wave. They were still shrieking his name—his and Loper's. Take Heart from Hart—Kill 'em, Cougar—All the Way, Saxons! Streamers were flying high, only somewhat bedraggled from the rain.

Kent kept waving.

Harry slapped him on the rump.

"My man, my man! What a party we're gonna have tonight!"

"Yeah, sure," Kent managed through his frozen smile.

He didn't want to have a party. All he wanted to do was soak the cold from his bones and the pain from his joints in a hot tub, maybe have a small scotch while he was at it. No—a big scotch. A giant scotch. And then he wanted to sleep on a firm mattress with clean, fresh sheets . . .

"Kent! Hot damn, we did it! We beat the Grizzlies!"

As soon as he landed on his feet in the locker room, Kent was swallowed in a bear hug by Sam Loper. Sam enthusiastically slapped his palms against Kent's ribs. "The last seconds! We pulled it out. We—"

"Boys"—it was the head coach interrupting—"there's little for me to say. You knew what you had to do, and you did it. Enjoy yourselves tonight, but remember we're going to have to work like hell next week. And Kent—don't you dare talk to me about retirement."

Kent smiled wearily. Everyone started talking at once again.

"Damn, did you guys do it!"

"We made it!"

"Whoo-eeee!"

"Loper and Hart all the way . . . Superbowl, here we come!"

Faces were swimming before Kent's own, most of them young, eager—and incredulously pleased. They were the faces of his friends, his teammates. Guys he worked and sweated with, guys that, for the most part, he liked. But why, he wondered, did they all seem to think that the only way to offer their congratulations was to slam against his abused shoulders and ribs?

"Hey, guys, thanks, but Loper's the quarterback. Go and beat on him for a while!" *Loper is also eleven years younger than I am*, Kent thought wryly.

Nothing was going to stay the enthusiasm in the locker room. Loper was heralded again, and every player congratulated every other player as champagne bottles were shaken and popped, spraying everyone. Then the news guys were in. Kent grabbed his clothes quickly and tried to escape into the showers. He knew there was one little whirlpool in there, and he intended to get to it.

Loper caught his arm. At twenty-five Loper was still young for the game. He wasn't particularly big, but he was as quick as lightning on the field, and had an uncanny knack for getting rid of the ball before the tackles could get near him. He had made history with his passing game. On the field he was a phenomenon. Off the field he was a nice kid. A great kid. Bright green eyes, sandy hair. *The perfect hero*, Kent thought. *And ripe for the fame, eager to accept it.*

He isn't old and tired and worn, Kent thought a little wryly; assessing his own attributes wasn't always an easy thing to do.

"Kent! Aren't you going to talk to the networks? They're clamoring for a word with you."

Kent placed an arm on Sam's shoulder. "Sammy, you do the talking. You're the quarterback. You're the man of the hour—and you deserve it! You go on out there and tell them what they want to hear. And remember, be humble! Everybody loves a humble winner."

"Kent—"

"Go on, Sam!"

"But you're the one—"

"Who happened to be in the way of the ball, that's all. Give me a break, Sam. I'm the old man of the team, remember? I've got to go soak the bones. Okay?"

"Yeah, okay," Sam said slowly.

Kent smiled as he turned around and headed for the door to the showers. Sam wouldn't have to act humble—he was humble. An All-American who deserved the title in every sense of the word. He was not only willing but eager to give the other guy his due. He also lived, ate, worked, played, dreamed, and breathed football.

I did that, too, once upon a time, Kent reminded himself. What had been getting to him so much lately? He knew he'd been instrumental in taking a fledgling team near the top. They even had a chance of reaching that pinnacle now . . .

I'm tired, that's all, he told himself. Maybe it was his age, although he knew that in the "real world" thirty-six wasn't considered that old. But nineteen of those years had been spent on the field, first in high school and college, then, at the age of twenty-one he had joined the pros, thanks to one man. A friend he had lost, years ago. He shook himself. He didn't want to get morbid.

Football, he thought, has give me a lot, but it's cost just as much. The words came to him unbidden. Yes, it had cost him his marriage, and in the years that had followed the divorce he had come to accept the fault . . .

"Mr. Hart, could I have a minute of your time?"

Someone else had his arm. A hand was on it—a gentle touch. A woman's voice had spoken, and it was a woman's hand on his sleeve. Long fingers, long nails covered in a silky beige polish. Soft hands, delicately boned . . .

He shook off the touch without really looking at her.

Women in the locker room! He would never get accustomed to it.

"Sorry. I'm headed for the showers."

Thank God there was a door! He stepped through it and closed it firmly behind him. A couple of the guys were already there.

"Hey, Kent! You old fox. They keep saying you're the greatest arm around, and I sure do believe them!" Bobby Patterson called to him from the shower.

Kent waved. "Thanks, Bob. You got some muscle there yourself, buddy," he answered Bobby, but he wasn't really paying attention. He was looking at the whirlpool, then sighing with pleasure and relief. No one was in it. The other guys were hurrying to shower and dress so that they could rush out and enjoy the homage of their fans and loved ones . . . or whatever spicy and beautiful women happened to be around, he added to himself dryly.

He pulled off his green and gold uniform, feeling a bit like a knight who had been encased in armor. A knight who had been unhorsed, he added. Man, was he beat!

Pads and braces followed his muddied, sweaty uniform to the floor. Whew! Was it going to feel good to crawl into that tub . . .

"See ya soon, Kent," Bobby called. Clad in his pants, he was hurrying out to his locker to don his suit, Kent was sure. They'd all packed double outfits, jeans and sweaters if they'd had to slink out of the stadium, three-piece suits if—miracle of miracles—they won.

"Yeah, see ya guys." He was, at last, alone with his aches and pains.

The warm water whirled and swished around his ankles. Ahhh. Kent sank down slowly. The water covered his calves, his knees, his buttocks. He sat, letting it swirl around his midriff, hot and pulsing, easing the aches and pains. He sank further, wetting his hair, cleaning the salt and grime from his face. He loved hot water, and he loved the healing jets that massaged his battered muscles.

"Just like a sultry maiden's kiss," he murmured aloud, smiling with his eyes closed to the steam and light.

"Humph," a voice said from just inside the doorway. Kent frowned. There had been a softness to the sound, something feminine . . . and yet there had been an edge to it as well. An angry edge? A feminine, angry edge—angry over his whispered words?

His eyes flew open and he stared at the door.

There was a woman there. His eyes roamed up and down her incredulously. She was fairly tall and slender, dressed in jeans and a gray turtleneck sweater. Her hair was plastered against her skull from the sleet that had fallen from the sky, but it stretched down the length of her back. Even wet, it was a blond color. Her forehead was high, and her eyes seemed huge. They were light . . . green or blue? Maybe a combination of both.

Kent stared at her several seconds before he realized that she was extremely attractive. Her face was beautifully boned. Her complexion was fine, although a little bluish right now; she seemed to be freezing. But if you set her before a fire and let all that pale hair dry around her, she would be . . . stunning.

Along with that thought came a burning anger in the pit of his stomach. He glanced at her hands as they clutched a brown notepad. She hadn't only intruded into the locker room —she had come straight into the showers.

"Oh, God!" he groaned. "Is nothing sacred anymore?"

"Mr. Hart—"

"Lady, get out of here."

"Wait a minute! All I ask is a minute of your time."

She seemed as aggravated as he, as if she didn't like football players and had very little interest in the sport as a great American pastime. So what was she doing here? Kent wondered.

17

"Lady, do me a big favor. Remove yourself before I take the initiative for you, okay?"

"Dammit, you muscle-bound ner—" She broke off her own speech and took a deep breath, apparently stiffening her spine as she did so. "If you would just listen—"

"The networks will all get their time."

"I'm not from one of the networks."

Kent frowned. There was a sense of something familiar about her, the sound of her voice, the classic beauty of her features. He sought quickly through his memory, but it eluded him. He shrugged, then leaned back in the tub, closing his eyes against her.

"I really don't care if you're a messenger from heaven. I want a little bit of peace. The same offer stands—get out or I'll throw you out."

"Mr. Hart, I'm from *World Magazine*. We'd like to offer you a nice sum for an exclusive—"

"I don't do interviews."

"Mr. Hart, I need this article rather desperately—"

"I don't do interviews."

She hesitated so long that he almost opened his eyes again. He didn't; he prayed that she'd go away.

When she spoke at last, it was with hesitation, as if she hated herself for the leverage she was about to use. "Not even for Dante Hudson's daughter?" Her question was softly asked.

Kent's eyes flew open, and he knew with certain clarity why she had seemed so familiar.

Sweet Jesus, he thought, she *is* Hudson's daughter!

CHAPTER ONE

Kent Hart in the flesh. Very much in the flesh. Except, of course, Katie had her back glued to the door, so she wasn't close enough to him to see much.

But she had done it. She had swallowed the emotions of half a lifetime—not to mention her pride—to come here.

He didn't look so very different, Katie thought. Not from the last time she had seen him—really seen him, other than a speck on a field or a helmeted form on the TV screen.

And it had been fourteen years since she had seen him last. She had been twelve; he had been . . . about twenty-two.

Katie could still relive that memory—as clearly as if it had been yesterday. Of course she could see it differently now. She wasn't a twelve-year-old anymore. But without even closing her eyes, she could recall that child and her feelings.

Time with her father—precious time, since it seemed to be little enough—was being interrupted. "You just gotta meet Kent, Katie!" Dante had told her. Dante, the best father a girl could have, a national hero . . . but more than that. He was young, barely thirty-two himself at the time, giving, warm, and entirely lovable. A young Nordic blue-eyed blond, he had charmed everyone, especially his own daughter.

Katie had been jealous. It had been her day with her father, her day to listen to the calls, then to astound one of the greatest quarterbacks who had ever lived with her ability—a twelve-year-old *girl's* ability—to catch the magic pigskin ball. But when her father had picked her up, it had been to tell her that they were going to meet Cougar—Kent Hart, the infalli-ble speed demon out of Alabama. He'd put a little-known college on the map in a big way. Not only had he the arms of an albatross and a grip like an eagle's talons, but he could run. "Lord Almighty," Dante had exclaimed to her that day, "that boy can *run!*" His grades had also been great. "Sheer genius!" in Dante's words.

Katie had hated the man before they'd even reached the football stadium.

Of course, he'd smiled at her. Kent Hart had smiled and ruffled her hair. Why not? He should be decent to the man who had helped him into the pros.

She'd hated to have her hair ruffled.

"Katie, show him your stuff!" Dante had commanded.

Katie had been ready, but for some reason, she had fumbled everything. Then she'd been sent to tackle Kent. "Tag foot-ball," Kent had said cheerfully.

But Katie hadn't been about to play a game of tag—espe-cially when she had realized that not even her extreme youth and healthy young legs could combat Cougar's speed. So, once she'd gotten him, she'd tackled him with all her wiry young strength. And when he had laughed and refused to relinquish the ball, she'd clawed his cheek with her fingernails. Hard. So hard that she'd drawn blood.

"Damn!" Had been his astonished response. And he'd shaken her with fury, then kept her firmly away at arm's length. "Dante! Call off this little she-cat of yours! I think I'm going to need a rabies shot!"

It was the last time Dante had ever tried to mix company with his daughter and his friend. It was painfully clear that they despised one another.

Oh, there had been jokes. Dante warning Kent that every-one was going to think he'd had a row with his fiancée. "Re-ally rough when you have to fight the girls off, eh?" Dante had teased. But he had been furious with Katie, so furious that he hadn't picked her up the next weekend, and she had learned to hate Kent Hart with a greater fury.

Oh, God, but that had been years ago. Long before her father's freak injury, before the game he had loved so dearly had quickly cost him his health, then slowly his mind. Long before he had finally died—old before his time, broken, a forgotten hero.

Returning to the present, she forced herself to draw in a breath and close a curtain on the past. She hoped that Kent Hart couldn't see how she was braced against the door for support.

"I'm Kathleen Hudson, Mr. Hart. Perhaps you don't remember me, but even with your own personal status, you must remember my father." Katie winced inwardly. She hadn't meant to sound so sarcastic and reproachful. It was just that she didn't want to be here, and she absolutely hated the fact that she had tried to compromise realistically with life and use a past association to get beyond all the walls of privacy Kent Hart built around himself.

Yes, she could see already that the words had been a mistake. He had brown, flashing eyes, so narrowed now that they seemed to burn with a red glint, ready to explode.

His hand—involuntarily, Katie was certain—moved to his cheek, his long fingers moving over it before falling back to the water.

"I could never forget your father, Miss Hudson. And"—he raised a dark and richly arched brow—"I don't think that I'll ever be able to forget you." His words were polite enough, but there was something very hard about his pleasant tone when he continued, "Every time I glance in a mirror, Miss Hudson, I get to remember you. Scars, you know."

She felt a little ill. Yes, peering through the steam that surrounded him, she could see that there were three scars, pale white lines that stretched from his cheekbone to his jaw.

It was time to apologize, she told herself. Perhaps remind

him that she had been a child. Laugh, flirt a bit—wheedle herself into his good graces . . .

Katie couldn't do it. She heard herself talking, and she hadn't even thought out what she wanted to say.

"I hardly think that those little scars can matter much. You're probably covered with them by now. How long have you been playing? Almost twenty years . . ."

He smiled at her, but the smile was as stiff as the strong line of his jaw. "Is that it?" he inquired acidly, ignoring her question. "You've come to count my scars for your article. That's why it was so almighty important that you see me, that you had to barge in where you were not invited—and definitely not wanted?"

Katie could feel the heat flaming her cheeks. Again she spoke without thought. "No, you ass! I barged in here because you think you're so high above humanity that you can't bother with common courtesy! I—" She broke off, dismally aware that she had just ruined the whole thing. She had put herself through a week of torment before coming here, and now . . . It didn't bother her so terribly much that she was going to lose the interview; it bothered her that she had come here at all, used her father's name, then bungled the whole thing in a spurt of temper.

Temper . . . it had caused her first disaster with him when she had been a child.

"I'm sorry," she murmured, involuntarily lowering her head and her lashes. She had wanted to at least apologize with dignity, meeting his eyes. Oh, come on, Katie! she chastised herself. Raff said that you could charm water from desert sands if you wanted to!

She looked up and smiled sweetly. "I really am sorry. It's just that you wouldn't bother to talk to me. You wouldn't even bother to look at me . . ."

His smile became warm in return. She wondered vaguely why his eyes still carried a little glitter, but she was getting too nervous to concentrate on his physical nuances.

22

"Sorry," he said softly. "Maybe I was a bit brusque. Be a good kid, will you, and come over here where I can see you? And you can toss me a towel."

Suddenly, she was feeling very nervous. She didn't want to get too close to the man, not after she had called him an ass.

"Perhaps," Katie murmured, "now that we've met, you could just meet me back out by the lockers."

"No, there will still be people around the lockers. Newscasters. I came in here looking for a bit of peace. Come on over—throw me the towel."

Katie set her purse and notebook on a bench and unhappily approached the whirlpool. The water jets and mist were all around him, so she could rationalize that there still wasn't anything indecent about it.

Near Kent and the tub was a shelf with a stack of towels. She managed to keep her eyes locked to his until she reached for a towel, but then she averted her gaze and threw it.

"Thanks," he muttered as the towel landed in the water.

When he began to stand, she found her eyes riveting to him again. "What are you doing? For decency's sake, sit down," she snapped.

He laughed, settling back into the water. "All right, but don't throw the next towel. Hand it to me. I'm wet—that's why the towel should be dry."

"You're supposed to be the greatest receiver in history," Katie mumbled as she reached for another one, "and you can't catch a towel?"

"I'd rather not take the chance," Kent said politely.

Katie felt a little flustered. She kept her lashes lowered and walked closer to the tub to hand him the towel.

Be nice, Katie, she warned herself, gritting her teeth behind a pleasant smile.

"Thanks," he murmured again as she came closer, extending her arm.

"Uh . . . sure. Listen, I'm really sorry about snapping at

you." She gave him a light—flirtatious?—laugh. "And I really am sorry about the scars. I was only twelve then."

"Mmm. And you've matured."

Was it a statement or a question? He had a husky voice, very deep. It seemed to touch her inside and ripple along her spine.

"Yes, well, it was quite a few years ago . . ."

"Yes, it was. A little closer, please, I can't quite reach. And I'd love to get a better glance at a matured woman."

Careful, Katie advised herself. He's famous for his conquests, so let him think he can con you, too. You know how to be sweet while keeping your distance.

"Here," she murmured, standing directly beside him. And then she gasped with outrage as she felt his fingers wind around her wrist, dragging her down to her knees beside him.

"Let go of me, you overgrown bastard! I swear every damn thing you hear about football players is true. And I knew from that first time I saw you that—"

"You knew what?" He grated out disdainfully, tossing her wrist aside. "You were a selfish little brat when I met you, and it doesn't appear that you've changed much since. Don't flirt with me, Miss Hudson. I like you better when you're an honest bitch."

Katie tossed the towel in his face. "All right. You want honesty? I think you're an overflown ingrate—and when you fall, I hope you fall hard. I didn't want to do an interview with you, but since my future seemed to depend on it, I thought I could overlook the past. Personally, I don't think there's anything to write about but, yes, I'm selfish enough to want a career for myself. Let's stick with selfish, shall we? I was wrong to dislike you for sharing my father's time—but I loved him! When you were gone, when everyone else was gone, *I was still there!* And if we want to get frank about it, my father actually did more for you than he ever could for me—"

"Hold it!" Kent snapped. He might have preferred his towels dry, but he distractedly grabbed the wet one and rose, wrapping it tightly around his hips to step with purpose from the tub. Katie didn't even realize that she watched him step from the tub, watched him as he strode angrily to her and sank his grip into her shoulders, shaking her as he had all those years before . . .

"You think I owe you because of Dante, is that it? Well, you're wrong, dammit. You owe me! You didn't have the courtesy to give him my letters. You didn't even have the courtesy to let me know he was ill. You just carried on your little charade. You didn't even let me know when he died—I had to read about it in the newspapers!"

"Let go of me—" Katie began, but the words died on her lips. Just as he had all those years ago, he shoved her away himself.

Suddenly, tears stung her eyes. Kent Hart *had* written many times. But she hadn't returned the letters unopened— Dante had. "Tell him . . . tell him we keep traveling," Dante insisted in his more lucid moments, and his beautiful Nordic eyes, turned rheumy, would sadden as if clouds had been flung over them. "Kent should never see me like this. Never."

"Dad, if he's your friend—"

"No. *No!*" Then Dante would be sorry that he had yelled at her. He would stare down at his hands, hands that shook. "I was a legend, Katie. A living legend. A true hero. I don't want that fantasy to die."

"Dad—"

"Ah, Katie! Did I ever tell you about the day when we turned around and beat the Redskins? It was twenty-one to three at the end of the third quarter, but we rallied! We rallied and beat them by two touchdowns. Two touchdowns! God, could I throw! And Kent . . . that man could catch anything and run like a jackrabbit. My Cougar. We were great together. What a game . . ."

Memory faded. So did Katie's burst of temper. She drew herself up and stared at Kent Hart's back, smiling bitterly. He

25

did have more scars. Four that she could see, across his shoulders.

She spoke more raspily than she would have liked, but a quiet dignity seemed to have come back to her, and the words were barely whispered. "My father didn't want to see you, Mr. Hart. He—he was very proud. He wanted the world to believe that he still existed with all his health and strength. I —I believe he always cared about you, though. Most."

She turned around, plucking her notebook from the bench and heading for the door. Well, the article was shot, and she'd probably be back on a local paper soon, doing the obituaries and interviewing more ladies who cooked for a town fair or kids from the high school athletic teams.

She'd only been given this chance because she was Dante Hudson's daughter. And the only person in the world Kent Hart might agree to do an interview with was Dante's daughter.

Sorry, Raff, she thought. You didn't know about the things that had happened. Dante's daughter is the last person in the world the man wants to talk to.

"Maybe"—his voice, as hoarse as hers, muffled as his back was still to her, made her halt, turning before she reached the door—"maybe we both owe each other."

Katie caught her breath, wondering if that meant that he'd do the interview. He turned around slowly, and she felt the heat of his dark eyes moving over her, as if he was assessing her. But before he could speak, the door opened suddenly and Sam Loper barged into the room.

"Kent—oh, sorry!" The young quarterback paused, looking curiously at Katie. "Hi."

"Hi," she responded a little uneasily. Women were gaining a grudged access to the locker rooms these days, and it had seemed all right to grit her teeth and walk into the showers to approach Kent when the other players had left. But now she felt totally out of place and deserving of the skeptical—and insinuative—way that Sam Loper was looking at her.

26

"Miss Hudson is a reporter from *World Magazine,* Sam," Kent said. Katie cast him a quick glance. It appeared that he was trying to save her—just a bit.

Except that he'd called her by name. Would Sam Loper recognize that name? Probably not. Loper was about her age. It was unlikely that he'd make the connection.

Apparently, the name didn't mean anything to him.

"Oh. *Oh!* Well, hello again, Miss Hudson." Sam Loper stuck out a hand and gave her a charming smile. Katie accepted his handshake and returned his smile.

"It was a wonderful game," she said. "You—uh—you were great." Loper was a good quarterback, probably a great one, just as the media was proclaiming. To do anything other than congratulate the man would have been totally churlish—even if he was looking at her lasciviously. Sorry, Loper, I'm not available. I've been this route before, she thought.

Sam Loper frowned suddenly, and she felt as if she liked him a bit better—even if he wasn't releasing her hand. "I hope this guy's been decent to you, Miss Hudson. He refuses to give interviews to anyone, and I know he can get a bit crude."

"Sam!" Kent snapped with aggravation.

Sam Loper was undaunted. "But listen, ignore him if he's a headache. I think it's old age setting in, you know? He gets cranky. But if you want—"

"Sam!"

"I'll be happy to give you an interview."

Katie tugged at her hand, smiling as she rescued it from his grasp. "Thank you, that's wonderful, and I would like to talk to you." She gazed across the room at Kent Hart's towel-draped form with only a slight sparkle of maliciousness touching her blue green eyes.

"You see, it's just because Kent is such an old-timer that we're trying to get an interview with him. He isn't the oldest player in the NFL, nor has he been playing the longest, but he's lasted on top in his position for the longest period of time, and that makes him quite an anomaly. Oh, not that you aren't. For a young man you've done wonders! And the future still lies ahead with lots of promise."

Bemused and a little irritated, Kent watched the interchange between the two. Sam was at his charismatic best. He liked women, and he had learned that his position—added to his charm—made him almost irresistible when he was on the hunt. And he was definitely on the hunt.

But it appeared that Hudson's daughter was wise and aware —and perhaps slightly amused herself. She was, in turn, charming, and yet there was a reserve about her that seemed to separate her from most other women. She was not the type to be swept off her feet by pretty phrases; she didn't giggle. Still, Kent had quickly realized that when she chose to, she could play the femme fatale for all the role was worth.

Sam Loper was the more in awe of the two—the bedazzled at last, it seemed, rather than the bedazzler.

But then, it appeared that she didn't think too much of football—or football players. Why should she? How could a mere player impress the daughter of the man whose name had once been synonymous with the game?

And she had lost him because of it.

"I can tell you a lot about our growling Cougar here," Sam Loper offered almost beseechingly.

"Can you?"

"Yes. He didn't agree to the interview, did he?"

She looked at Kent. He kept smiling, although he was beginning to feel like a piece of furniture being discussed. Old furniture at that.

"No, he hasn't agreed," she said softly.

"*He* hasn't made his mind up yet," Kent said dryly. "*He* would very much like to get dressed if you two don't mind. *He* will let you know, Miss Hudson, if you'd care to give him some time to think."

"Certainly," she replied sweetly.

Sam opened the door for her. She smiled at Kent wryly and went through it. Sam winked at Kent and followed her. The

28

door closed, then opened again as Sam stuck his head back through.

"Will we see you at the party?" he asked Kent.

"Sure, why not?" Kent replied.

He didn't move as he watched the door close a second time. He could hear Sam's voice telling Kathleen Hudson something. He heard her laugh—not a giggle but a nice laugh, a little bit husky, with a feminine touch. An honest laugh, not a bit silly.

The sounds faded away, and Kent reached for his clothing. He was reflective as he dressed, wondering why he had agreed to go to a party he wanted nothing to do with.

He paused with a sock half on, fully aware of why he had done what he had.

It had been obvious. Sam was going to invite Hudson's girl to the party, and Kent hadn't wanted her there with him. Not alone.

Alone? The party would be full of people . . .

"What is this?" he wondered out loud, annoyed with himself. He answered himself in silence as he pulled the sock the rest of the way onto his foot. She was Hudson's daughter, and she was very, very attractive. And because she was his friend's daughter, he believed, he felt some kind of urge to watch out for her.

She really didn't look as if she needed protection . . .

And Sam Loper was certainly no . . . no attacker of innocents. And who was to say that she was an innocent anyway?

If she wanted to have an affair with Sam Loper, what business was it of his?

I'm making it my business, he thought grimly.

His silent argument with himself continued, no matter what logic told him.

If she didn't want to get involved with Sam, all she would have to do was tell him so.

But Sam Loper could be persistent. And he had a habit of

taking women lightly because he was accustomed to them falling all over him.

Be fair. You've done the same thing yourself, he reminded himself.

Years ago! was his mental protest.

No, now, too, added the other faction of his silent, inner battle.

But only because his marriage had been such a disaster. Because not only had he and Paula been hurt; Anne was still suffering the effects of their breakup.

"Hudson's daughter," he said aloud. Yeah, whether she needed it or not, he was going to look after her. He owed Hudson, not because of his career but because of his friendship. Dante had shown him all the ropes; he'd been there when Kent had needed him. He had been more than a great quarterback; he had been a great man.

Kent's mouth compressed tightly as he slipped into his shirt. Lady, you are wrong about one thing, he thought. If I'd known there would be any way in hell to help Dante—or even just to be near him—I would have been there. You denied the end to me.

He didn't really know what the end had been, only what he had discerned from reading between the lines of the newspaper clippings. She'd had him cremated before anyone had known of his death; his ashes had been scattered somewhere in northern Wisconsin.

Anger took hold of him, a hot feeling that riddled and swept through him against his will or conscious thought. "Self-righteous bitch!" he muttered. Then he paused again, this time with his jacket halfway on. He knew he would do the interview for her. She was Hudson's daughter. And she seemed to want it badly—very badly.

But, he decided grimly, she was going to pay a few dues to receive it.

Kent patted his pockets to check for his wallet and keys, then he turned to leave the showers behind. But as he neared the door, he passed the shaving mirrors and caught sight of his own reflection.

Dark eyes, dark hair, tanned, kind of craggy features. Some lines around the eyes . . .

And those tiny, almost indiscernible white scratch marks that ran down his cheekbone.

He touched them absently. He never thought about them anymore; who would have thought that the little wildcat would have come back all these years later to haunt his life?

"You *will* come to the party, won't you?" Sam Loper inquired, stopping in the now almost empty stadium to catch her free hand and smile wistfully.

Katie hesitated, stalling. If there was anything that she really didn't want to do, it was spend the evening with a bunch of triumphant football players. She'd had enough of that scene lately.

But Kent Hart had said that he was going; he had also said that he was still thinking about giving her the interview. Wouldn't it be a good idea to stay as close to him as possible until he gave her a firm agreement?

Maybe not, she thought fleetingly. She didn't seem to have a talent for controlling her thoughts when she was near him. Usually, she could appear pleasantly interested in anyone; Kent Hart seemed to have her number all sewed up.

She smiled, hedging. "Aren't you guys still in training? Next week is a big game—and if you take that one, the following game will be even bigger. The Superbowl. You can't go any higher than that."

Sam Loper laughed, flushing a little. "Yeah, well, we're supposed to be lying low, but we're only human, you know."

Yes, you are, Katie thought, but I wonder if you really know that yourself.

"Actually," Sam continued, "the party is a little bit illegal. I mean, the coaches sure won't be invited. But there's this guy who's a Forty-Niner now who used to be a Saxon. He's got a beautiful place a little south of San Francisco. We just kind of all decided to get together. We've got tonight and tomorrow, then it's back to the grind, so we might as well get in a little R and R."

"Yes, I guess you might as well," Katie agreed pleasantly. Wine, women, and song for the conquering heroes, she thought ruefully.

"Will you come? We're really not a wild crowd. Not half so wild as the papers make us out to be."

She hesitated again. She had been to just such a party last week in New York, one that hadn't actually caused her to break off a relationship—that decision had been made before the party—but the atmosphere of the party had certainly added to the chaos and strain of the situation.

And long before New York—long before she had even been an adult—she had been an out-of-sight witness to a few such parties. She had seen one destroy her parents' marriage.

Ancient history . . . But was it? The years changed, but did anything else?

"Please? Say you'll come. You—we—can always leave if you aren't enjoying yourself."

It was either the party or dinner alone with a lot of introspective wandering that she didn't really feel like enduring. And, she reminded herself, she still did have a chance of getting the interview with Kent Hart that was so important to her boss.

Who would have thought, she wondered a little bitterly, that she would have come to crawling—no! She wasn't crawling! Yes, sorry kid, you're crawling—to the college kid her father had patronized all those years ago just to make a go of her own career?

"Well?"

"Sure, I'll come. Thanks for the invitation. What time?"

"Now."

"Oh, I can't come like this. I got drenched during the game."

"I'll take you back to your hotel, wait, and we'll go whenever you're ready."

"Well . . ."

"Really, it will be easier that way. I know the area, and I've got a car." He grimaced. "The car dealers don't mind a little publicity—whether the quarterback is their own or not! And we can stop and grab dinner along the way and . . ."

"And what?" Katie asked sweetly.

"Get to know one another a little."

She had to turn away from him before he saw her smile. This was one quarterback who had learned to make all the right moves.

"Hmm," she murmured with her back to him. "Well, all right, if you don't mind all the running around . . ." She turned to face him again, curiously. "I would have thought, though, that you would have been inundated with fans and friends by now."

He smiled, and she thought again that even if he was a little bit of a self-assured Don Juan, he was a nice enough guy with his heart in the right place.

"I told the others to go on ahead. I didn't think that Kent would agree to company tonight too easily, so I stayed behind to convince him that he wasn't too worn out to party."

"Oh. Well"—Katie shrugged—"I guess we're ready, then. Where's this car of yours?"

"Out front, but we'll slip around the back way, just in case. You are a fan, Kathleen . . . aren't you?"

She smiled, feeling ancient even though they were about the same age and Sam Loper was probably worlds ahead of her in certain kinds of experience.

"Katie," she told him lightly. "And I—of course I'm a fan. Football has always been part of my life."

The last was stated with a very dry undercurrent, but it was unlikely that Sam Loper caught that note or could even begin to understand it.

Kent Hart would have understood, though, she mused as she linked an arm with Sam and followed him back through the stadium.

Perhaps he would have understood all too clearly.

CHAPTER TWO

Sam Loper was an amiable companion. During the drive from the stadium to Katie's hotel, he touched lightly upon a number of subjects—the weather in California, what living in Florida was like, politics, and his involvement with a nuclear freeze group. Katie enjoyed him, yet she was still amused by him. He drove with one hand, at first stretching his free arm behind her on the seat, then around her shoulder. She caught his hand, lifted it, and set it on the steering wheel.

"I'm sorry," she told him, "but I'm a big believer in two-handed drivers."

He grinned, clutched the wheel with both hands, then cast her a quick and covert glance that was very astute. "You're really not after the quarterback, are you?"

"No." Katie laughed.

Sam shrugged good-naturedly. "They're usually after the quarterback," he said with a rueful shake of his head.

"Sam"—Katie felt compelled to shift in her seat and look at him—"I do like you. You're a nice guy. I just try not to make it a habit to 'go after' anyone for what they do."

"Aha! A 'for what you are' woman, eh?"

"Something like that," Katie agreed.

"But you are after Kent," Sam added wisely, and Katie sighed.

"I have an editor who really wants an article on Kent Hart," Katie told him.

"Well," Sam told her, flashing a pleasant smile, "I'm going

35

to harass the old Cougar until he decides to give it to you. That seems to be the only way I'll get him off your mind and me on it."

Katie smiled. This didn't seem to be a good time to tell him that she would just as soon not have *any* football player on her mind. After her father's life, she should have learned. She *had* learned. But then she'd decided that it wasn't fair to judge a man by his profession, and she'd gotten involved with a football player. And then there had been last week's horrendous and embarrassing breakup.

"If I'm not mistaken," Katie murmured, "I think you take a left at the next corner for the hotel."

She received another of Sam Loper's quick glances. There seemed to be a secretive little glimmer to his eyes.

"You are going to ask me up, aren't you?"

"No," Katie replied with a laugh.

"But if there are any fans in the lobby, I'll be swamped!" Sam complained woefully.

"Hide out at the newsstand," Katie suggested.

Sam's smile fell, and he muttered something, but he took her rejection well. And the quaint Victorian lobby was almost empty, so Katie couldn't feel too much guilt for her blunt refusal. Not that she felt he would press himself where he wasn't wanted; she just wanted to keep a distance.

"Fifteen minutes. Please!" Sam begged. "You wouldn't want anyone to see me walking around alone—and waiting!—would you?"

"Certainly not!" Katie responded, and then they both laughed. Katie hurried to the elevators. She noted that Sam did walk hurriedly into the newsstand and hide his face with a paper.

She wasn't in the least concerned about making a fifteen-minute time limit; the little traveling she had done so far had taught her to change in a matter of minutes. But once she reached her room, she hesitated uncharacteristically, wondering what to wear. She wanted to look her best.

36

Why? Because she wanted to try to charm Kent Hart when she saw him again? No, he had already caught her at that act once, and he hadn't liked it one bit. But still . . .

Well, if she wasn't going to charm him into acquiescence, she had to somehow do it with dignity. And to do that, she wanted to feel as confident as possible.

Katie hurried to her closet, chewing nervously on the rim of her thumbnail. What had she brought? A short, white cocktail dress, but with the weather having turned so cold, she would look absurd. She hadn't really come prepared . . . That wasn't true. She had come prepared for a business trip. She was just learning that there was more than one way to go about business.

Katie hesitated a minute longer, then spun around, grabbing her purse. She had seen it—the perfect dress for this type of occasion—at the second-floor hotel boutique. It was overpriced and beyond her budget, but she hastily assured herself that being in debt to the credit card companies was an American way of life. She was going to take more than fifteen minutes to get ready, but she promised herself that she would make it up to Sam Loper by talking about quarterbacks in general and Sam Loper in particular all through dinner.

The elevators moved quickly; there were no other customers in the boutique. Katie swallowed back her last minute mental warnings that she was being an idiot and pulled out her charge card. She was back in her room with the dress in seven minutes.

She took her shower in less than three, muttered out a multitude of oaths as she tripped into pantyhose, then slipped into the new dress with two minutes to spare for the hairdryer and a touch of makeup.

She obviously wasn't going to make it in two minutes, but she wasn't going to be more than five minutes late. And stepping back from the floor-length mirror on the closet door, Katie tried a little dubiously to convince herself that the time and money had been spent wisely.

The dress was a simple knit, but it was indigo-blue and floor-length. It had long sleeves and a vee neck, and it managed to be sexy while still perfect for a chilly night. With her hair dry and no longer plastered against her face, it spilled out against the deep navy with a pale gold shimmer, and her eyes reflected the deep blue of the dress. It wasn't really dressy, just wintry, and it emphasized all the right things.

Katie turned away from the mirror, more than a little irritated with herself. She shouldn't have to be playing games—with Kent Hart or herself. If he'd any decency at all, Kent would be more than willing to help her. Not only that, but he should be battling for a public image. After all, how many more years could he expect to play before his knees gave way or his body became so battered that it could no longer fly across a field? He should want the exposure so that he could retire from the game and sell some macho product on televison.

And he should simply be willing to help Dante Hudson's daughter, no matter how much Dante Hudson's daughter hated coming to him for help.

Katie sighed. It was her own fault. She should just forget the interview. It just seemed so incredibly stupid to give up on what could prove to be the turning point of her career. A career she had begun late because, at the end, she had been the only person left to care for Dante Hudson . . .

Tears stung her eyes; he'd been dead for almost four years now, but it still hurt. The emptiness, pain, and loneliness were still with her. He had been dependent on her in the end; she hadn't realized until he died just how dependent she had been on him.

Katie gave herself a shake and glanced at her watch, wailing out an "Oh no!" She'd left Sam Loper downstairs with his nose in a newspaper for almost half an hour.

Spilling items all over the place, she transferred her things to a small purse from her larger leather bag and grabbed her

38

waist-length jacket of white rabbit's fur. Without another backward glance she hurried out of the room.

Sam Loper did still have his nose in a newspaper. She had to touch his shoulder twice to get him to turn around.

"Katie!" he exclaimed. "How could you do this to me? Leaving me here all this time with the shopkeeper certain that I'm a—Whoa! Never mind. Look at you . . . it was worth it!"

Katie laughed and turned around in the aisle between the magazines and the paperback books. "Like it?" Her voice sounded a little more eager than she wanted. Maybe it was good, since she had chastised herself with a reminder that Sam was being decent enough to deserve a certain amount of flattery.

He gave her a soft whistle, refolded the newspaper, placed it back on the stack, then hurriedly gripped her elbow. "Let's get out of here," he told her. "I don't want to be swamped by fans, but if they were so dazzled by you that they didn't recognize me, I'm afraid my ego would suffer quite a blow."

Katie chuckled. "Sam Loper, I don't believe that for a minute. Your fans would never look past you."

"Let's get going anyway—I'm anxious to share an intimate dinner with a beautiful woman of ever-increasing mystique!"

Katie kept quiet, smiling as they hurried back through the lobby and out to the hotel's portico, waiting there only moments while the valet brought up the car. Sam was smooth with his lines, but even aware of it, Katie couldn't be insulted. He might have said the same flattering thing a thousand times, but he still said it with warmth.

She kept her promise to herself and asked Sam all kinds of questions as they began their ride south along the coast. It wasn't until they had stopped at a small, intimate oyster house and their drinks had been served that he decided to query her.

"I've known a lot of women into football," he said, sipping at his beer, "but you have an uncanny understanding of the game. How come?"

Katie froze. There really wasn't any reason not to tell him —and yet there was. She didn't want to be introduced that evening as Dante's daughter. Not that she wasn't very proud of the fact, but she would be questioned about her father, and the questions would hurt.

She lifted her beer glass to touch his nonchalantly. "Goes with the territory, I suppose. If I'm going to report on sports figures, it pays to know something about the sport."

"Yeah, but you really know what I'm talking about."

"I've watched a lot of football. Sam"—she hesitated, assuring herself that she had repaid him for her tardiness several times over—"why is Kent such a pain in the rear about interviews? I don't get it. What's the big deal?"

Sam shrugged. "Back to Kent, huh? Well, remember, I'm persistent."

Katie smiled.

Sam continued. "I can't really answer that—not completely at any rate. It happened about twelve years ago . . . before I knew him."

"What happened?"

Sam looked a little uncomfortable, as if he really hated discussing a friend even in the pursuit of a woman. "No big thing," he said at last, then reflected, "and no *one* thing, at that. He just kind of got rolled up in the news. A photographer took a picture of him coming out of a restaurant with a woman and threw it all over the front pages of one of those sensationalist magazines. Kent's wife didn't appreciate it. From what I understand, she'd been getting edgy to begin with. He hadn't really been doing anything to begin with, just opening the door for one of the cheerleaders. But you know how the press can be. They had him involved in a half-dozen affairs before he ever got home. His marriage went downhill fast, and the press stayed with it until the end. As I said, I don't know the details. He just told me once that the press is going to write what it wants anyway—why tell them anything?"

Katie sipped her beer and nodded slowly. Maybe Kent did have a legitimate excuse for being such a pain. Once ripped to pieces, anyone would be wary.

"Maybe I can get him to trust me," she murmured.

"Anything's possible," Sam told her. She noted that he was watching her with more than a curious interest. "Why do I get the feeling that there's more between the two of you than meets the eye?"

Katie swallowed a little guiltily, then laughed. "Believe me, Sam, I think the only thing between Mr. Hart and me is a fair amount of animosity."

"That's strange," Sam replied, setting his elbows on the table and staring at her. But his eyes fell from hers and followed the neckline of her new dress. He took a little breath. "I can't imagine Kent being antagonistic toward any woman with your obvious assets—oops. Sorry . . . I really didn't mean that the way it sounded along with the way I'm looking. I mean—"

"Let's order, shall we?" Katie interrupted.

"Yes. Yes!" Sam murmured.

They decided on oysters on the half shell and prime rib. Katie caught Sam looking at her peculiarly again and asked him what was wrong.

"I don't know," he told her sheepishly. "I just . . . feel like a fresh kid around you." He reached across the table and took her hand in his. "What is it about you?"

Stunned, Katie stared back at him, then she smiled slowly. "Sam, that was really awfully, awfully nice, but it isn't anything about me. I think I'm proving to be a more intriguing chase than you're accustomed to."

He shook his head, meeting her eyes in such a way that she felt she had truly found a friend. "There isn't really going to be a chase, is there? I've found a woman who absolutely fascinates me, and yet I know it isn't going to go anywhere. Damn that Kent!"

Katie lowered her lashes quickly, then wondered why. She

met his eyes again. "It really doesn't have anything to do with Kent. Just—"

"A woman with a past!"

"We all have pasts." She laughed.

"True, but now you're more intriguing than ever." He smiled and released her hand.

They both returned to their food, then Sam put down his fork and clasped his hands around his glass as he talked.

"Kent Hart is more than a great receiver—he's a great guy. A team player all the way. We may not know too much of what's going on with him all the time—he's kind of a private person—but he's always there when someone else is in trouble. I know of three marriages that would have ended in divorce if Kent hadn't been there to remind both the players and their wives what they were about to throw away. Another player was going to be cut, but Kent got word of it and spent his spare time working the guy back up to snuff. He's a disciplinarian—hard sometimes, but hard on himself. He won't make appearances to earn extra money, but he's there on his own for disadvantaged kids. If you're trying to dredge up some dirt on him, you won't find a guy on the team willing to help."

Katie listened in amazement to Sam's quiet, intense speech; his fingers were knotting more and more tightly around the glass. It was costing him to come out with such a warning, and she liked him all the more for it. She was forced to wonder about the man who could draw such loyalty from a friend.

"Sam," she said softly, "the last thing I want to do is dredge up dirt on anyone." He didn't look entirely convinced. "Really. I'm on the spot myself. I wound up being a bit late trying to get a career going. I didn't get out of college until a year ago. I started with a New Hampshire newspaper, doing the obituaries. Then I got to cover the garden parties, and then I decided to pick up and head for New York. Sam—I really needed a life. As it stands, I'm kind of on the line here myself. If I can get a good article from Kent, I'll have a full-time staff position. If not . . . well, I'll be doing obits and garden parties again. I swear I'm not about to drag anyone through the mud!"

Sam smiled. He picked up his fork again. "Katie, you're all right. And if you're certain you don't want to elope with me tonight, I'll live up to my original promise and help you battle the ole Cougar."

Katie smiled. "Thanks, Sam."

Sam cleaned his plate of the prime rib. Katie couldn't quite do that, but she reminded herself that she wasn't a growing quarterback. Sam had dessert; she settled for coffee. He talked affectionately about his parents, and she carefully kept that focus on him, avoiding references to her own background.

When they left the restaurant, Sam suddenly seemed hesitant.

"What's the matter?" Katie asked.

"I don't know. Yes, I do. I'm wondering if I should have invited you to this party."

"Why? I appreciate the invitation."

"Because . . . well, because the guys get rowdy sometimes. And I just felt . . ."

"What?"

"I don't know. A strange feeling. Déjà vu or something. Dumb, probably."

Katie shrugged, slipped an arm through his, and started leading him toward the car.

"Sam, I have a strange feeling, too, that whatever it is, I'm going to have weathered worse. Let's go, shall we?"

Kent could hear the music blaring long before he came into the elaborate drive.

The house, he noted with admiration, was set in the alcove of a hill, high and protected. It was a nice place; modern, it seemed to nestle against the cliff and enhance the natural rock with an exterior full of glass and wood trim.

A perfect den of iniquity, he thought with a little grin. Then

43

his grin fell, because he had run really late, having carried on a conversation with his thirteen-year-old daughter on the phone for over an hour. And he was thinking about another man's daughter—Hudson's daughter. He had a funny feeling about the night. To the best of his knowledge the coaches didn't know a thing about the party. That, along with the victorous game, meant that things were going to get wild. And wild . . . well, she might be over twenty-one, but Kent just didn't want Hudson's daughter involved with anything too wild.

Kent parked at the end of the drive; he didn't want to get blocked in, should he decide he wanted to leave early. Which he probably would.

The walk up the long driveway felt good to him. The air was really cool here, nice. It was a hideout, almost like the one he kept in the Rockies. Almost, he repeated to himself with a laugh. Actually, the only similarity was the mountain air. This was a bachelor pad right out of a magazine. His was a rustic wood cabin that had only recently acquired indoor plumbing. But that was the way he wanted it—he went to the mountains to be alone.

Kent banged against the door, but no one answered. It was obvious that even a bang couldn't be heard. He pushed the door open, closed it behind him, then stood in the tiled entry for a minute to assess the scene before joining it.

Down a few steps to the left was a carpeted conversation pit with a copper and stone fireplace. Couples were seated on cushions and chairs around the fire, talking and laughing. To his right was a living room decorated in modern chrome and glass. More couples were there, dancing. Beyond the living room was a huge buffet table; beyond the table was an elaborate, curling bar with carved, high-backed stools.

It was there that his eyes found Kathleen Hudson. She was perched on a stool like a queen holding court. She was in a long blue dress, a color that made a striking display of her Cinderella hair as it spilled over her shoulders in a cascade of

44

platinum and gold. One long leg was crossed over the other; she had kicked off her shoes, and one stockinged foot curled occasionally with a ridiculous elegance as she talked and laughed. Somehow, Kent thought with irritation, that one foot was more arousing than any of the ample displays of cleavage and legs about the room.

Holding court . . . That was exactly what she was doing. Her fingers were curled around a champagne glass that she sipped from occasionally between spurts of laughter and words. Sam was standing behind her, an elbow protectively leaned on the bar as if he sought to make sure no one could make an advance from the rear. But before her and around her . . . well, it seemed like half the team had decided to pay homage. There was an air about her—an aura of sweet but touch-me-not dignity.

That thought didn't help his irrational annoyance much. Just like the subtle, elegant appeal of her nyloned foot, that touch of remoteness gave her an even greater appeal. The guys around her were fascinated—hanging on the melody of her laughter like a pack of drooling lapdogs.

She's playing you all for a pack of fools, Kent thought. And you're all being suckered in. She has no intention of giving any of you more than a pat on the head . . .

So why was he worrying about her? It was like thinking he needed to protect a small but deadly black widow.

Maybe, maybe not. The Sarasota Saxons were, on the whole, an okay group of guys. But they'd been in training and off liquor for a long time. And tonight they were drinking. If they got sloppy, even a pedestaled princess could be in trouble.

"Kent! Oh, Kent, you came! Now the party can really begin!" Long arms tangled around his neck and full breasts crushed to his chest along with the words.

Distracted, he gripped the arms about him and turned his eyes downward to the velvet-eyed brunette who had spoken. Connie Azzizi was the ex-wife of a football player, a dark beauty who liked the game—and the players. Her alimony checks could take her wherever she wanted to go, and she had a friend on every team. She was a nice woman; generally Kent liked her and her company. Connie might not have any scruples—but neither did she have any pretense.

But right now he wasn't feeling much patience for Connie. She was obstructing his view of Miss Hudson and her court of admirers.

"Hi, Connie," Kent murmured, holding her hands so they couldn't strangle him with affection. "Good to see you."

Connie frowned. "Well, if you're so damned glad to see me, Kent Hart, you might pay a bit of attention to me!" Connie pouted.

"What? Oh, sorry," Kent apologized. "What have you been up to, Connie?"

"It's football season," Connie replied. "I've been flying around to catch my pick of the games. And you're still not paying the least bit of attention to me. Why don't you come to the bar and get a drink? Maybe I can get you a little sloshed and then seduce you."

Kent gazed down at her and laughed. That was part of Connie's charm. No one ever knew if she was serious or not. She was a bit of a reigning queen herself; it was always her choice.

"I'm not drinking tonight, Connie, but I think I'll get a soda."

"Aha! You're willing to get close to the bar—and our lovely little reporter, eh?" Connie teased.

Again, Kent pulled his eyes from Kathleen Hudson to stare at Connie. She was smiling genuinely, without malice.

"Maybe," he returned.

"You're the one she's after, you know."

"So she told me."

"You've met her?"

"Yes, right after the game."

"Wonder why I've never seen her before?" Connie mused.

"She knows how to talk football, knows the plays and the players. But she says she doesn't really cover the game—just people."

Kent hesitated. Obviously, she wasn't telling anyone who she was. He could probably burst her pristine bubble by casually blurting out the truth. Oddly enough—with the way she was irritating him, and she was irritating him beyond all bounds—he didn't want to do that. If there was anything about her that seemed to be honest, it was the love she had felt for her father. She'd be inundated with questions—painful questions—if he revealed her identity.

It was surprising, though, that a few of the older guys hadn't made the connection. She had a look of Dante about her, the Nordic coloring, her sea-changing eyes—blue tonight, a blue he could see clearly all the way across the room. And though her features were slim and refined, even they spoke of Dante. They were chiseled without flaw, full of character and determination.

And guile, he reminded himself. She wasn't interested in one of the men she was dangling about like puppets. Not even Sam—who seemed to have it real bad for her.

Sam—of all people. Well, he thought, that's none of my business. So what am I doing? he asked himself for the hundredth time.

It all boiled down to one answer in his mind: She was Dante's daughter. It didn't matter a lick where she had been for the last fourteen years—or with whom. Kent felt like her guardian right now, and it was a feeling he just couldn't ignore.

He was stopped as he followed Connie across the room to the bar. The party seemed to have split into two groups, with the married couples on the dance floor and the free-wheeling singles in the conversation pit and around the bar.

It was the dancers who stopped him, calling out to him. Bobby Patterson's wife, Joanie, paused in midstride to slip from her husband's hold and give him a quick kiss on the

47

cheek. She was a beautiful woman—and a beautiful mother and a beautiful wife. Bobby knew it; he wasn't about to lose her. Nothing that went on around them bothered either of them because they knew they had each other.

Jim Norcross, a defensive tackle, stopped him next with a quick greeting. Sally Norcross made Kent promise her a dance later. She was a tiny blond and very much in love with a husband who was very much in love with her.

Kent waved them back to dancing and started weaving his way along behind Connie again, reflecting on the couples who were out on the dance floor. There were a lot of good people out there, a lot of top-notch, caring relationships. He tended to be a cynic, and it wasn't fair to his profession or his friends. Marriage was up to the individual. His own had gone sour, but that didn't mean that love couldn't exist. It did—a lot of it.

Then Kent wondered why he was thinking about love and marriage. He'd been that route once and had failed royally. Divorce—and the admittedly wild years following it—had sobered and hardened him. He liked being a loner who touched base with earth and women at his own pace.

"Hey, the Cougar made it!" Sam had somehow managed to take his eyes from Kathleen Hudson to lift a hand in greeting and slam it down hard on Kent's back as he reached the bar. Kent groaned inwardly. The whirlpool had helped him a lot, but he had still been the bottom pin in a massive pileup. Sam's touch was not a gentle one.

"Hey, Sam," he said quietly.

"I'll get your soda," Connie offered, slipping behind the bar.

Greetings were called out in general. Kent noted that Kathleen Hudson spun around on her stool, her eyes—crystal, crystal-blue tonight—raised to his.

There were voices all around them, but Kent didn't hear them as he returned her steady gaze. "Good evening, Miss Hudson."

48

"Good evening." Her voice was low, silken, husky.

Don't play the sultry bit on me, he wanted to snap. He looked up to thank Connie for the soda she handed him, then leaned against the bar, watching Kathleen Hudson again. "Enjoying yourself?" he asked her.

"Immensely," she responded coolly.

There was a challenge in her eyes that he met evenly. What the hell are we doing? he wondered. Just what is the challenge? Sweetie, you may have been hurt with your father, but you got hard somewhere along the line. You know exactly what you want and how you intend to go about getting it, and you'll deal with any obstacle in your way . . .

He lowered his voice slightly. "I wouldn't have thought that you'd enjoy an occasion like this."

"Depends on the company," she answered sweetly.

He sipped his soda, raising a brow. "Oh, I thought it was my company you were seeking?"

She smiled. "Yes. But not for enjoyment."

"Cool as a cucumber, aren't you . . . Miss Hudson?" he queried lightly. "That's what they say a good quarterback should be. But ask our friend Sam, here. He'll tell you that there are times when the quarterback gets sacked—no matter how good his defenses."

She listened to him and then leisurely sipped her champagne before answering. "I know my plays, Mr. Hart."

"Do you? I wonder. An experienced player can sometimes tackle the best of the rookies."

"But I'm not a rookie, Mr. Hart."

Now what the hell did that mean? Kent wondered, furious with himself. He was growing really hot under the collar, and it just didn't make any damn sense. Experience had taught him to control his temper; years of being a bit distant had made it so that nothing could anger him. But he was getting angry now, all the more so because it didn't make sense.

"Kent!" Sam turned from the others to join into their conversation. "Have you decided to give her the interview? She's promised no mudslinging."

"Has she?" Kent inquired. Good—he sounded cool. Almost indifferent. Hell, he *was* indifferent. No, he wasn't. "And do you trust her, Sam?" he asked.

"Hell, yes! I trust Katie completely," Sam replied good-naturedly.

Katie, was it? Kent stared at her politely.

"Come on, Cougar!" Connie suddenly exclaimed from across the bar. "Give the girl a break. Give her a nice interview. What will it cost you?"

Once, he thought bitterly, it cost me a lot. But that wasn't the point here—not anymore. He smiled. "I'm thinking about it."

"Champagne, champagne—make way for more champagne!" Tony Low, their host, came through the kitchen to the bar area, champagne gushing from the bottle. "Hey, Cougar! You made it! How about some champagne?"

"No, thanks, Tony. I'm off the sauce tonight."

Tony didn't press him. He started doling out the champagne.

Kent twisted around and saw that a number of the married couples were leaving. And a number of the lovers from around the fireplace were disappearing up the winding staircase in the back of the room.

Then he heard a shout from outside, and one of the Saxons' second string offensive backs came rushing in, shaking off water and laughing.

"She did it! Jean Harkin did it! Stripped naked and flew into the pool—said you kept it heated, Tony!"

"It's heated," Tony replied.

"Yahoo!" someone shouted. "Skinny-dipping time!"

"Tony!" Connie yelped, "you're spilling champagne all over me!"

"Hey, it's okay! I'll wash you off out in the pool," Tony replied deviously.

"Get the quarterback, get the quarterback!" someone else shouted.

"No!" Sam protested to no avail. It started to look like a pileup around the bar. Laughing away, Connie was leading that pileup. "Ah, come on, Sammy, we'll all go if you go. Then we'll come back for Kent."

They were all laughing ridiculously as the party turned into one big skinny-dipping free-for-all. Kent realized that he had gotten there very late, and a lot of drinking had been going on. Sam—still protesting—was raised into the air. His tie went flying, then his jacket followed. The group began to move toward the back of the house.

He glanced quickly at Kathleen Hudson. She was still sitting regally on her stool. Her eyes portrayed amusement and tolerance. She didn't intend on doing any skinny-dipping herself—such things would be beneath the queen—but she didn't seem at all alarmed.

You little idiot! he thought. These guys aren't vicious, but they'll come after you in the spirit of the thing, and you'll be bare in that water before you get the chance to tell them you just aren't in that spirit. I should let them.

"Get Kent!" Connie was shouting. "Someone get that hunk out here!"

"And Katie. Get that sexy blond!" came a male shout.

She was laughing. "No, thanks. It's too cold for swimming."

Kent shook his head with disbelief. Half the crowd was returning for them.

He didn't hesitate another second. He tucked down a shoulder as if he had the ball, rammed it lightly to her waistline, and lifted her over that shoulder, clutching her legs.

She was taken so completely by surprise that he was halfway across the room before she could draw breath to shout at him.

"What are you doing, you idiot? Put me down! Kent Hart, put me down. I don't want to go anywhere with you. Stop it—

51

you're acting like a lunatic." She was trying reason. "I mean it. You're behaving like a gorilla." Reason didn't cause a falter in his step. She pounded furiously against his back. "Dammit! Put me—"

He opened the front door and slammed it behind him. Her fists were pounding against his back with such a vengeance that he groaned.

"Am I hurting you?" she grated out in a fury as he started walking down the drive. "I hope so, because I mean to! You let me down. What the hell is the matter with you? My opinion of you hasn't been the highest, but now—Oh!" She stormed as his quickened pace sent her nose flying into his backbone. *"Dammit—you let me down this instant or else I'll tear you to pieces!"*

She *was* tearing him to pieces. Now she was trying to claw through his sweater to rip into his back. Kent grated his teeth, and suddenly his temper flew. All he could remember was the child who had scratched him years ago.

Ah, hell!

He heard shouts and laughter as the crowd came out the door after them. And she was hindering his speed.

"Son of a bitch!" he suddenly exploded. She was trying her old tactics. He could feel the scrape of her nails trying to take hold through his shirt and sweater.

That did it. He slammed his open-palmed hand with a strength born of fury against her rump, delivering what he knew to be a stinging blow.

She let out a little scream, then she was at it again—but verbally, not physically.

"I'll kill you!" she garbled out unreasonably. "I'll strangle you . . . I'll tear you to pieces—"

"Fine. Just do it once we're out of here!" Kent snapped back.

The footsteps behind them were coming closer. But he was a runner, even with added weight, and hers wasn't that much.

He reached his car, opened the driver's door, and shoved

her in with little grace. She was immediately trying to get out the other side, but he was quicker than she. The key was in the ignition as he slammed his door and hit the automatic locks. She was still swearing away a mile a minute and working feverishly at her door as he wheeled his car around and sped down the driveway.

CHAPTER THREE

She was capable of going on and on—and on, Kent realized. Katie Hudson continued her verbal attack, her voice rising as her oaths surpassed those of the most seasoned player on the field. How had Hudson raised such a shrew? he wondered.

He was on the highway, going a good sixty miles an hour, and she was still playing with the damned door handle. A headache was growing inside his skull, pounding with a force that matched her venomous words.

He lifted a hand from the wheel. *"Stop!"* he ordered, his voice sounding something like an aggravated roar. It apparently had some effect on her, because she shut up for a minute. "I swear to God," he continued with exasperation, "I can't believe Dante could have raised such a stupid child!"

"Stupid child?"

Wrong choice of words—not because they weren't true but because they got her started again.

"I'm not a child anymore, Mr. Hart. I'm an adult. Twenty-six years old—"

"You may be a chronological twenty-six, but I'm beginning to believe you're a mental two!"

"You asinine muscle-bound ape! You—"

"Get your fingers off that door handle! Only a stupid two-year-old would do such a thing in a car going sixty miles an hour."

"Stop the damned car!"

"I will not."

Katie flung herself back into the seat, crossing her arms over her chest and locking them there. She wasn't stupid, but she was so infuriated she felt almost insane, ready to do violence—and possibly kill them both.

Calm down, Katie! she pleaded with herself. She knew she was in what her father had termed a "flaming fury." It was a state of mind so far gone with anger that reason flew away with the wind. She was fighting furiously with herself, but she couldn't cool down. Never in her life had she been treated so —so barbarously! So totally without dignity or respect. So—

"All right!" she snapped out. Her voice was low but not controlled. Each word fell like a taut whipcrack. "I'm going for a coastal drive with an aging madman who thinks that primal tactics are in. I should report you to the NFL. To the police. What the hell is the matter with you? You're crazy! You've been knocked down so many times that you have no mind left. You—"

"Shut up, will you?" Kent grated out. "Can you really be that stupid? Or are you blind?"

"What are you talking about?" Katie raged, struggling very hard to keep her hands from his neck.

"Idiot!" The word rumbled warningly in his throat. "Don't you realize that you were about to be good-naturedly stripped by a dozen roaming hands and thrown naked into a pool?"

"Don't you be an idiot!" Katie retorted. Calm yourself! she pleaded mentally. No good. She hadn't even known she was capable of being this furious. "I would have said no—"

"You would have said 'no'?" he yelled at her incredulously. "Just a simple 'no' from a catty little tease and a pack of half-smashed two hundred pounders would have been down on their knees—"

"I'm not a tease! And I don't want anyone down on his knees! I would have—"

"They would have forced you!"

"Bull! They aren't vicious brutes! You're the only one who has forced me to do anything."

"Dammit, they aren't vicious brutes, but they are men. They're loaded, and you were acting like a tease, sitting there all night gathering them around you as if you had something to give."

"You bastard! You weren't even there half the night. And don't you dare presume to tell me anything about me—"

"I call it like I see it, lady."

"Well, you call it however the hell you like! But stop this car and let me out of it—now!"

"Here? In the middle of the road?"

"I wouldn't care if we were in the middle of a damn desert."

"Bitch!" he muttered, the sports car jerking with the vehemence of his word. "I should have let them. I should have let every single one of them paw you to their heart's content."

Katie was shaking. Was it true? Would the laughter, drink, and spontaneity of the moment have been too much? No! She'd never met a man who was really a beast—except for this one!

She turned on him in the seat, her voice dripping scathingly. "That's right. You should have just left me alone. What business is it of yours? Maybe I love to skinny-dip! Maybe I would have been the first one out there if Jean what's-her-name hadn't started the surge. Maybe I even like being pawed. Maybe I'm just crazy about hands all over me—" She broke off, amazed, when the car jerked off the road and came to a screeching halt. He was going to do it; he was going to let her out. She reached for the door handle again, only to freeze when his voice lashed out at her with a razor-edged warning.

"Touch that handle—just touch it—and I promise on my life that you'll have hands all over you!"

Oh, she was dying—dying!—to ignore him. Dying to rip open the door and give him nothing more than the contemptuous and indifferent glare he deserved!

But he was shaking just as much as she was. So intense that it seemed he might explode at any second. His fingers were gripped around the steering wheel so tautly that his knuckles were white. And though he appeared slim because of his height, Katie knew that he was totally composed of hard muscle and sinew and his shoulders could have served as battering rams.

And she had learned firsthand that he was capable of moving on whim or insane impulse.

She locked her teeth together so hard she was certain they would splinter and break, and she folded her hands together so tightly that her nails dug into her palms. She barely felt them.

She stared straight ahead, praying that she could get hold of her own temper, praying that she could reason with this madman.

"Miss Hudson," he said at last, staring straight ahead into the darkness of night just as she was, "if I disrupted an evening of fun and pleasure for you, I'm sorry. I—"

"I went with Sam Loper!" Katie snapped out, then she groaned inwardly, begging herself to shut up. Involuntarily, she turned to him, certain that his eyes were on her. They were. Deep, dark—and yet blazing with a heat that reached all the way inside her and made her tremble. Then his hands flew off the wheel with exasperated strength and fell back to it with a force she was certain would break it.

"Maybe I really was wrong! Maybe you wanted to be in that pool with Sam—and maybe after that you wanted to try out every player on the—"

"Maybe I did!" Katie shouted. Her hands jerked apart; she didn't mean to do it, her left hand just flew sideways in the most ridiculous gesture she had ever seen. She hit him in the chest with her knuckles. The irony of it was that she couldn't have hurt him in the least—and without even that satisfaction, she fueled his temper to a very dangerous level.

He didn't touch her, but his voice went very low, slow and threatening. "Do you know what I would have done the day you scratched me if your father hadn't been there? Do you

57

know what I should have done anyway? Found a switch and taught you a lesson. Well, maybe—since we're on maybes—maybe it isn't too damned late!"

Oh, God, Katie thought fleetingly, what was happening to her? She could barely think, much less think rationally. She had never been so angry, and she had never felt eyes touch her in such a way. She still trembled. She felt an unearthly strength and a horrible weakness, all at once. She wanted to think before she spoke, but she couldn't. Words spewed from her like dripping ice to combat the fire that seemed to burn all around her in the tumult of her emotions.

"Are you threatening me, Mr. Hart? If so, bear in mind that it's illegal—"

"Illegal?" He stared at her incredulously, then all of a sudden he began to laugh. "Illegal!" He looked up as if seeking help from heaven. "Illegal! She's in the middle of nowhere with an irate man almost three times her size, and she's talking about *illegal!*"

"I'm not at all amused," Katie warned, then stopped herself quickly because he was, at least, laughing. If she could just get him off guard, she could get out of the car and onto the highway, where someone would stop and get her away from him. "Ah!" She forced herself to smile—and to think. She drew in a deep, shaky breath. "Kent, I'm sorry. Truly sorry. I see now that you were saving me from sheer stupidity, and I'm terribly grateful, really I am."

He looked at her again. In the dim light she could see only the flash of his eyes and the square line of his jaw.

He was silent for several seconds, then he asked pleasantly, "You do understand why I carried you out of there?"

"Of course. I was just so—so stunned that I responded stupidly. I am sorry. Please forgive me." She had lowered her voice to a silky tone. She knew she was attractive in the hugging knit dress—even if she was enshrouded by a certain amount of darkness. Katie only hoped her cologne was still infusing the air with a light and provocative scent and that she was convincing Kent Hart that she really was sweet, vulnerable, and properly chastised. If he would just respond like the average male, she could even hope that he would forget what she had called him.

"Really?" he queried softly.

"Really," she whispered in return.

"I'm forgiven?"

"Of course." Katie tensed and waited. She thought she saw a white flash of perfect teeth against a crooked grin, then he looked ahead again. His left hand was on the wheel, his right was twisting the keys in the ignition.

Katie had seen the automatic locks. She reached for hers and flipped the button. In a flash she opened the door. But his hand was already reaching her, snaking out instantly.

"Kathleen." His voice lashed out at her. His epithets—vehement enough to rival hers—continued in a muttered fury.

He had known. He'd known exactly what she was doing!

"Oh, God!" Katie gasped out. In that moment she was truly convinced that she had crossed a very dangerous man. She eluded his fingers by less than a hair'sbreadth and leaped from the car, slamming the door behind her. The wind was very cold now and slashed around and through her. Her coat, shoes and purse had been left at the party. She didn't dare take the time to worry about them. She started running blindly for the highway.

Oh, thank God! She could see headlights coming!

Katie ran into the road, tripping over her hem and gasping for breath. She waved madly at the approaching vehicle, hope causing her heart to thunder hard. She was almost free . . . she had almost escaped him. The lights were coming closer and closer . . .

And then, with horror, she realized that they were coming too close, too quickly. She was in a blue that blended with the night, and the driver couldn't possibly see her. Any second now she would be run over. And she couldn't move! She felt blinded, blinded and held in a deadly freeze by the flaring headlights that were almost upon her!

"No," she heard herself whisper in horror. But then, from the corner of her eye, she sensed movement, a streak in the night. And then the breath was knocked from her as she lifted in a whirl of motion and thrown to the ground. The thud of the impact riddled her, but she felt it, and it was easy . . . she hadn't been hit by the car. She had been lifted and hurled to the ground . . . with Kent Hart.

They had landed on an embankment, a slope that was softened by wet, springy grass, and were now rolling in that grass, over and over, together. Then they reached the narrow valley where impetus halted, and they both lay, breathless, panting, inhaling desperately . . .

The moon came out. It poured over them. Katie realized that she had almost killed herself, but he had saved her. And in that moment, she came to a rationale that her earlier temper would have never allowed her. Kent had been right. He knew the team; he knew the party. And men who were basically nice guys could, with a little too much champagne and in the spirit of fun, get carried away.

He really had meant to protect her from the overzealous partyers.

She closed her eyes and smelled the fresh grass around her. She had to apologize and mean it and hope that he would believe her this time. "Kent—" The whisper didn't quite come out. Unfortunately, it was enough to spur him into action.

Suddenly, when she had just regained her breath, she lost it again. He straddled over her with a tense vengeance, pinning her wrists to the ground, his rugged features twisted into a mask of fury. He was shaking—she could feel it. Oh, she could feel it! And she knew that she had really terrified him and that, yes, this time she deserved his anger. She wanted to say something, but when she opened her mouth, the words refused to come. She formed them with trembling lips. "I'm sorry."

"Sorry? *Sorry!* Oh, God! I warned you not to touch the door . . . I warned you not to touch it!" He was leaning closer and closer to her. She was afraid that he meant to break her in two.

"Kent," she whispered.

She felt the heat of his eyes, and then she felt his breath touch her mouth when he said, "You almost killed yourself!"

And then it was not the caress of his breath that whispered against her lips but the touch of his mouth. Forming to hers, hot and moist, trembling and compelling. She felt his tongue, pressing entry between her lips, persistent against her teeth. The kiss was not brutal, cruel, or punishing. It was forceful. Tears stung her eyes because she gave to it easily. She wanted it. Oh, she wanted it! Like a child held against a storm, she wanted his arms, the hunger of his lips on hers, the passion that had so suddenly rocked them in the aftermath of danger.

His grip on her wrists relaxed, then his hands slid along the length of her arms. Katie felt his tongue move deeper and deeper into her mouth, and the warmth that encompassed her grew as if he could fill her with his heat. She felt his left hand tangle into her hair as his right palm caressed her cheek, cupped it, held it. She didn't know when she had moved, but she became achingly aware that she was holding him, her arms locked around his neck, her fingers dancing feverishly over his shoulders and back, playing into the deep rich hair at his nape.

He kept holding her, his hand grazing her cheek, sliding to her shoulder, slipping between them. His fingers explored the hollows of her shoulders, traced the neckline of her dress, fell lower to her breast.

This was it—the feeling that had touched her insides, racing and coiling low in her abdomen, and it was wonderful. It had been anger, it had been fear, but now it was desire. And whether it was foolish or not, Katie couldn't begin to deny it. She clung to him, savoring the forceful movement of his lips, the hunger in the persistent thrust of his tongue. It was rich, warm, and moist . . . and so close. She loved the scent of him; she was adrift in it and somewhat delirious with all there was to feel, to cherish. The hardness of his hips, his body pressing against hers, real against the knit that kept little of him from her. His hand . . . against her heart, cupping her breast, moving slightly, fluidly, his palm a merciless taunt against her nipple, and yet so good that she whimpered against his kiss, clinging to him with greater abandon.

Kent rolled with her still in his arms, refusing to relinquish the onslaught. Willingly, eagerly, she followed him. His hand coursed over her waist to her hip and back to her breast. Again it moved, exploring more slowly this time, fingers teasing her ribs, her stomach, the little hollow by her hip. His lips moved slowly from hers and fell to the pulse beating erratically in her throat. And he was touching her hip again, her waist, rounding over her buttocks, sliding around them to fall again on her abdomen, low where the heat found its base, and causing her to tremble anew and sob out something entirely uncomprehensible. He touched her breast again, his thumb finding the peak of her nipple, rubbing.

"Oh, God!" she cried out, and it was a sob again, because it was so good and . . .

And because she was lying in a grassy ditch, practically groveling for the sensual attentions of a man she had once sworn she never wanted to see again. A man she had really only met today as an adult, one who had quickly become a bitter enemy.

But when he withdrew his touch, Katie felt the loss instantly. A deep loss. She was cold again, frightened, and bewildered. Without opening her eyes she knew that Kent was still beside her, leaning on his elbow, watching her. What would she find when she opened her eyes? Contempt? Possibly. What else could she expect?

"Katie." He said her name softly.

Misery clutched her. She didn't want to look at him.

"Open your eyes, Katie."

You aren't a coward, Kathleen, she reminded herself. And what could it matter? Her life would go on . . . Yes, thanks to his actions out on the road.

She opened her eyes and looked at him searchingly, too shaken for anything resembling pretense. But she didn't find contempt in his eyes. Katie found nothing that she read, only a somber darkness, pinning her soul. And in the moonlight her heart seemed to take a sudden lurch, then ache. She saw the hard lines of his profile, the character in the set of his jaw, the uncompromising line of his mouth. She had never realized quite how handsome he was. Perhaps he wasn't really handsome; his appeal went deeper than that. It was in the sound of his voice, the fire—and the wisdom—in his eyes. When he was angry . . . passionate . . . or tender.

He stood up, offering her his hand, helping her to her feet. "I'll take you to your hotel," he told her quietly. He put an arm around her shoulder and led her toward the road. Minutes later, she was in the bucket seat of the sports car, no longer angry but torn by emotion again.

Kent drove in silence, a silence that was broken only when they neared the city and he asked, "Where are you staying?"

A little dazed, Katie glanced his way, then finally came up with the name of her hotel. He nodded and kept driving.

When he came up through the entryway, Katie assumed he only meant to drop her off. She learned that he meant to walk her in when she reached for the door handle to let herself out.

"You and that damned door," he remarked irritably. The point was moot—a valet was already opening it for her. She stepped out, aware that Kent had left the keys in the car and was accepting a ticket, as well as the slightly awed congratulations of the valet on the day's game.

She started up the steps without him but quickly felt the touch of his hand at her elbow.

"I can go up alone," she murmured.

"If you do, you'll be in for a few problems. You're barefoot

63

and you haven't got a room key. Shouldn't we go to the desk?"

Why did he have to be so damned logical? she wondered resentfully.

They walked to the reception desk together. When Katie asked for a key, the girl asked for her identification. Katie tried to explain that she didn't have her purse—which was why she didn't have her key—and therefore didn't have any identification.

She was growing frustrated when Kent broke into the conversation, laughing with definite charm and telling about their quick escape from a "slightly" wild party.

It annoyed Katie that the girl behind the desk was practically purring in response. Then she realized who Kent was and begged for an autograph. Kent politely wrote his name. Katie received a key.

"Aren't you going to say thanks?" Kent asked against her ear as they walked away from the desk.

"No," Katie snapped. "If it weren't for you, I'd have my shoes, my purse, *and* my key."

"I'll get them back for you tomorrow," Kent replied as they headed for the elevator.

Katie was about to tell him she could reach her room alone, but she never got the chance. A little boy who couldn't have been more than seven or eight years old came racing toward them crying, "It's him! It is him! The Cougar—Mom, it's him!"

Katie couldn't help but smile at the child's enthusiasm. His eyes were wide with awe and admiration, but he stopped a foot away from Kent, as if his sudden proximity to his idol had made him suddenly shy. He spoke in a whisper to himself this time. "It is the Cougar!"

"Hi," Kent said, stepping forward and bending down on a knee to offer him a handshake.

The little boy looked at the hand touching his as if it were magic. "Hi," he breathed.

Katie glanced past them as she heard the sound of hurried footsteps padding across the carpet. A woman was approaching with another, smaller boy in tow. She was in her early thirties, very pretty if a little harassed, and obviously very distressed. She caught the little boy by a shoulder and pulled him to her, staring at Kent a little awed herself and looking very apologetic.

"I'm so sorry, Mr. Hart. You really are the Cougar, aren't you? I'm—I mean, we're fans. From Sarasota. We flew out for the game. I told Matthew that he could get closer. I didn't mean for him to bother you. I know that you don't care much for the press and the like and I'm so sorry—it's just that he's such a fan—"

"Please!" Kent interrupted with a quiet laugh, rising from his knee. Katie noted that his tone remained quiet and a little reflective when he spoke again. "I'm not fond of the press, but I'm very fond of children, and it was a real pleasure to meet Matthew—and his mother and his little brother, I presume." He smiled at Matthew. "You live in Sarasota, huh?"

It took Matthew a second to find his tongue. "Yes, sir!"

"What's your last name, Matthew?"

"Jenkins. I'm Matt Jenkins, sir!"

"Are you with us even when we're down?" Kent teased.

"Oh, yes!" Matthew assured him solemnly.

Kent ruffled his hair and looked over Matthew's head to his mother again. "Mrs. Jenkins, call our main offices in March if you get a chance. Some of us do a workshop with local kids during the summer, and I'd love to see Matt there. If you call the offices, I'll have left his name and they'll set it up for Matt."

"Oh!" Mrs. Jenkins exclaimed. "Oh, I—thank you so very much."

Kent gave her a crooked smile and wave, taking Katie's elbow again. But Mrs. Jenkins was gazing at her now. "Oh, and thank you, too, miss, for allowing the interruption."

Katie was totally startled by the woman's sincere words.

She didn't want to tell the nice Mrs. Jenkins that she was welcome to take Kent Hart and go hang him!

And apparently Mrs. Jenkins was assuming she was much more to Kent Hart than what she was.

Katie managed a weak smile. "He loves kids," she mimicked a little stupidly, remembering then that she was "the press" of which he wasn't quite so fond.

The press, yes, but she was also Dante Hudson's daughter. Then, too, she was the woman who had almost committed a stupid form of suicide before rolling around in a ditch, passionately entwined in his arms.

Mrs. Jenkins waved and pulled her son away. Katie found herself propelled into the elevator.

"What floor?" Kent asked her. Ridiculously, she couldn't remember. With impatience he plucked the key from her fingers, checked her door number, and punched a button.

She couldn't help but stare at him as the elevator silently moved along. He'd really had a nice smile for Matthew. He did like kids—a lot more than he liked reporters or women or both.

Or maybe it was just her, and very possibly she deserved his feelings. We started off wrong, she thought a little wistfully. I couldn't help remembering the past, and I didn't give him a chance to forget it.

The elevator door slid open, and Kent led her along the hall. When he slipped the key into her door, she thought in a moment's panic that he intended to come in. He didn't. He prodded her through the doorway but didn't follow.

"I have plans for tomorrow evening," he told her brusquely. "But I'll bring you your things in the morning. We can take a drive along the coast and have brunch or something. I don't know if you can get what you want in one morning, but you can make a start if you like."

She could read nothing from his stoney expression and dark eyes. It seemed that he didn't intend to refer to their strange, intimate circumstances earlier. Katie felt a constriction in her

66

throat. She certainly wouldn't make any reference to it either. She couldn't anyway. She didn't seem capable of speech. She nodded.

"Ten o'clock?"

She nodded again.

As if satisfied with the end of the evening, he turned around and started down the hallway. Katie stood still, oddly entranced by the breadth of his shoulders, his thick, tousled dark brown hair, and his long strides. She was startled when he spun around suddenly.

"For heaven's sake, Katie, close the door. And lock it. You're an absurdly trusting woman!"

He stood impatiently, hands on his hips as he waited for her to obey. Katie felt an instant streak of belligerence—she'd been managing just fine on her own for years—but quickly smothered it.

Why was she always so tempted to fight him? she asked herself with dismay. It was ridiculous. She needed an interview with him; he had agreed to do it. It wouldn't hurt to close the damn door and lock it—she would do it eventually anyway.

"Good night," she said quietly. She closed the door and locked it, expecting him to come back any minute and check up on her. But he didn't. Eventually, she walked away from the door and tiredly fell on the bed, an arm draped over her eyes.

Oh, dear Lord, it had been a strange day! It felt as if a lifetime had passed . . . So many things, so many emotions . . .

And the worst of it all was Kent Hart. She could still feel his eyes, his touch, his caress. And if she thought about it, she could feel the burning sensations all over again, the aching and the longing, the need for his touch to go on and on . . .

Oh, Katie, stop it! she groaned to herself. He's Kent Hart; I spent years hating him, and not too much has happened to change that! Oh, but yes, she argued, it has! He saved my life,

I've seen him be kind, and his teammates are absurdly loyal to him.

And he kissed me.

Her fingers moved to her lips; she felt a trembling start up again. She rolled over, slamming a fist into her pillow. Oh, God! It was ridiculous! She had just gotten out of a relationship with a football jock!

Relationship. Had it really been a relationship? She felt that she had exchanged more, experienced more, felt more with Kent Hart in one night . . . And maybe she had.

What about him? It had really been nothing but anger and a surprising surge of desire. It hadn't even meant that he liked her.

Dante. Dante stood between them. A ghost, the man they had both loved. But that love had turned them against each other and refused to let them forgive . . .

"Oh, hell!" Katie gasped aloud. Her voice was frighteningly like a sob again. Frightening . . . yes, it had been terribly frightening when he had touched her. Her response had been so instant, so intense, and it had left this yearning, this aching.

"No, Katie," she murmured aloud. And then the phone began to ring.

She stared at it, not wanting to answer. Maybe it would stop. No, she thought with a sigh. It was Raff, and Raff never gave up.

Katie wearily pulled herself up and answered the phone. "Hello?"

"Katie? Raff here!" Katie listened to his cheerful greeting; she listened, too, as the touch of steel came into Raff's voice. "Did you get it?"

"I think so," she replied carefully.

"What?" Raff demanded. "What kind of an answer is that? Katie Hudson, this is Raff here. I know you could charm a baby into buying dentures—and the man owes you, remember? Now, did you get the interview or not?"

"I've got something," Katie muttered. She went on quickly

before he could start at her again. "I'm seeing him tomorrow, Raff. I'll have something."

"We need an in-depth article, Katie," Raff said impatiently. He lowered his voice to a slightly crooning sound. "Katie, honey, I'm not the big cheese around here. The powers that be want a ten-page spread on the Cougar. You go out there and get it now, okay? Sweet-talk the man. You'll have him eating right out of your hand."

Yeah, sure! Katie thought bitterly. You sure as hell don't know much about Kent Hart!

"Katie, you with me, honey?"

"Yes, I'm still here."

"Okay, honey. Do what you have to do, got it?"

She took a deep breath, her anger simmering. "Are you suggesting I put my morals on the line, Raff?" she inquired coolly.

"No, no, honey!" Raff protested over the wire. She heard his wary chuckle. "I'm just telling you to get the job done."

"Fine. I'll do my best," Katie said stiffly.

"I'll hear from you soon," Raff closed. He didn't add a good-bye, he just hung up.

Katie slowly replaced the receiver. She lay back on the bed again and burst into tears.

She thought she had buried her pain, but now it was with her again as so many things—memories, conflicting emotions, confusions—were all dredged up. Sometimes she felt as strong as steel. She had, she thought, learned to manage very well. Until today.

Somehow, it had taught her all about emptiness again.

CHAPTER FOUR

Katie was ready much too early.

Kent hadn't really said where they were going, only that they would probably have brunch somewhere. That left her wondering if she had dressed properly. She shrugged as she scrutinized her reflection in the long mirror. She had donned a pair of maroon corduroy jeans and a soft white sweater with delicate embroidery about the neckline and sleeves. This was California—laid-back, she assured herself. She should be okay whether they roughed it or wound up someplace that was a little elegant.

So, deciding that her outfit was fine left time on her hands, and she was sick to death of thinking about the man she was about to see.

Katie sat down on the bed and poured herself a cup of coffee from the gold carafe she'd ordered when she had wakened. This was her fourth cup. She held her fingers out before her after she poured the coffee and set her cup down on the nightstand. They shook slightly—she was overdoing the caffeine and making herself edgy; dumb, but she couldn't seem to help herself.

It was just as dumb to think about Kent Hart, and she didn't seem to be able to help herself on that score either.

Face it, she told herself, I came into this thing with a bad attitude. I had him judged and pegged—I certainly wasn't expecting to take hold of a keg of dynamite.

She had been sure that his behavior had been totally boorish and obnoxious when he had wrenched her so crudely from the party. But she now realized it was more than possible that she'd had a few too many sips of champagne and had become too trusting of the situation. She knew that parties could get out of hand—it had just never occurred to her that she could be forced into anything. And why not? she demanded of herself bitterly. Hadn't she more or less been forced into *this* situation?

No! No! Because it was still her choice. She could say the hell with the damn story anytime she chose. Of course, she would also be saying the hell with an incredible job.

In the long run, what would it matter that she had set aside her pride—and a few of her scruples, she had to admit—when it would make her entire life better?

It was the inflection in Raff's voice that had bothered her so much. That she should really be willing to set aside anything to get to Kent Hart . . . That thought caused her to laugh dryly. If Kent Hart could be bought by a face or figure, surely some other aspiring young woman would have used her assets by now. Not many women reached their midtwenties with Katie's inexperience these days. But then, few women spent years in virtual hiding, in loving attendance upon a dying man.

"I'm doing all right," she assured herself out loud.

Those years had been good for her, really. She'd had time to age and mature a little before finding herself a player in the dating game. She couldn't be easily swayed; she knew very well how to say no and mean it—and still come out of the situation being friends.

Well, that wasn't exactly true. There was one man with whom she was no longer friends. The man with whom she'd broken off, just last week. But it hadn't been right! she told herself. For all that he had been charming, bright, handsome, and full of laughter, something had been missing. Very missing, she decided with a sigh. The breakup should have hurt her; it should still be bothering her. But she could hardly remember what he looked like.

How could she remember anyone's face when the features that would come to her mind's eye were Kent's?

"Oh, what is the matter with me?" she wondered aloud. One night, one kiss absurdly shared in a bed of grass, and she felt as if she would never be the same again. How many kisses just like that had he enjoyed over the years? And he was known for making touchdowns once he had the ball in his hands.

Katie stood up and walked resolutely to the mirror. She stared at herself and spoke out loud. "Number one, Kathleen Hudson, you do not like football players. Nothing personal, just the name of the game. Number two—and listen to me, Katie—you are nothing to Kent Hart except for the obnoxious little brat who scratched him fourteen years ago. He must have loved Dante—that's why he feels that he owes you. And that's exactly what you wanted. Now Katie, we're on to three. The man is dynamite. They don't call him Cougar for nothing. Only a fool would come close enough to feel the strength of his pounce. He knows how to toss you around like a sack of potatoes. We're talking the pros here, Kathleen. You thought you were good, but you've got amateur rating. Go out there, young lady, get your interview, say 'thank you very much,' and get away! There's a whole lifetime ahead of you to find a man who doesn't think you're a ball that needs to be dragged over the goal line!"

I like him, a silent voice replied. I never thought that I could, but I like him. I'd admire him . . .

You fell in love with him—like any dolt of a fan!

No. I could have fallen in love with any one of these guys.

A firm rap sounded on her door with such sudden assurance that she jumped, praying that she hadn't been speaking out loud. Then her heart began to race.

Get it together, kid, she warned herself dryly. Let's come up with some assurance of your own and a little dignity here.

72

The rap sounded again, harder.

She curled her fingers tightly into her palms, released them, and walked to the door, hesitating less than a second before opening it.

"Good morning," Kent said briefly, sweeping by her.

She hadn't expected him to come into the room. She would have made the bed and straightened up. But he was in the room. Katie closed the door and turned around to look at him, speaking quickly.

"Is this—I mean, are the jeans okay? I didn't know what you . . ." Her voice trailed away. It was obvious that the jeans were okay; he was wearing blue denims and a red plaid cavalry shirt. She swallowed a little uneasily, thinking that he filled the room with the strength of his presence. He seemed very tall and composed of well-designed steel. The cut of the shirt enhanced the breadth of his shoulders, and the leather belt about his waist betrayed its trimness. He looked good. His hair was still damp from a recent shower, his jaw was freshly shaven, and his eyes . . . were both dark and brilliant. He was rested; he looked much younger than he had right after the game, very alert and only slightly wary.

He was carrying a shopping bag, which he now extended toward her. "Your purse, shoes, and some white hairy thing that I assume to be a coat," he told her laconically.

Katie took the bag from him, careful not to touch his fingers. "Thank you," she said, ignoring his amused jibe. She walked past him to set the bag on the dresser and pull out her purse. "If you'll just give me a second, I'll switch my things into my leather shoulder bag."

"Take all the time you need," he told her.

Katie started transferring her belongings from one purse to another. She noticed inadvertently that he was watching her when she caught his eyes on hers through the dresser mirror.

"Where are we going?" she asked politely. "There are so many things to do in the area."

He appeared to be a little startled by her question. "I wasn't

73

planning on doing anything really touristy. I'm sorry, maybe you'd like something like that? We *could* go to Fisherman's Wharf—"

"No, no," Katie protested, "whatever you've planned is fine. I—I've been here before."

His smile was a little crooked. "Come to think of it, the day just might be a little touristy. I think I'm taking you to the most beautiful spot along the California coast—and there are many."

Katie made sure she had her notebook and a number of sharpened pencils. "It sounds wonderful," she murmured.

Then she looked up into the mirror again. His eyes were still on her, catching hers in the reflection. His arms were idly crossed against his chest, but it seemed that his entire stance had stiffened. It was as if Kent were looking at her but seeing more than her.

Then she understood, because she felt ripples rake through her, like hot, sweet oil filling her body. The bed . . . the unmade bed . . . stood between them, and she suddenly knew that he was imagining the two of them there, just as she was.

Her breath seemed to catch as heat flared in her cheeks, and she was ridiculously frightened that she was going to lose all strength and melt to the floor. Her heart skipped and pelted, and her fingers froze at their task. She could not tear her eyes from his; nor could she stop herself from wondering, from longing to know, just what it would be like to feel all the sensual things taking place in the picture in her mind, things that were reflected in the midnight fire of his eyes.

How long did she stand there? She didn't know. At last she wrenched her eyes from his, straining not to cry out, as if he had indeed held her physically. She dropped a lipstick and her compact, but at least she had freed herself from his magic gaze. Did he clear his throat, or did she just imagine it? Or had she imagined the whole thing? They had to get out of the room.

Kent stepped around the bed, walking to her. "Can I help you?" he asked.

"No, no, I'm fine. I've got everything," Katie said quickly, and to prove it, she hurried ahead of him to the door, not looking at him as she threw it open and preceded him into the hall. "We'd better get going, I guess," she added nervously.

He followed her out. Katie started hurrying down the hall.

"Shouldn't you lock the door?" he asked her.

"It, uh, locks automatically," she responded over her shoulder.

He was right behind her, pressing the button over her shoulder. They stepped into the elevator.

It seemed very small. She could suffocate in a place this tiny, Katie thought. She still couldn't look at him; she didn't really need to. He wasn't ten inches away, and every breath she took held his pleasant, masculine scent. He shifted from foot to foot; she could feel the power of his muscles as he did so, sinewed thighs, broad chest, arms that surely rippled with that slight movement . . .

It was hot in the elevator. She closed her eyes, and the most ungodly daydream invaded her mind: the power failing; and the elevator stopping between floors, trapping them together in the small heated space. She would fling herself at the door at first, praying for rescue and release, but it wouldn't come. And he would tap her on the shoulder, and she would turn around, and she would see that look in his eyes again. A look that stripped her and tossed her upon an unmade bed with rumpled and inviting sheets. Suddenly, she would forget everything; everything that stood between them, the absurdity of wanting a man she hardly knew so badly . . . Just as his look stripped her of clothing, it would dissolve her sense and logic, and she would cry out, flinging herself into his arms. Bared of all lies, she would admit that she couldn't understand it, but she wanted him . . . to touch her, to teach her . . . to show her what his love could be about . . .

75

The elevator door slid silently open and she opened her eyes, startled.

"Katie, ground floor," Kent murmured, taking her elbow.

She didn't know whether to laugh at herself or die with the embarrassment that filled her mind.

"Sorry," she replied. "I—I guess that I was wandering." Did he hear it? Did he hear that she could barely breathe?

He led her out of the elevator, and she took a deep, stabilizing breath. There were people milling about the lobby, and suddenly she was totally bemused. Kent was an attractive man, no more, and, dear God, she would never throw herself at anyone, much less in an elevator!

She managed to smile at him—and herself—as he led her through the lobby and out the front door. His sports car was driven up by a valet, and they were shortly weaving their way out into traffic.

Katie gazed at him then, having completely retrieved her natural poise. "Where are we going?"

"Along Route 1. Have you been there?"

"Yes, but it was years ago."

"Well," Kent responded, "perhaps it will almost be new to you then. As magnificent as the first time."

As magnificent as the first time. The words seemed to echo in her mind. The first time . . . magnificent.

She stiffened in her bucket seat and rolled down the window. The wind rushed in to tangle her hair and cool her face.

"Would you mind if I ask you questions while you drive?" she asked.

"No."

"A few of them will be just for the record," Katie said a little apologetically. "You're thirty-six, right?"

"Right," he replied blandly, his eyes on the road. "My birthday is June twelfth; I understand that means I'm a Gemini . . . No, I'm not at all into astrology . . . I graduated from UCLA . . . Yes, I went to summer school to qualify early for the draft. I was picked up in the second round by

76

Pennsylvania—mainly because I was given such a buildup by their first-string quarterback at the time, Dante Hudson. That was almost fifteen years ago. But then you know that, don't you?" He shot her a glance that glittered with hostility, then returned his gaze to the road. "And I'm sure you know about my birthday and my college and lots of other trivia. You're the type to do your homework well. I'm also certain you know that I was married once, that I have a thirteen-year-old daughter. You probably know where I live—even the brand of jockey shorts I buy. It's all on record somewhere—and reporters are great at snooping out the records. So you still want an article. Well, you've already got your facts, so what you really want is a 'How does Kent Hart *really* live?' article. How has he managed to stay alive all these years? Does he eat Wheaties? Live entirely on organic foods, or secretly survive on yogurt? You're not going to get that in a morning. What you will get is my decision on just how far we're going to go with this."

He glanced at her quickly again, and she could feel his hostility. What was it about the man? she wondered furiously. He could cause her to imagine the most erotic flights of fancy and then turn around and make her imagination run to a new picture, one of herself throwing ice water in his face, then attacking him with an iron spike just for good measure.

"Your decision on how far we're going to go?" she gasped out, her anger causing her voice to rise. "Dammit!" She stared straight ahead, clenching the seat with both hands to maintain control. "What the hell is this? You told me you'd give me the interview—that's supposedly what we're doing. That's what you said last night. That's what—"

"I said I had some time this morning. I also said it might not be enough but that you could get what you could. Well, that's true. But the interview is going to start with you—not me. And when I get some of the answers I want, so will you."

Katie locked her teeth together hard. What kind of a game was this? Didn't he know what last night had cost her? They should have just been able to sit down today—remotely, distantly—and gotten the whole interview over with; it wouldn't take that long.

"What about me could possibly interest you?" she muttered irritably. "I assure you I've led a boring life. I—"

"You're missing the scenery," Kent interrupted. She watched him as he gazed into his rearview mirror, put on his blinker, and carefully maneuvered off the road to a wide shoulder set there by the state of California just for viewing pleasure.

Kent opened his door; Katie did likewise.

She hadn't been paying much attention to the scenery. Now she couldn't help but do so. To her right was the road, with higher cliffs rising behind it. To her left—very, very close to her left—was nothing. No railing, just a sheer drop-off.

Kent lifted a brow. "Are you afraid of heights?"

"No," Katie replied. She stepped around the car and stared up to the cliffs, then down to the lashing waves far below them.

"Isn't it beautiful?" Kent asked her softly. And she knew that he meant it; there was a wistful quality to the deep male cadence of his voice. And when his voice touched her, she felt and saw it all, too. The sheer crystal beauty of the sky, lightly touched by drifting white clouds, soft and elegant. The jagged cliffs above and below them with their rugged majesty. The sparkling, shimmering clash and lulling thunder of the waves, rising, soaring, falling . . . far below.

"Yes," she murmured. "It's a lovely spot."

He gazed at her a second, then laughed. "Lovely? No, 'lovely' means . . . soft, delicate. This is . . . powerful. It can be 'beautiful' and 'grand,' but 'lovely'?" He moved fluidly behind her, resting one hand on her left shoulder, leaning his elbow on her right shoulder to extend his arm past her nose and point out to the water. "Look, Katie. Far out. Do you see them?"

"See them?" she murmured. His words, his breath, were brushing her cheeks, the lobe of her ear. She felt his hardness close behind her and found it almost impossible to remember that they were incapable of talking for more than ten minutes without flaring into an argument.

"See what?" she asked. The sky was melding into the water; oddly, she could see nothing but a shimmering haze.

"Whales. Two of them—right out there. See? One has just surfaced."

Yes, she could see it now, far off in the distance. The huge, gentle sea creature, a part of the natural magnificence of the scene, rose with a gushing fountain of water that caught the sunshine.

The great creature fell back into the water. Kent chuckled behind her, and a tingling sensation played havoc with her spine.

"Here comes his mate," he told her, and sure enough, a second whale seemed to leap straight up and out of the water, spout a gusher to rival Old Faithful, then fall back with a shimmer of sun-created golden sparks.

"They look so small from here," Katie murmured, awed by their graceful magnificence.

"They're immense," Kent replied. "It's just that we're so far away." He released her shoulder and turned back to the car.

Katie kept staring at the water for a minute. She shivered; without him the cool breeze seemed to sweep right through her sweater. She hurried back to the car.

"How was that for a tourist treat?" he asked, turning the ignition and easing back to the highway.

"That was something," Katie replied.

"Are you a nature lover?"

She glanced his way uneasily, sensing there was more to the question than his casual tone might indicate.

"It depends on how you mean that. I like hills, trees, water, pretty flowers. I'm not particularly fond of insects, snakes, or mud pits. Why do you ask?"

"Oh, just because I preferred to carry on our little—interview—alone."

"Oh?"

He glanced her way quickly, expertly steering the small car along the curving road.

"I thought we'd have a picnic. Any objections?"

A picnic? "No," she replied, hoping he couldn't sense the uneasiness in her voice. "Yes. I'm the reporter, and you've just informed me that I'm going to be the one going through the third degree."

He grinned a bit deviously, she thought. Or maybe it wasn't a devious grin, just a sardonic twist of his mouth that indicated he was one tiger not about to be pulled by the tail. Katie gazed out the window to her right, pretending to watch the scenery. She had known yesterday, and then again last night, that she had strayed into dangerous waters. She didn't seem able to flirt her way around anything with him; she did nothing but singe her wings at any attempt to manipulate him. As Sam Loper might say, the old Cougar had been around a long time; no woman was going to wind him around her finger.

"I think it's fair, don't you?" he queried.

"No," Katie stated flatly. "I'm not a public figure."

"I don't intend to make public any of your statements."

She didn't answer him. They continued to ride in silence for several moments, then Kent startled Katie by pulling off the highway onto a narrow dirt path she would have never recognized as being any kind of road. The small car bucked against the incline, increasing Katie's nervousness. But Kent seemed to know what he was doing; he coaxed the car along, then instead of ascending, they began descending.

She gazed his way suspiciously. "Are you sure we're headed for a picnic ground?"

"Don't you trust me?"

"No."

He laughed good-naturedly. "Well, trust me—this once

anyway. Don't you have any sense of adventure? You'll never make it as a reporter if you don't."

"Oh, my sense of adventure is just fine. However, I don't consider myself suicidal."

He smiled. The path kept descending. There were pines all around them, then Katie noted a break in the pines. They were almost right on the ocean. Sandy beaches were strewn with massive rocks; cliffs and sand and colorful scruff bushes seemed to blend into one another.

"Like it?" he asked, pulling the car to a stop right before the excuse for a road ended and became pure sand.

Yes, of course she did. It was the type of place one dreamed about. The sand and the sea, the sun and a cool breeze. A gentle scent of freshness and salt. It was the type of place they advertised in travel brochures, secluded, remote . . .

He was watching her closely, she knew. She turned to him politely, gripping her door handle. "Where are we? This can't be a public beach?"

"The property belongs to a friend of mine," he said briefly.

They got out of the car, and Katie looked around while he opened the car's small trunk.

"Want to give me a hand?"

"Sure."

He gave her a huge worn quilt to carry and picked up a wicker picnic basket himself and started toward the beach. Katie tried to follow his long strides, but sand kept filling her shoes. She paused to take them off; he waited patiently, then started walking again.

"This suit you?" he asked.

"Yes."

They were about thirty feet from the water, sheltered from the breeze by a stark rise of rock.

Kent set down the basket, then helped her with the quilt. He used her shoes to hold down two of the corners, then pulled off his sneakers for the remaining two.

Katie didn't sit right away; she pretended a great interest in the water, crossing her arms and shivering a little as she stared out at the waves.

"Are you cold?"

"No, not really."

"Have a glass of wine. It might warm you up."

She turned around at last. He appeared languidly comfortable, leaned on an elbow, his length stretched over one side of the quilt with a wineglass in his hand. He offered it to Katie.

She sat gingerly on her own side of the quilt, annoyed with the cynical amusement in his dark eyes. "Wine in glasses?" She inquired cattily, accepting the glass. "I was expecting beer bottles."

"Ah, yes! And I could open them with my teeth, right?" he asked her.

Katie shrugged. "It would go with the macho image."

"Do I have a macho image?"

"Aren't you supposed to?"

"My day for the questions, Miss Hudson," he told her, stretching out to pick up the second glass of wine he had apparently poured while she was watching the ocean, lifting it to touch it to hers. "I asked you—do I have a macho image?"

"Yes, I suppose so!" Katie snapped irritably. "Men who drag women around over their shoulders don't usually get reputations for being gentlemen."

"And what about women who like to sit around waiting to get stripped by a number of men?"

He would look wonderful right then with his damned wine dripping all over his face, Katie thought, her temper—so easily kindled by him—rising dangerously again. She did, however, manage to refrain from tossing the contents of her glass over his head.

"I refuse to go into it again," she said coolly. "Perhaps I was wrong, but you were obnoxious."

"I tend to be obnoxious that way—assuming that young women don't want to be attacked."

"Don't assume anything about me in the future," she told him.

"So, there is to be a future?"

Katie cast him an exasperated glance, then decided he was right—she could use the wine herself. She gulped down half the glass in one long swallow. It was a smooth wine, a bit dry, and it gave her a quick and pleasant rush of warmth.

"You said you were asking the questions today. If I answer them, I'm assuming you're going to give me a chance to ask mine."

"That's true," he murmured, sipping his own wine and watching her assessively, his dark eyes hiding all the conclusions he might have come to regarding her. Then his gaze left her as he inclined his head toward the picnic basket. "Are you ready for brunch?"

More because she wanted something to do than because she was hungry, Katie opened the basket. Plates and forks were neatly strapped to the sides; brunch consisted of rolls, fruit, and various sandwich meats and cheeses.

Feeling his eyes on her once again, Katie pulled out the breadboard at the bottom of the basket and began arranging the food.

"What do you want to ask me?" she snapped out after his prolonged silence began to wear on her nerves.

"You can start with telling me about your life since you were twelve years old."

Katie compressed her lips. "I dropped out of high school when dad was injured and went with him to Europe, where he saw one doctor after another. They all thought they could do something for him . . . None of them could. His spinal cord was damaged, then he developed a cancer that attacked his nervous system." Katie spoke flatly, but then she had to pause, taking a deep breath. "By the time I was nineteen we both knew the chase was finished. Dad just wanted to . . . to hide out. We moved up to New Hampshire, where I finished high school. After my father died, I went to college, then spent a year writing up obituaries and garden parties for various small papers. I decided to go to New York. I did some game coverage there . . ." She paused again, buttering a roll while she gazed at him covertly from beneath her lashes. Had he heard anything about her life in New York? She didn't think so. His expression hadn't changed—it was grim, but it had been grim since the beginning. And his eyes were just on her. He was listening attentively to everything she said, still performing some kind of a secret assessment. "Then"—she drew in a deep breath—"I sold a freelance article to *World* and was invited to do another. After that, well, they decided they wanted an article on you."

"Because they knew who you were?"

"Yes."

"But you wanted to refuse."

Katie stopped buttering the bread and looked at him. "Obviously."

"Go on."

"You've got it. That was my life."

"All right, I'll ask more direct questions, then. Why didn't you answer my letters when you knew damned well your father was too sick to do so?"

Katie stared at him incredulously. She picked up her wineglass and finished off the liquid, watching him over the rim of her glass. "Dammit, that's not fair! I was very young and trying to make him happy. I was following his wishes, and—"

"You were still busy hating me, judging me, because you had become jealous of me as a kid?"

"No!" Katie flared. "If you'd really cared—if you'd cared at all!—*you* would have come to him. Our trail wasn't hard to follow. You must have known he'd been hurt in that last game. You had to know! If you were his friend, you would have seen through his lies. Don't blame me because you couldn't spare any of your precious time!"

She'd pushed it too far. Kent was no longer stretched indolently over the blanket; he had moved like mercury, sitting to face her, clenching his fists as if he longed to reach out and shake her. His mouth was a compressed line, white and stark in the copper hardness of his jaw; his eyes looked like gleaming jets.

He did reach out a hand. Katie started, certain he intended to strangle her and that she was an idiot to be sitting here with him on a deserted beach, goading his temper.

But he didn't touch her. He reached past her to the picnic basket and pulled out the wine bottle and refilled her glass. Her fingers were trembling.

"Hold it steady!" he snapped as the glass wobbled. He replaced the wine bottle, sipped from his own glass, then set it down carefully on the quilt and folded his hands over his crossed legs. "I've been an anathema to you for the majority of your life, but a magazine suggests that you come after me, and you do."

There was contempt in his tone. So much so that Katie found her temper flaring once again. "Yes! I need a job. And though I can survive off obituaries, I'd rather not spend my life that way. I want and deserve a chance for a career. Don't you dare presume to judge me. What was your last contract for? A million? More? You're doing exactly what you want to do, and you're swimming in money, so don't look down your nose at the peasants who have to work to survive! The entire world can't get paid outrageously for playing a stupid game!"

For a minute she thought she had made him so angry that his powerful hands *would* close about her throat, but then, surprisingly, he laughed.

"Yes, I suppose I am paid outrageously for playing a game. But I still don't understand this—not completely. Surely your career can't hinge on one story?"

"A lot of careers have hinged on one story," Katie replied with a sigh, allowing her lashes to fall as she stared down at her glass. "Am I done now? Have I left anything out?"

"I'm sure you've left out lots of things," he told her dryly.

"And, no, you're not done yet, but I've only got a few questions left."

She glanced up at him uneasily, then made a pretense of bored disinterest and shrugged. "Go on. Let's get this over with."

"All right. This still doesn't quite cut the mustard. I might have been one of your father's best friends, but I'm notorious for being rude to the press. I only ever speak when it has a direct bearing on a game and is crucial for the goodwill of the team. Why would these editors of yours decide that I was going to turn around and be a nice guy to you?"

"Because of my father."

"Not good enough. I have this feeling that you were supposed to come out here, use your father's name to get to me, and then use your own considerable assets to get to the nitty-gritty."

"What do you mean by that?" Katie flared.

Kent arched a brow, his disbelief and cynicism unmistakable. "Oh, come on, Katie. There was no suggestion that you just might be able to seduce out of me what they wanted?"

"You really are an arrogant bastard," she told him heatedly.

"Hey—you just said your career was at stake. I'm just trying to find out how important it is to you."

"I was right to hate you when I was twelve," Katie retorted. She was really angry now. It was all she could do to keep her voice level and her nails out of his flesh.

"Katie, I'm extremely fond of honesty. Lie to me, and you won't get a thing."

She lifted her chin, her eyes hard as flint, her tone icy. "I never intended to seduce you."

He laughed again. "No, maybe you didn't. But your editors intended for you to." He sobered slightly, looking at her curiously and, as strange as it seemed, caringly. "That's harassment, you know. You could fight it."

She suddenly felt drained of anger. "Possibly," she murmured, "but it's impossible to prove innuendo. And with my luck I'd lose a court battle and be out of a job with no prospects for even a future in obits."

He gazed at her several seconds longer, then rose with a supple grace and walked down to the shore. Katie stared after his long, broad back, wondering a little desperately what was going on in his mind. At last she could bear the anxiety no longer; she stood and followed, feeling the cool sand against her bare feet.

She didn't touch him, but he knew she was behind him. Kent turned to her, and his speculative dark eyes gave away none of his feelings. "We've got to head back as soon as we've eaten." His voice seemed to grate, as if that fact made him a little angry.

Or was it just she who made him angry?

"But you want a full-length, knock-'em-dead article, and if you're willing to go for it, I'll see that you get it. Tuesday we have to be back in Sarasota; Wednesday we head out to Denver to warm up for the last playoff game. Come out to Denver. I won't be able to see you much before the game, but when it's over, win or lose, I'll be going up to my place in the Rockies for a few days. I can give you all the time you can possibly handle then."

He didn't speak angrily or sardonically, nor did he touch her. But he looked at her, the ocean making his eyes so dark that they were jet again, a jet touched by fire. His eyes seared into her, warming her, making her tremble and shake. His words hadn't been a dare, and yet a challenge had been issued. Katie didn't want to be challenged—she wanted to run. He made her blood run hot and cold with unwanted excitement; he could ignite her temper to a roaring blaze, then turn that fire to something else . . .

His lips curled into a taunting grin. "Are you afraid of me, Miss Hudson?"

"Yes," she told him truthfully, making him laugh.

"If I'd been going to tan your hide, lady, I would have done so fourteen years ago."

"Humph," she murmured. She lowered her lashes and stared down at the cool tide, now running up to her toes.

"Ah, poor Katie!" he teased. "We'll have to see, won't we, if you've got the spine to go after what you really want?"

That did it. She pulled her eyes back to his and planted her hands firmly on her hips.

"Oh, I've got the spine, Kent Hart," she said regally.

He laughed again. And then, before she quite knew what was happening, his arms were around her. She was pressed to the hardness of his body, feeling all its sinewed strength. She tilted her head back to protest, but the parting of her lips only served as an invitation to his. Firm, warm, compelling, his mouth mastered hers, and her protest died unspoken. The waves bounced around them; the breeze was cool; all she knew was a delicious heat and the strong, searing seduction of his tongue in her mouth, coaxing hers firmly to play in return. His hands, moving on her with such assurance, made her feel liquid and weak, and she groaned deep in her throat as they unerringly loved her breasts through her sweater, then found her naked flesh beneath it and the lace of her bra . . .

His lips moved from hers, trailing little kisses over her cheek then down, where his teeth nipped and raked lightly against her throat. She heard his whisper, erotically warm and moist against her ear, "So . . . you are willing to seduce me for a story."

She went dead still. Heat left her as if she had been blanketed by ice as she heard the amused contempt in his voice. Furiously, she jerked away from him, tripping in the sand. When Kent reached down to help her, she venomously slapped his hand away.

"Don't! You son of a—"

"Does that mean you won't be coming to the Rockies?" he interrupted her. Only the midnight sheen of his eyes portrayed anger; his voice was rich with sarcasm.

Katie was halfway across the sand in a moment. She retrieved her purse and shoes and started walking to the car, snapping out over her shoulder, "I don't know what it means yet. Except that I pegged you just right from the very beginning. You're totally despicable."

Laughing, he followed her, preferring to ignore the fact that she had no intention of helping to pack up their uneaten meal. He did so himself. Katie walked on to the car, ripped the door open vehemently, then sat rigidly and waited.

Kent took his time. It was several minutes before he approached the trunk of the car and threw the basket and quilt into it. When he was seated beside her again, she didn't even glance his way.

He started up the car but seemed to have no qualms about looking at her.

"Despicable?" he asked.

"Totally," she enunciated coolly, hating the laughter she heard in his voice.

"My God, you really are good, then."

"At what?" she demanded with fury and exasperation.

"Seduction," he replied blandly.

She twisted, temper and sanity lost, ready to blacken both his eyes if possible. He caught both her wrists and smiled at her as she strenuously fought his hold, then went rigid.

"Fact one about Kent Hart, Miss Katie Reporter. I never abuse women—unless they abuse me."

She lifted her chin in silence and waited with miraculous patience, considering the cauldron inside her, for him to release her.

"You still need the information, don't you?"

"Oh, I could write a lot about you right now," she seethed.

"But it wouldn't be what your editors want. So, are you still on the story?"

"I can only give you one guarantee, Mr. Hart."

"Oh?"

"Yes."

Kent kept his smile in place as he stared into her eyes. They were sea crystals, a rage of shifting blue and green. Pride, rigid and fierce, tensed her delicate features. Why? he wondered. Why am I taunting her?

His conscience answered him fully.

He had wanted to protect Hudson's daughter, but the greatest protection that she needed was against him. He wanted her, desperately, painfully. She was a sweet potion that he had tasted briefly, and a gnawing, driving hunger for her now tore at his body, taunting his insides. He had taken her into his arms to shake her up, but he had been the one trembling, ready to make love to her on the sand under the sun and sky.

Both of them—bought and sold.

He couldn't refuse her—all he could possibly do was make her turn from him . . .

"I can guarantee you, Mr. Hart," she said with words that touched him like jagged ice, "that I will be old and wrinkled and dead before I'll ever allow you to touch me again!"

Kent released her and laughed. The sound grated in his throat; it held no humor. He turned the key in the ignition, and the sports car roared to life.

"It will be interesting, Miss Hudson," he drawled, "to see if that's true."

"Oh, it will be," Katie vowed. "It will be."

CHAPTER FIVE

Kent returned Katie to her hotel by one thirty; by two thirty he was standing in the airport waiting for his flight to be called.

Sam Loper was with him. Sam just didn't believe that anyone should fly off without someone there to say good-bye.

"You're crazy, you know," Sam was telling him good-naturedly. "You'll get to Philly tonight, and you'll have to fly back to Sarasota tomorrow. That's a lot. We'll have a week of hard training and then—if we're real, real lucky next weekend —we'll have two weeks of hard training before the Superbowl. After that you'll have all the time in the world. Why don't you just wait? Annie would understand. You could even see her next week, leave right after the game."

Kent shook his head. "I made my plans for next weekend. And I promised Anne I'd see her tonight. I don't let her down."

"Yeah, I guess that's good," Sam said, no longer attempting to dissuade Kent from the trip. He frowned suddenly. "But what's up next weekend? You mean after the game on Saturday, I take it."

"I'm going up to my place in the mountains." He shrugged. "We'll already be in Denver. I might have a whole pack of time," Kent chuckled, "but if we do make the big game, I'll still have a couple of days before intense training again."

"Want me to come with you to the cabin?" Sam asked. "It might be just what I need. Mountain air, fishing—"

91

"Not this time." Kent answered quickly.

Sam looked at him suspiciously. "What's up?"

"I don't know, maybe nothing."

Sam gazed at him quizzically for a minute, decided Kent wasn't going to say any more, and suggested that they walk closer to the gate. Kent's flight was called over the loudspeaker, and Sam offered Kent his hand.

"Say hi to Paula and Annie for me. And Ted."

"I will," Kent promised. He grinned. "And lie a bit low yourself tonight, will you? I hear things got even wilder after I left last night."

Sam shrugged, then grinned sheepishly. "Not that bad. And I have plans for a more personal outing this evening."

"Oh?" Kent raised a suspicious brow. Intuition was warning him that something was up in Sam's mind that he wasn't going to like.

"I'm going to go and apologize to Miss Hudson for the rowdiness of the party. I'm going to beg to make amends and—"

Kent dropped his overnight bag and grabbed Sam by the lapels of his jacket. "Sammy," he said heatedly, "that's one woman I want you to leave be. She's not . . . an ordinary groupie."

"Kent!" Sam explained with surprise, amazed at the intense anger that tautened his friend's features. He grasped Kent's hands, aware that Kent had age and muscle over him but not afraid. He gripped Kent's hands. "Hey—if she's special to you, just say so. I wasn't going after her in that way to begin with. Anyone can see that she isn't ordinary."

Kent gave himself a little shake and released Sam. "She isn't really special to me, Sam. I'm sorry."

Sam watched him curiously for a minute. "Kent, I like her. I really like her. I was just going to take her to dinner." He paused, then lowered his voice. "Honest, Kent, just dinner. I'd be keeping an eye on her for you, actually."

Kent shook his head again. "It isn't that, Sam. I just don't want her in any more situations like last night." He hesitated. "She's the daughter of an old friend of mine. He's dead now. Do you remember Dante Hudson?"

"Dante Hudson?" Sam repeated, then he whistled softly. "Sure, what quarterback doesn't get a million lessons with his name in them all. She's—Katie's his daughter?"

Kent nodded.

Sam lifted his hands. "I promise, no parties, nothing wild. And I'll keep my hands to myself."

Kent lowered his head and smiled. Sam was a good friend. Kent had just denied that he was staking a claim himself, but Sam was still going to watch out for Katie Hudson—for him.

Maybe it wasn't such a bad idea. He'd know she wasn't going to get in any trouble that night, anyway. Of course, for the next week—well, it would depend on what she decided to do. He honestly didn't know whether he wanted her to disappear from his life or remain and drive him half mad.

"Hey, you'd better get on that plane," Sam warned.

Kent nodded. He gave Sam an open-palmed tap on the shoulder. "See you tomorrow night before curfew."

Sam nodded. Kent hurried to board his plane.

It was a long, long flight. Listening to music couldn't stop him from thinking, nor could he get himself interested in the movie being shown. There were some excellent articles in the magazines being passed around, but he couldn't keep his concentration steady for more than a paragraph.

Hudson's daughter . . .

At twelve she had been a beauty. Tall and slim, all legs like a young colt. Even then her features had promised perfection; her hair had been like a wild, golden halo. Kent had wanted to like her because he liked Dante so much. He would have gladly and willingly loved anything in Dante's life.

But from the moment he'd seen her that day, he'd known she was bound and determined to hate him. He remembered understanding—a little. But he'd also been too young then himself to bend over backward with toleration. Especially after she had clawed his cheek.

He smiled a little wistfully, remembering how Dante had warned him that everyone would think he'd had a lovers' scrap. Because of Katie's nails, he had endured a lovers' scrap. He and Paula had been engaged then, and she'd been furious, certain that he'd been fooling around. He'd finally convinced her that he hadn't. Or at least he had thought he'd convinced her that he hadn't.

Kent leaned back in his seat and closed his eyes, a smile filtering onto his lips. It seemed strange now that he was such good friends with Paula. Their divorce had been a vicious one, made so mainly by the press. They both kept believing what they read without bothering to ask each other. Paula was made to believe he wanted to take Anne from her; Kent was made to believe she meant to refuse him visitation rights by accusing him of a lewd and disgusting life, harmful to his daughter.

It was amazing that they'd ever gotten it settled, that they'd ever been able to sit down and acknowledge that they weren't right for each other, that neither of them was a horrible person. Paula had never been a nag or a witch, just as he had never been the adulterer she had come to believe.

It had been ten years since then—ten years in which they had learned to care deeply about one another as friends. Just as they both cared with all their hearts for their daughter Anne. And Ted Haskell, whom Paula had married a year after the divorce, was a man with a totally giving, mature, and refined character. He knew his wife loved him, and he felt no insecurity. Kent had always wanted marriage to be a forever thing; his hadn't worked out that way, but at least their lives —his, Paula's, Anne's, and yes, Ted's—had worked out in the next best possible way.

Kent taught Anne to love and respect Ted, which she did. But she was his daughter, too, and she knew it. If there was one thing Kent did in his life against all odds, it was to uphold all his commitments to Anne. He had promised to see her tonight; he was going to do so.

But tonight . . . tonight he was wishing a bit that he wasn't facing such a tight schedule. He wished he could have called Anne and asked her if she would mind waiting another day. He hadn't been ready to leave. He'd wanted to spend more time with Kathleen Hudson. Even with Sam's promise, he didn't want her in California. Why? It was stupid. How the hell could he know what she usually did in New York? She was what? Twenty-five? Twenty-six? Old enough to date, he reminded himself.

He didn't want her dating. He didn't want her out with any man. Not even Sam, who had made a promise that—being Sam—he would keep. Kent wanted her himself. So badly that sitting in the wide-bodied jet with the air-conditioning vent right on his face, his body still went hot and rigid with the thought of her. The woman he was belatedly convinced that he had to protect.

Damn! He groaned silently. She had admitted today that she had been told to get the interview with him at any personal cost. Of course, she had denied her own collusion. But she appeared to hate him; it was obvious that she often forced great control upon herself to keep from giving him a set of matching scars on his opposite cheek. But then, when he touched her, she moved like fire and honey in his arms, seducing away his good intentions and will . . . and all reason.

Where was the truth? Did she despise him? And was she willing to act out the innocent enchantress for the sake of her all-important career?

He didn't know. He just didn't know. She denied him, but she enwrapped his desires with far greater talent than any woman he had known before her.

Kent sighed, totally frustrated. He had tried to infuriate her today. He had wanted to infuriate her because he hadn't wanted to find himself guilty of an affair with his dead friend's daughter. Hell, he owed Dante's memory more than that . . .

95

But at the same time he was also wishing that she would follow him to the mountains. Then they would find out once and for all if what was passing between them was something born of hatred or something real, that special chemistry between a man and a woman that he had given up on after his divorce.

Showdown, he thought. Would it happen?

Oh, get her off your mind, will you? he pleaded with himself. He picked up a magazine and forced himself to read.

Eventually, the plane brought him to Philadelphia. It was eleven o'clock when he paid the cab driver and walked up the brick path to his ex-wife's stately old home. Paula had assured him that none of them was worried about the time; he knew that her assurance had been no lie when, despite the hour, the night, and the high banks of snow on the lawn, the front door burst open.

A bundled streak with long dark hair came flying toward him.

"Daddy! You're here! You did come! Oh, Dad!"

Kent dropped his bag and caught his daughter's flying form as it pelted against his. He wrapped his arms tightly around her, lifting her from the ground, hugging her furiously.

"Annie, oh, Annie!"

For a full minute he held her close, whispering her name, running his fingers through her dark hair. She was life and warmth and the greatest love he had ever known.

At last she pulled away from him. Her eyes, a sparkling hazel like her mother's, stared into his like glittering diamonds.

"Oh, Dad! You were great! Ted watched the game with me —and Mom, too, but you know how she is—and Ted kept saying the only chance in hell that Loper had was to get that ball to you! I was so proud when you made that touchdown!"

Kent grimaced and set her down at last. "Don't you say 'hell,' young lady," he chastised softly. "And I'm not sure you should be so proud of me. I ran my legs off because I didn't want those goons falling on me—which they did anyway."

"Oh, Dad! You're so funny!" Anne said, giggling. She slipped her hand into his. "Come on, Mom and Ted are waiting at the door, and Mom will start complaining that all the cold air is getting in."

Grinning, Kent retrieved his overnight bag and followed Anne up the path to the old steps. Paula and Ted were both in the doorway.

"Kent! Get in here before we all freeze!" Paula chastised, smiling. Anne and Kent exchanged knowing looks and a quick laugh. Ted reached for Kent's bag, and Paula quickly closed the door behind them all, still scolding Kent as she took his coat and kissed his cheek.

"Come on in by the fire," Ted said, and Kent followed him into the delightful old-fashioned parlor. He sat on the plump sofa, his arm around his daughter, who curled beside him.

"Great game, Kent, really great game!" Ted said warmly.

Kent smiled. Damn, but he did like Ted. Maybe it was possibly because he and Paula had really fallen out of love with one another. Or maybe it was just Ted. His daughter's stepfather was a tall, slim man with pleasant blue eyes, gaunt features, and a smile that spoke of honesty and a gentle nature. Ted was a prominent attorney, a true pillar of society. He had avoided any possible problems by coming to Kent before he had married Paula and setting all his cards on the table. He had, without being broached on the subject, promised to love and care for Anne with all his heart—and welcome her natural father into his house at any time. He was an amazing man, Kent thought affectionately.

"Thanks," he said, then shrugging, he admitted to Ted, too, that his effort had been for self-preservation.

Paula swept back into the room at that moment, carrying a tray of warm muffins and hot chocolate.

"Self-preservation!" She sniffed. "You should be thinking

about more than a little self-preservation, Kent. You should start thinking about retirement."

"Paula, I'm not that old—"

"Old has nothing to do with it, not in the true sense of the word," Paula reminded him. He felt a little uneasy, since she was accurately touching upon a number of his own recent thoughts. "You've been front line forever!"

"Most men last three or four years in your position. Ten tops," Ted commented.

"Oh, I'll probably retire soon," Kent murmured.

"While you've got a body left?" Paula asked dryly.

"Ouch!" Ted said, laughing. "She's sure on your case tonight."

Paula sat on the other side of Anne and pushed back a sweep of her rich chestnut hair. "I'm not on his case," she protested to her husband. "I've just been watching the lineup." Paula proceeded to outline the "if they beat" path to the Superbowl. "And Kent, if you meet up with Pennsylvania, I'll really be worried."

"Because you won't know who to root for, huh?"

"No, I'm serious!" Paula declared. "That defensive tackle—what's his name, Ted?"

"Paul Crane," Ted supplied, filling his pipe with tobacco and packing it down lightly with his thumb.

Paula looked at Kent again. "That's it—Paul Crane. He's been on a lot of the sportscasts lately, saying that the only way to beat the Saxons would be to knock you and Sam Loper right out of the game."

Kent sighed and shrugged. "Oh, come on, Paula, you know a lot of the players talk that way."

"Yes," Paula insisted, "but this man means it, Kent. If you face him, he's going to try to cripple or kill you!"

"Paula, there are rules to the game," Kent reminded her gently.

"Great. They get a penalty while you're wheeled to the hospital."

"Dad won't get hurt by any big lug, will you, Dad?" Anne piped in.

He looked into her earnest eyes and gave her a hug. "I'll try not to!" Kent promised with a laugh.

"Anne, bedtime," Paula said suddenly.

"Oh, Mom, Dad just got here—"

"And I'm letting you stay out of school tomorrow because of it," Paula reminded her daughter.

Anne looked at her father pleadingly.

"Bed when your mother says so," he told her.

As a last-ditch effort Anne looked at Ted. He laughed. "You think I'm the soft spot, huh? No way. Up to bed. We've got nice things planned for tomorrow."

Anne gave up. She kissed her father, then her mother, then Ted. Emotions riddled through Kent. After Anne disappeared up the stairs, he looked at Paula and Ted.

"I really want to thank you both," he said quietly.

Ted laughed and lit his pipe. "For what?"

Kent grinned. "It isn't every man who can feel at home in his ex-wife's new home."

"Well, you're welcome any time," Paula said matter-of-factly, folding a piece of her plaid skirt. Then she looked directly at him. "But haven't you thought about having a home of your own?"

"I have two of them," Kent defended himself, "one in the Rockies and one right on the beach in Sarasota. You've seen them both—"

"And neither is a home," Paula stated. "You need a wife."

"Paula," Kent protested, looking to Ted for help. Ted shrugged.

"Paula," Kent continued, "you were there, remember? Marriage didn't work for me."

She waved a hand in the air. "We weren't suited to one another to begin with. You need someone with a little more . . . spirit, I guess is the word. A woman who fights back. I could become a cringing, soppy doormat too easily."

"You were not—"

"I was," Paula said, "or I never would have let a few newspaper articles ruin our marriage. But that's past history." She paused, then continued in a slightly different vein, "Kent, if the Saxons do go to the Superbowl, there will be a lot of reporters coming after you."

"I've already got one on my tail," Kent murmured.

"Oh?"

He shrugged, then decided he did want to talk—at least a little. "A girl—woman, that is. Dante Hudson's daughter."

"Oh!" Paula exclaimed. She was quiet for a minute. "If she wants an article, you're going to have to give it to her, Kent. You'll never forgive yourself if you don't." Paula laughed suddenly. "Wasn't she the one who scratched up your cheek?"

"The same."

"How the years fly!" Paula murmured.

"That they do, my love," Ted agreed. He gazed at Kent. "You don't sound happy about this."

"I'm not. I think that I wish she would have stayed in New York. Loper brought her out to a party the other night, and, well, Paula, you've seen a few of those parties."

Paula raised a brow. "She can't be a child anymore, Kent."

"I know, but . . ."

"Something's telling me our football hero dragged the young lady out of the party," Ted said.

"Did you?" Paula pressed, laughing.

To his embarrassment, Kent found himself blushing. "Uh, yeah, I did." He lifted his hands. "And now . . . well, now, I'm not really sure what she's up to."

"You're the Cougar," Paula reminded him.

"An old cat," he countered.

"But still the most cunning on the mountain. Maybe I should call her and warn her," Paula mused.

"Don't you dare!" Ted warned his wife.

"Well, are you going to give her an article?" Paula asked.

Kent shrugged. "I've invited her up to the Rockies next weekend."

"I definitely better call her up and warn her!" Paula exclaimed with a laugh.

"I've already tried that myself," Kent muttered. "I just wish I knew whether she deserved a warning or not. Maybe I'm the one being . . . stalked."

"Well," Paula said, "I guess I'm going to have to take your side in this one. She's a big girl now. If she comes at you with claws bared, she'll have to expect to get scratched back."

"Maybe you're right," Kent mused.

"I think I want to meet this woman," Ted said suddenly. Then Kent caught him exchanging a glance with his wife.

Am I wearing my feelings that clearly? he wondered. Both of them knew that he wanted her—and were apparently interested in the outcome.

Paula yawned. "I'm going to bed. I assume you two are going to stay up and discuss sports and the American legal system for the next hour. Just don't stay up too late. We planned a big day tomorrow for you and Annie."

"Sure, we'll turn in soon," Kent promised.

"Your bedroom is ready," Paula said. She brushed his cheek with a fond kiss, gave her husband a much more promising one, and disappeared up the stairs.

Kent did stay up with Ted for another hour, and they did discuss sports and the law.

Kent was glad of the company. Because when he did go up to the guest bedroom, he didn't sleep. He lay awake, hot and uncomfortable, consumed with thoughts of Katie Hudson.

What was she doing now? It was one o'clock here, but only ten in California. Had Sam taken her back to the hotel room? Was she safely in bed—alone? Was she dreaming of a lover? Planning on returning to one? Or were there many lovers in her life?

He groaned aloud, suddenly aware that if Katie Hudson didn't come to him, he would be going to Katie Hudson.

His prayers weren't really directed to heaven when he murmured out loud in the night—they were to an old friend.

"Dante, forgive me. All I can think about is bedding your daughter . . ."

When his own daughter slept in the same house. A pretty, bright, loving little girl . . . Just like Katie Hudson had been.

Except that his daughter still had a mother and a great stepfather. Katie's mother had deserted her after the divorce. She had spent the years with a kind but elderly aunt, and she had lived for her father . . .

Kent jumped out of bed. They were all going to think he was crazy when they heard the shower running at this time of night. He had to cool himself down somehow.

While Kent was visiting Independence Hall with his daughter, Katie was dragging herself into the sixth floor offices of *World Magazine*.

In New York it was two o'clock, but back in California it was only eleven. And after her early-morning six o'clock flight, she felt as if it were still the middle of the night—anywhere.

I stayed out with Sam too long, she decided regretfully as she attempted to give the receptionist a sunny smile and assure her that both the trip and the game had been wonderful.

Katie then hurried through the narrow corridor to her own office, a five by five patch of space that could barely hold a desk, chair, and typewriter. But then, she wasn't really on the staff yet, so she was probably lucky to have that space with its thin paneling and glass partitions.

She sat down, dropped her note pad on her desk, and put her purse in the bottom drawer, then closed her eyes and rubbed her temples, hoping that activity would give her a sudden burst of energy—or at least the desire to be alive and awake.

Julie, *World*'s tall, elegant, and nice receptionist, tapped on her door, speaking cheerfully. "Brought you some coffee, Katie. Hate to say it, but I think you need it."

Katie opened her eyes and accepted the mug with a grateful smile. The editors at *World* might not think that she was there to stay, but Julie had welcomed her. Julie had given her the *World* mug with her name scrolled across it.

"Thanks, Julie, you're a doll," Katie murmured. "I guess I'd better drink this quickly and look as if I'm doing something."

Julie waved a hand with beautifully manicured fingers in the air. "Raff is still at lunch. Sue Morgan is on the desk for me and will ring back if he shows up. I'm just dying to hear all. Tell me. What was he like?"

"Who?"

"'Who' she asks!" Julie laughed. "Kent Hart."

Katie stared at her coffee while she sipped it and shrugged. "He's . . . okay."

"You spend a weekend chasing Kent Hart, and all you have to say is that he's okay?"

"Julie, you know I didn't want to go, and you know why."

"Yes, because of your dad, and that's foolish, Katie. And if he's only 'okay,' why do you look so bad?"

Katie had to laugh. "Thanks a lot! I look so bad because I was out with Sam Loper, not Kent Hart."

"Oh! Sam Loper, now, huh? Hmm . . . well, I must say, even if he's not quite as intriguing, he's still a cutie. A real cutie. And all I ever get is stockbrokers!"

Julie moved into the room. She was about three years older than Katie and, Katie felt, much more sophisticated. She moved through life with an amused tolerance and a very shrewd intelligence.

"I didn't exactly 'get' Sam Loper," Katie replied dryly.

Julie leaned against the single bare spot on Katie's desk, arching a slim dark brow. "The young lion of the NFL takes you out, and you barely sound interested? Katie!" She laughed again. "You're dating schedule sounds like a *Who's Who* article, and you'd rather be going after ancient war heroes!"

"More character there," Katie murmured.

"So what's Loper like?" Julie pressed.

Katie could smile freely then. "A doll. A perfect gentleman. He opens car doors, watches for traffic, talks about his sisters and brothers, loves animals—"

"Kate, you sound like a mother that's proud of her son."

"That's a little how I feel about Sam."

"Six feet of bronzed muscle, the cutest tush I've ever seen, and she comes up with a maternal complex!" Julie groaned.

"You haven't asked me about the article yet," Katie reminded Julie dryly.

"Why bother? You attract football players like a free ball in the end zone. I'm sure Hart succumbed sweetly."

"No, not exactly," Katie murmured.

Julie's smile fell. "You're kidding! He refused to give you the article?"

"No, not exactly that either—"

"Oh, thank God! Raff is really set on this one."

Katie felt herself pale with tension and anger. "Damn Raff! I'm thinking the damn job isn't worth it!"

"Calm down, honey," Julie advised sympathetically. "Think past the moment, okay? The pay is good here, and you're talented. In the years to come, you could bypass Raff and then fire him! Think of it that way. Now, why don't you explain your 'not exactlys'?"

Katie sighed, finished her coffee, and set down the empty cup. "I saw Kent Hart on Saturday night and Sunday morning. He asked all the questions. If I want a real interview, I have to go to his place in the Rockies after the next game."

"Oh. Oh!" Julie started to laugh. "Well, I guess you collected Kent Hart after all!"

"Julie, it's nothing like that, I assure you," Katie said uneasily. "I think the man hates me—but he does feel he owes my father." Was that true? she wondered. Kent *acted* as if he hated her, and yet she could still feel the touch of his arms, the hardness of his body . . .

A blush rose to her cheeks when she thought about his hands on her. She closed her eyes and ran her fingers through her hair, hoping Julie wouldn't notice the heated color in her cheeks.

"Anyway," she continued, "I guess that means I head out to Denver next."

Katie's phone extension started to ring. She cast Julie a startled glance, then reached around her typewriter to catch it quickly.

"Raff's on his way," Sue Morgan told her briefly.

"Thanks," Katie said quickly.

Julie was already standing. "See you later!" she told Katie, two steps taking her to the door. "Oh"—she paused with one hand on the frame—"just a warning—Paul Crane has called you at least a dozen times. He must have thought I was lying about your being out of town." Julie hesitated. "If you're really breaking it off with him, make sure that he knows it. I don't want to sound like a mother hen, but I don't think he believes it's over between the two of you, and . . . I don't think I'd want to really tangle with his temper, if you know what I mean." Julie turned around suddenly, looking down the hall. "Raff! Look who just came in!"

"I know she's here, Julie."

The male voice sounded annoyed, but that didn't faze Julie. She winked at Katie, then strolled past the approaching man.

Raff Chapman took Julie's place in her doorway for a minute, then moved to Katie's desk, leaned against it, and crossed his arms over his chest.

"So, kid, how'd it go?"

He sounded friendly enough. But Katie knew him fairly well by now. Raphael "Raff" Chapman was a slim, attractive man in his late thirties. He always wore just the right suits, and his dark looks were impeccable. His one driving force in life was ambition; he was determined to make *World* the biggest and best publication in the country. Generally, he and Katie got along fine. He was too ambitious to be schemingly chauvinistic. She was sure that he usually didn't even see his writers or employees by gender—they were all just a work force to get *World* moving in his direction as best they could.

"Fine," Katie replied evenly.

"Have I got an article?"

"I think so. He said I could talk to him at his place in the Rockies after the next game."

"Hmmm." Raff stared at her for several moments, his dark eyes narrowed and reflective. "Good. Good."

Katie felt her temper begin to simmer as intuition told her his thoughts. He was assuming that she had started an affair with Kent Hart, and he thought it was just a fine way to get an article. Of course, he wasn't going to say so, not when he knew her thoughts on the subject.

"Good, good," he repeated as he stood up and placed a hand on her shoulder. "You shouldn't have come in right from your flight. You look tired, and you have to fly out again."

"What?" Katie demanded, shaking off his touch as she spun her chair around to stare at him.

"Sarasota. Julie will get you a dinner flight. First class. I'll see that you have all the passes you need, and I'll arrange for you to fly out to Denver with the team. I think they're going on Wednesday."

"Raff," Katie protested, "if Kent Hart starts to think of me as a leech, he won't want to talk to me!"

"You don't have to bother him. Just watch him. Observe him with his teammates. See how he really behaves in training and find out where he gets his stamina."

"Wait a minute, Raff—"

"Katie . . ."

Something about his tone caused her to pause. She actually thought there was some warmth in his eyes.

"Katie, I think you should be out of town for a while anyway. Paul Crane keeps trying to get in touch with you." He turned to leave her. "Go home and pack now. Keep me updated at least every other day—or I'll call you. Stay as long as you like in the Rockies, and if the Saxons should make the Superbowl, keep following them. Your expense account is unlimited. Okay? Good. I'll talk to you soon." He was halfway down the hall before he finished speaking.

Katie stared after him, wondering if she shouldn't throw something after him and tell him what he could do with the job.

But he had sounded concerned because of Paul Crane. Well, he should have been concerned. It had been his fault that she had gotten involved with Paul to begin with!

She half rose from her chair, then sank back to it. She was so tired! Sam had made her feel like a child again last night; they had laughed and joked, and it had all been so easy. There had been no threat of anything deeper than a friendship, and it had been so nice. After the tension of being with Kent, it had been wonderful!

Katie wasn't concerned with Paul. She had meant it when she had said she didn't want to see him again. But she was concerned with the idea of following Kent Hart. Kent was a threat, in every sense of the word. Ah, hell. What did it really matter? she asked herself with dismay. If she was going to follow him to the mountains, she might just as well get to know him a little better before taking that plunge.

Katie realized suddenly that her palms were wet, and little tremors were skating along her spine, just because she was going to Sarasota . . .

She groaned aloud and covered her face with her hands. Damn Kent Hart! He touched her, then denied her; loved her, then despised her. She didn't know herself around him.

And yesterday . . . yesterday he had made a point of seeing her. He had taken her into his arms, kissed her as if she were everything in his world, then practically told her she was a prostitute for a story and hurried off because he'd had previous plans. And the greatest insult to her self-esteem was that after all that she'd been riddled with jealousy because his plans had most assuredly involved another woman.

"Damn!" She slammed a fist down on her desk—and with the action the tremors left her. Kent Hart was not going to best her. Not in any way, shape, or form. She was going to get her story, and she was going to walk away without hesitating.

He might be Kent Hart, the illustrious Cougar, but she was Dante Hudson's daughter.

CHAPTER SIX

Katie was glad when the phone rang. She had almost fallen asleep in the hot bubble bath she had decided to indulge in before boarding a plane again.

Dripping water and bubbles, she grabbed a towel and hurried from the bath to the phone on the nightstand in her bedroom. Certain that it was Julie calling with some last-minute instructions, she wanted to beat her answering machine to the punch.

But then, when silence at first greeted her breathless greeting, she grew uneasy.

Rightfully so.

"Katie? You *are* there. Those liars at that *World* office said you were out of town again!"

She held the phone away from her ear at the sound of the angrily shouted words.

"Paul. Hi," she murmured, wishing that she'd left the answering machine on. "I am going out of town again in less than an hour. I . . . did get your messages. I planned on calling you later."

"Long distance?" he asked bitingly.

"Paul, *this* is long distance."

"Not that long a distance."

"Long distance is long distance."

"Stop it, Katie. You know what I mean!"

She went rigid, considering the possibility of just hanging

up on him. But Julie had been right—Paul Crane didn't believe that she had called it quits for good.

"Katie?"

"Yes?" she inquired dully.

"I—I called to apologize." That was said softly, contritely.
Katie closed her eyes tiredly and lay back on her bed, envi-
sioning the man who was speaking. Paul was a respected
tackle on the Philadelphia team, a man of the hour just like
Kent Hart, because his team was also a likely prospect for the
Superbowl.

Katie's second article for *World* had been a short spot on
the Philadelphia Titans, the team that had looked like gold
since the preseason. It had been early fall when she and Julie
had driven down to Pennsylvania, attended a practice session,
and met the players.

Julie had spent the drive convincing Katie that she was a
fool, stereotyping people in a cruel and uncharacteristic manner by claiming that she hated football players in general.

And maybe—just maybe—she had begun to date Paul in
order to prove Julie wrong. Or maybe she had just decided she
liked Paul. Katie *had* liked him. He'd been as pleasant as his
blond all-American good looks. He had driven to New York
for their first date, and they had spent the day at the Metro-
politan. On their second date they'd gone to dinner. Next,
they'd attended a play, then a hockey game.

But somewhere in there she'd known—or perhaps it had
been from the very beginning—that he just wasn't right for
her. Katie always had the strange feeling that she was some
kind of challenge to Paul. And last week, when she'd been to a
celebration party with him, he'd decided to put the pressure
on. The majority of his teammates were all necking with their
dates, necking with more enthusiasm in public than Katie
would have enjoyed had she been with the absolute prince of
her dreams.

Paul was—according to football statistics—six feet three
and two hundred and sixty-five pounds; fighting him off was

not her idea of a pleasant evening out, especially when he'd been drinking a little too much. When he'd realized she was going to make a scene and embarrass him in front of his friends, he had at last driven her home, going from Pennsylvania to New York in record time and swearing abuses the entire way.

No man, he'd told her, would tolerate "her kind" of female. She was one entire female lie with blond hair and curves; dating her was like dating a cold-blooded fish.

Katie hadn't even answered him. She'd listened to him, gotten out of the car, and told him that she didn't want to see him again.

"Katie, dammit, are you listening to me? I know I was drinking too much . . . I know the atmosphere was a little crazy. But listen, honey, I'm not really an exhibitionist myself, you know? I was wrong, Katie. I should have taken you someplace quiet where we could have been alone. Katie . . . we were seeing each other enough just to make me crazy—do you understand?"

She sighed at last. "I understand. I like you, Paul, but it's just not—"

"Oh, good, you're not mad anymore."

"Paul, it isn't a matter of 'mad.' Don't you see? The chemistry wasn't there. We wouldn't have made it anyway."

" 'Wouldn't have made it'? 'Chemistry'?" he repeated as if she had clearly lost her mind. "You don't need ten miles of chemistry and forever afters to behave normally and follow a little instinct!"

"Paul, that's what I mean. We're on opposite wavelengths—"

"No, Katie, don't you understand? I can have lots of women—"

Good for you, she decided silently, glancing at her watch while he rattled on. She had to hurry to make it to the airport on time.

Then she started to wonder if the things he was saying

might not be true? Was she a cold fish? No! She didn't feel cold at all when Kent Hart touched her.

Paul was trying to apologize—in his way. He just couldn't imagine anyone not falling over backward to be with him.

"Paul," she interrupted him, "I really have to go."

"Katie, this can't be it. I have to talk to you . . . I have to see you in person."

"Okay, okay," she said rashly. "I'll see you as soon as I get back. I'll call you."

"Alone, Katie, please. Give me a chance, and we'll work things out."

"I'll talk to you, Paul. That's my only promise—"

"Oh, it will be more than that!" he assured her with a smug chuckle.

"Paul—"

He hung up on her. Katie stared at the phone in amazement. Damn. She should have made herself clear. To let him think there was the slightest possibility of any kind of a future between the two of them hadn't been fair or right.

She sighed. It probably didn't matter very much. He was probably only interested in her because she wasn't willing to fall at his feet. He would get over her quickly. She smiled. It would likely be insulting just how quickly he *would* get over her.

But will I get over Kent Hart? she found herself wondering.

"You've no right to 'get over' the man—you barely know him, and you don't want to know him!" she told herself out loud.

It was a lie. In a few short days living had become a lie.

Katie stood and finished drying herself, then prayed she had enough clean clothing to pack all over again. She dragged her suitcase out, then suddenly stopped, still in her towel, and walked out to the small living room in her apartment.

Yes, it was small but nice, abounding with plants and books and antique picture frames. She'd worked hard on the apartment, just as she'd worked hard on her life since her father's

112

death. She'd been so far behind women her age. All that she had been able to do was attempt to take giant steps forward, with career goals in mind.

And now . . . now it all seemed so cold, as if she'd been afraid of warmth. But when Dante had died, she'd had nothing more than herself and a determination to survive.

Katie felt hot tears spring to her eyes; she brushed them away furiously. Oh, God, this was getting ridiculous! She hadn't cried since the day she had buried Dante until the other night, and now she was at it again! Everything was out of proportion. Her steadfast plan for life was wobbling all around her. And it had been a good plan, she assured herself; she hadn't even questioned it until she'd seen Kent Hart again.

He made her think, and he made her feel. He made her yearn for unknown things she hadn't known she was missing.

Katie grated her teeth together.

"I will get over him," she commanded herself out loud. "I will best him, and I will get over him."

"You don't like football players," she reminded herself.

But when she was at last out of her apartment and in a cab to Kennedy Airport, she admitted to herself that a lot of her thinking represented misconceptions and cop-outs. She didn't dislike football or football players—she disliked what had happened to her father.

Her involvement with Paul hadn't been Raff's fault—it had been her own. And if she became any more deeply involved with Kent Hart—well, that would be her own fault, too.

Thinking about it made her heart pound quickly. Her palms grew damp, and liquid shivers ran along her back. She swallowed. For the first time in her life, Katie didn't know what she wanted. Yes, she knew what she wanted, but she didn't dare admit it to herself. She wanted Kent Hart to touch her again, to sear her lips with his kisses.

Don't even think that way, Katie! she warned herself. What

happened to the calm, cool soul who despised the man with a totally analytical mind?

She shook her head slightly with disgust as she realized that she was at the airport. She paid her cab driver, turned in her luggage for a claim check, and hurried to the check-in counter.

She was dismayed to discover that her flight was not direct. There was a stop at Philadelphia with a thirty-minute layover. She would arrive not in Sarasota but in Tampa, where she could arrange for a car for the thirty- to sixty-minute drive south to Sarasota. It was ridiculous, but being in the dead of winter, everyone seemed to be traveling south, and it was the only flight she was going to get. Well, she thought, at least Raff had arranged for her to travel first-class.

Once seated on the wide-bodied jet, Katie kicked off her shoes, ordered a rum and Coke, and leaned back to relax. She decided immediately that she liked the first-class section of the airplane. The chair was comfortable enough to nap in, and she was, for the moment, all alone. Economy was filled, but first class was empty enough for each person to be alone in his or her two-seat row.

She wasn't quite as thrilled when the jet took off and the pilot announced that the wind currents were rough, apologizing pleasantly for the inconvenience. Katie listened to every nuance of his voice. Did he sound scared? No. She decided to watch the stewardesses. As long as they kept smiling, it had to be okay.

But still she couldn't relax. By the time the plane set down in Philadelphia, she had to argue with herself to keep from crawling off it—and she flew all the time.

She ordered another drink, deciding she'd just spend the night in Tampa and drive to Sarasota in the morning; halfway inebriated was going to be the only way to endure the rest of the trip.

She sipped at her drink as the passengers from Philadelphia boarded the plane, staring out the window as men added baggage below. She barely noticed at first when a coat was tossed on the seat beside her; when she did, she was just mildly annoyed that she wouldn't have privacy for the second leg of the flight.

Then she saw the arms that had tossed the coat down—and the face and body attached to those arms.

"Oh, no!" she gasped. She wasn't at all sure if the groan that followed was one of horror because she was totally unprepared for a confrontation and growing languorous from the rum or because, with one simple look, Kent Hart had made her ridiculously warm and nervous.

Kent was as surprised as she, but his reaction held no confusion whatsoever; he was annoyed. He didn't take his seat. He stood in the aisle to rail at her, his hands on his hips.

"What the hell are you doing here?" he demanded icily.

Katie braced herself and tried for a frosty smile to match his tone. "Flying," she flipped sarcastically.

"Damn. What did they assign you to be . . . a leech?"

"Don't be absurd. How could I have possibly known you were going to be on this plane?"

"Because reporters are worse than private eyes," he retorted angrily. "You probably got the information from Sam. You just couldn't stand it when I walked away from your almighty interview for something else in my life!"

"Oh, my God!" Katie said low and heatedly. "You are a sick, arrogant bastard! You're the last thing in the world I'd discuss with Sam Loper, and I really couldn't give a damn where you go or what you do!" Her voice—as always around him, it seemed—began to rise. Katie lowered it again quickly when she saw a stewardess coming toward them. More people were boarding the plane, and Kent made a large obstacle in the aisle.

The pretty stewardess spoke to Kent, her dimples flashing as she smiled. "Mr. Hart, is anything wrong? Perhaps we could arrange for different seating if there's a problem?"

115

Katie didn't know why, but she would have been absolutely mortified if he had asked for another seat.

He didn't. Nor did he seem to respond to the gushing stewardess. He muttered out a "Sorry!," ran a hand through his hair, and sank into his seat.

He stared straight ahead. Katie stared straight ahead. People continued to board the plane. She heard people muttering excitedly after they'd passed them, people who recognized Kent. But they all seemed discreet; no one stopped to demand an autograph. The only bad moment that occurred was when two teenagers went by. Delayed in the aisle just behind Katie and Kent, the two girls began to whisper and giggle.

"God! Is he handsome!"

"Oh, much better in the flesh!"

"What a body!"

Katie felt like smirking—she knew Kent was suffering a severe flash of embarrassment.

But her turn was coming. No one, it seemed, was safe from the girls' speculations and observations.

"What about the woman?"

"Think she's his wife? She could be . . . she's something, too. Think she's a real blond?"

"Don't be silly—her hair is obviously bleached! And he's not married, so you know she has to be his mistress! Or a 'fly by night affair'!"

"Well, she's lucky anyway . . ."

Lucky? Katie thought. She wanted to die! No, no—it wasn't that serious, she amended in what constituted a silent prayer. One didn't even think the word "die" when flying on a night like this!

I want to crawl under a chair . . . that's what I want to do! she thought. Not die, God. I didn't mean that!

She felt Kent's eyes on her, so strongly that she had to turn to him. She was certain that she would snap something out . . .

But there was amusement in his eyes. It was so apparent that they had both heard the girls.

She didn't yell or snap. She started laughing.

He reached out and touched her hair, curling a strand around his finger. "Is it bleached?" he asked with mock seriousness.

"Does it look bleached?" she demanded dryly. At least he was talking about her hair, she thought with relief—he could have picked up on the giggled words relating to their sexual status.

"I don't know," he said slowly. "I'll think about it."

Katie tugged the lock back from his grasp. "Don't touch. People who accuse me of vile things are not allowed to touch."

She realized how badly her words sounded the minute they were out of her mouth. She saw the corners of his mouth twitch, and she knew that she was in trouble. He lowered his head and leaned toward her so that he was almost whispering in her ear. "If I say nice things, I get to touch? Is that rule just for me—or anyone?"

A rush of blood heated Katie's cheeks, and she almost cracked her plastic glass, the tension in her fingers was so great.

"Get your head over in your air space, will you please, Mr. Hart?"

"What are you doing here, then?"

"I told you—flying."

"It has nothing to do with me?"

She snapped her head around so quickly that he felt the touch of her hair against his cheek.

"Obviously it has to do with you. I'm on my way to Florida, but I had no idea you'd be on this flight."

His eyes were very intent and dark. A frown was deeply etched into his brow; he was tense but thoughtful. Returning his stare, Katie inadvertently did a little assessing herself. He was exceptionally striking tonight. His dark hair was a little damp, as if he had recently showered, jaw newly shaven and pleasantly scented with a soap or cologne that spoke subtly of something very male. He looked rested and almost relaxed. His jeans hugged his lean hips and long, sinewed legs; the tailored shirt beneath his gray cardigan was light and contrasted with the healthy bronze glow of his features. His mouth was compressed, too severe now, but when he did smile . . .

Her heart skipped a beat.

He sighed at last, folded his hands together, and shrugged. "It would be interesting to know exactly when you were telling the truth."

"I really don't run around lying," Katie retorted.

"Isn't it a lie every time you smile—at me?" he asked.

She sighed with exasperation. "I do have a sense of humor."

"Oh, I'm sure you do," he murmured cryptically.

A minute later they were taxiing out to the runway, and a flash of lightning suddenly arced through the sky. Katie cringed, digging her fingernails into the seat and closing her eyes. It was all she could do to keep from screaming.

The plane came to a stop, and the pilot came on the air to announce that due to delays from the weather conditions they would be on the ground awhile longer.

Kent noticed Katie's hand first as it gripped the plush divider between them. Her nails, long with that peach and bronze polish, were digging into the upholstery. Then his gaze moved from her long, sexy legs to her blue A-line skirt and her soft silky blue blouse. It was then that he noticed her ashen face. Her eyes, reflecting the blue of her outfit, were huge in her pale and delicately lovely face. She was sitting stiffly, not about to bend.

And more than he had ever longed to do so before, he wished he could reach out and hold her, promise her that it would be all right.

"Are you afraid of flying?" he asked quietly.

"No—not usually," she replied with a little smile.

Kent gave her a small smile. He couldn't resist the temptation—the ache in his heart to reassure her was overwhelming. He placed his hand over hers, dwarfing it, then tugged it from its viselike grip on the armrest and held it warmly.

For a moment he felt resistance. Then she seemed to give in with relief. Her fingers curled around his.

"It won't be that bad," he whispered to her, and she nodded.

The wait wasn't that long. The plane began to taxi again, the stewardesses took their seats, and they were soon up in the air. The pilot's voice came to them again, warning in a casual, reassuring tone that it was going to be a slightly bumpy ride. They were free to move about the aircraft but should keep their safety belts fastened when seated.

Kent tugged slightly at Katie's hand. "Want another drink?"

She moistened her lips. "Please."

The stewardess rushed to them quickly when Kent lifted his hand. To Katie's annoyance the pair began to carry on a flirtation—at her expense. Kent explained that Katie had suddenly acquired "flying nerves."

To Katie's mind, it took the stewardess too long to stop laughing and go about her business.

Kent caught her eyes, his own filled with mischief. "What's wrong?"

"Nothing."

"Ah, come on, Katie. You're angry. Oh—I'm sorry. I guess it looks bad. Me chatting with our brunette friend when I seem to be with you."

"Don't be absurd." Katie acquired the presence of mind to jerk her hand from his. She stared at him, dangerous sparks crystallizing in her eyes. "You forget that I traveled with my father. You'll never acquire his following, Mr. Hart."

Kent laughed easily. When the stewardess brought their drinks, he merely thanked her. Katie's temper wasn't appeased; the smile that accompanied his thanks could melt steel.

"How was dinner with Sam?" he suddenly asked.

"Fine," she said shortly. "But if I'm supposed to be the spy, what are you doing with all the information?"

"Sam mentioned dinner to me."

Katie didn't respond. The airplane suddenly dropped, leaving her stomach up where it had been.

"It was just an air pocket," Kent assured her gently. Katie finished her drink quickly. The rum burned her entire system, but at least it seemed to replace the organs she could have sworn she had lost.

"This could be a fun evening," Kent teased her.

"A fun evening?" She shouldn't have gulped down the drink—her head was spinning madly.

"Or many evenings . . . your choice."

Katie looked at him. His eyes were very dark, sparkling with mischief. He was excessively handsome, though, and his voice was doing things to her spine again. Or was it just that her head was spinning so badly? She gave him a wicked smile in return, one that just touched her lips.

"What are you talking about?"

"Let me see, what were your choices? You can be my mistress, or a 'fly by night affair.' What's your pleasure?"

"Another drink to dump over your head," Katie said sweetly. But she wasn't feeling at all vengeful.

They were interrupted, as dinner was brought. Something really nice with steak and seafood. Katie knew she couldn't eat. First-class food and she couldn't eat, she thought woefully. But she really couldn't, and so as Kent commented on how delicious it all was, she stared out the window, telling him he was welcome to enjoy hers, too.

"Thanks, but no thanks."

"Hey, you're a growing football player."

"No—I'm full-grown already. Too grown to overeat."

The trays had just been taken away when it seemed that a

vicious bolt of lightning came near to wrenching the plane from the sky. Katie paused and shut her eyes. Kent took her hand again.

"Honey, it really is safe," he whispered gently.

"Then why do so many planes crash?"

" 'So many' don't," he told her.

As if on cue to his words, the bumpy rise and pitch of the plane seemed to cease. Katie opened her eyes.

"We're flying out of it," he told her. "Want another drink?"

"Yes," she murmured. "No—I shouldn't."

He shrugged. "What are you worried about?"

"Stumbling off the plane."

She felt a tremendous warmth from his smile. "I'll carry you."

His shoulder seemed very large and very strong. She didn't think about it, though; she just leaned her head against him. "Maybe I should sleep."

He laughed. She heard him thanking the stewardess again, and then he was pressing another drink into her hand.

"Finish that and take a nap. You haven't got anything to worry about. You were planning on following me to Sarasota anyway—I'll drive you instead."

Katie smiled languorously and sipped her drink. The plane seemed to be staying in the air, she was becoming drowsy, and she felt that she had all the security and strength she might need from the warm, muscled body that sheltered hers. Had she really clawed him once? It all seemed so silly now.

She finished her drink and pressed the glass back into his hands, fumbling a little as her eyes were half closed. He accepted it wordlessly. She curled more comfortably into her chair, using his chest and shoulder as a pillow.

She barely felt his fingers stroking through her hair. It was just a soft caress, as sweet as the sleepy euphoria seeping over her. His warmth, the beat of his heart, the rise and fall of his breath—all served to give her greater comfort.

She must have slept, because she was startled when she

heard him clearing his throat. Then he picked up her hand, and she realized it had been lying intimately on his inner thigh. Very intimately.

She started to rise in horror, a deep blush staining her cheeks.

Kent laughed and caught the nape of her neck, pressing her back against him. "Relax, Katie. You're fine. I was just suffering a minor torture."

Katie closed her eyes and kept her head against him; it was better than facing him.

She felt his lips gently nuzzling her hair and cheek. "Oh, I can't wait to get you home."

She let out a strangled gasp but felt the laughter in him again, mocking her swift, outraged reaction. She sat up and stared at him; he moved the divider between them and slipped an arm around her, pulling her down to rest more comfortably.

"Sorry," he murmured. "My word of honor—I've no intention of attacking you. Tonight anyway. Go back to sleep."

His hand was on her back, his fingers moving soothingly, seductively along the length of her spine. Nice, so nice. If she were a cat, she would be purring. And yet . . . it was exciting, too. She didn't want to sleep; she wanted to luxuriate in that thrilling touch.

She closed her eyes and tried to fight the feeling. She was being such a fool. Katie started to move, wondering if he could sense her fear.

"Katie!" His exasperated murmur was soft, actually gentle. "Honey, I swear to you that I'm not going to attack." He was silent for just a second, then his voice came to her again, even more softly, more huskily: "When I do attack, you're going to be awake—and totally aware of every little move I make, reciprocating touch for touch."

She opened her eyes, wanting to tell him he could whistle "Dixie" for a year and she wouldn't reciprocate a thing.

But she didn't. She just lay there in a bit of a haze and

studied his features. His dark eyes were intent on hers, there was a slight curl to his mouth, and the character etched in fine lines about his ruggedly carved face was fascinating.

"What were you doing in Philadelphia?" she asked suddenly.

He smiled. His dark lashes fell over his eyes for a second, and when they opened again, it was only halfway. They carried a demonlike glow of fiery amusement. Sexy, Katie thought. And sensual . . .

"You really don't know?"

"No." Her eyes met his, sapphire radiance combined with an earth-green honesty. A slight shudder coursed through him. Dear Lord, he thought, Dante Hudson had created a beautiful child. A child who was a woman now. Dazzling, stunning . . . warm and alive against his body and soul.

He brushed a lock of her hair from her cheek, smoothing it over his leg. "I went to see my daughter."

"Oh," Katie said, and smiling very smugly, she closed her eyes and went back to sleep.

CHAPTER SEVEN

Katie woke up feeling lethargic. Beyond her spacious room she could hear the languorous roll and lash of gulf waves. She smiled. She was right on the beach. The hotel was an expensive one, but Kent, in bringing her here, had reminded her that since *World* was determined she get the story, *World* deserved to pick up the tab.

Katie carefully opened her eyes. The drapes kept the light muted in the room, but she assumed it was early morning. She closed her eyes again, wondering if the lethargy would recede. Well, if not, it was simply the price she had to pay—and well worth it because she hadn't screamed out loud at any of the lightning.

And yet she knew that it had been more than four rum and Cokes that had kept her calm. It had been Kent.

"Katie, girl, you've lost your mind, your senses, your reason, and your logic!" she whispered aloud, but she was smiling indolently as she did so. Kent Hart, beloved of the multitudes, was being very decent toward her, and she, in return, had done an absolute somersault. She was in dangerous territory. God alone knew how many women he had touched, but he had touched her, too, and not even a hangover could keep her from feeling as if she were drifting in the clouds.

She shook her head slightly, trying to remember why she had hated him so much at the start. Because of her father. But her father, too, had loved Kent.

I do not love him, she told herself strenuously. I have just decided that I can find this assignment a lot more fun than simply bearable.

Katie forced herself to sit up, and as she did so she sobered suddenly. She had gotten to where she could think of nothing else but Kent Hart, and that wasn't good. She wasn't a fool; she knew there couldn't be anything between them. If and when she fell in love, it was going to be with one of Julie's stockbrokers—an armchair quarterback, the type of guy who had some friends over to the house for the big games, then turned in his sweatshirt for a three-piece suit on Monday morning. Someone stable, capable of loving only one woman —and all in one piece.

There was a knock on her door. Katie frowned, aware that a curious thrill danced like quicksilver into her system. Was it Kent? No, it couldn't be. Kent Hart was probably at his house, sipping coffee, eating a nutritious breakfast, and dressing for practice.

The knock sounded again. "Room service!"

Katie crawled out of bed, rummaged at the foot of it for her robe, and moved to the door. Her head took only one dangerous lurch, but her frown embedded itself more deeply into her forehead. She hadn't ordered room service.

She opened the top latch, and the thrill left her system. The young man standing outside her doorway was dressed in the hotel's neat red and blue uniform.

"Good morning," the young man greeted cheerfully.

"Good morning," Katie responded, "but I didn't call for room service."

The young man laughed. "It was called in last night, compliments of Kent Hart."

"Oh," Katie murmured.

"May I bring the cart in?"

"Oh, of course."

Katie opened the door and moved into the room. The man pushed in the cart and dexterously pulled the vanity chair before it. He lifted a silver cover.

"Bacon, eggs, potatoes, muffins, orange juice—and lots and lots of coffee. That was the order." He touched the chair again, pulling it so that Katie might take a seat. "Miss Hudson?"

Katie gazed at him as she took the chair. He was young—no more than nineteen, she guessed—and he was watching her with a speculative fascination. She realized that he was making the same assumption the giggling girls on the plane last night had—that she was either Kent's mistress or a "fly by night" affair. And looking at her now, Katie thought dryly, the young man was trying to divine just what Kent Hart saw in her; she was surely showing the effects of constant travel and a bit too much to drink the night before.

"Thank you," she murmured, taking the chair.

"My name is Mike," he told her.

"Thank you, Mike." Katie reached for the coffeepot, but Mike was quick to serve her. She thought then that he was waiting for a tip.

"Let me find my purse—" she began, but Mike cut her off.

"Oh, no, Miss Hudson. Everything is taken care of."

She gazed at him curiously, but not so curiously that she wasn't reaching for the coffee. The languor she felt was becoming annoying.

And apparently her direct gaze was a little disconcerting, because Mike suddenly flushed.

"I'm sorry. I just assume that you know him rather well, and I was hoping—I know this is really presumptuous and awful, but could you get his signature for me on a jersey?"

Katie laughed. "Sure." She realized then that her easy comment had probably just branded her as something that she wasn't. She quickly added, "I really don't know Kent that well. I'm a reporter doing an article on him. But I don't think he'd mind signing a jersey for you."

"Thanks!" Mike said eagerly. Katie saw that he didn't believe a word about her not knowing Kent well. She shrugged, knowing she would only get herself in deeper by protesting more.

"Oh," Mike added, pausing as he opened her door to let himself out, "there's a note on the tray."

Katie nodded and looked down to see the envelope with her name written in large but surprisingly legible cursive letters. She ignored it, sipping her coffee until Mike was out of the room.

The liquid shivers had begun in her heart again. When the door closed, she picked up the note.

It was brief, but it held a hint of . . . something. Something she just wanted to accept and not question. She read the few sentences over twice:

Katie,
Thought you could use the coffee. Team meeting in the morning—why not head for the beach? Practice in the afternoon at the stadium if you want to be there. We're on curfew, but early dinner if you'd like.

Kent

Katie refolded the note and smiled, then became annoyed with herself for smiling. I'm falling for this man, she thought, and that is a stupid, stupid thing to do. He's a charmer—but he's also a dangerous man. The Cougar, sleek and beautiful, but always watchful, shrewd, and alert. He was toying with her. Like a cat with a mouse. When he was ready, he would leave her, clawed and bleeding . . .

No! she protested in silence. She was Dante's daughter, and she couldn't believe that he hadn't cared for her father.

But, she reminded herself soberly, he had also told her that he believed she was willing to do anything for her story. She had to prove him wrong—and keep her head ruling her actions as she did so.

Katie drank two cups of coffee before starting on her food, then decided that she was ravenous.

As she ate she decided to follow Kent's suggestion. It might be winter in the rest of the world, but the day was a balmy seventy-five, and she was going to acquire a bit of a tan. Then she could go to the stadium and quiz his teammates about him.

It was about three o'clock when Kent saw her, and she looked like a spring breeze. Her dress was a white shirtwaist, belted in bold red. She had acquired a rosy glow from a morning in the sun, and the white against her flesh was stunning. Her sandals were red, as were her striking earrings, her bag, and the ribbon that held her hair back in a gold cascade.

He almost missed the pass that was being thown to him. The ball was thrown straight into his chest by Timmons, the second-string quarterback. All Kent had to do was gasp and clutch to receive it. It did, however, take him a second too long to start running, so he really had to double up his effort to avoid his own defense.

Someone—Coach Griffith, he thought—called out that they could take a break. Panting, Kent buckled down to rest on the balls of his feet. Timmons said something to him; he smiled in return. A second later he saw that Sam was headed his way.

Sam was a mess. The coaches would cool down so as not to injure their own players once they reached Denver, but today they were trying to prove how hard the game of football could be. Sam had been up and down like a yo-yo; his jersey and pants were stained in a hundred places, and his features were slick with sweat and grime.

"You look like hell," Kent told him.

"Yeah, but I look like younger hell than you," Sam retorted. He started to hunch down like Kent, lost his balance, and landed hard on his rear with a shrug that clearly stated that as exhausted as he was, it didn't matter.

Sam wiped a hand across his eyes and looked at Kent. "She's here, you know. Hudson's daughter."

Kent grinned. "Yeah, I know. I invited her."

"You did? Well, good for you." He paused a minute. "You know, you're really testing friendship, Kent. I exercised self-control to the limit the other night—after you kidnapped *my* date from the party."

Kent laughed. "You know damned well why I rushed her out of that party."

Sam shrugged. "Yeah, I do, and that's why I wasn't mad. So what's the story with you two?"

Kent grinned. "I don't know." He paused a minute, then said, "Want to come to dinner tonight?"

Sam laughed. "I'm not allowed to come to the Rockies, but I'm being invited to come to dinner? I don't get it."

"I don't either," Kent muttered. But he did. Every time he saw Katie he was more tempted to . . . something. Having Sam around would keep him in check—and keep them both from falling into another argument. He was playing for time.

"Yeah, I'd like to come," Sam said. He glanced shrewdly at Kent. "But what are you up to? You're dragging me along for good measure now, but you want to be alone with her at the cabin. I'm supposed to remember she's off limits, but you're out to seduce her."

"No, I'm not."

"Bull!"

"I'm not," Kent protested calmly. "I'm out to see if she's determined to seduce me."

"Same difference, isn't it?" Sam asked dryly.

"No," Kent told him quietly, "not in this case."

One of the coaches called them. Groaning a little, they rose and went back to work.

Later, Kent saw Katie briefly before he headed into the showers. She flashed him a smile that made every one of his muscles shudder and grow taut.

"Working hard?" she teased.

He grimaced. She might look and smell like spring, but he was about as fresh as week-old bread.

"Yeah, we've been working hard. Are you hungry?"

"Hmm, I could be."

"Sam's coming to dinner with us."

"How nice." She said the words with enthusiasm, but she looked a little perplexed.

He smiled. "Have you been working hard?"

"Very. I talked to your owner, your manager, two of the coaches, two front ends, a tackle, and a right guard. So far I haven't gotten one of them to say anything nasty about you."

Kent laughed. "Team loyalty. What do you want? Besides, you're a reporter—you'll figure out something nasty to say all by yourself."

Her smile seemed to freeze, but Kent felt no regret for his words. He'd been the route before and was convinced that his words were true. But he was peculiarly annoyed, and he wasn't sure if it was with her or with himself. "See you soon," he told her briefly, and he left her in the bleachers and headed for the showers.

The showers were almost empty. Well, Kent thought with a shrug, it made sense. Husbands were anxious to get home to their families; the single guys were in a hurry to either relax or make a little time on their last night home. By tomorrow night they'd all be in Denver.

But Sam was still there—in what appeared to be a somnambulant state in the shower.

"Hey, don't drown," Kent warned him, grabbing a huge bar of soap.

"Hmm?" Sam asked, startled. "Oh . . . Kent. I was just thinking."

"About what?"

"Gambling." He turned to Kent. "You know, last Sunday some of the guys took a junket out to Vegas."

"Yeah?"

130

"They say there's already a lot of money going down on the playoffs and the Superbowl."

Kent shrugged and watched Sam curiously with narrowed eyes. "There's always a lot of money going down on the games."

Sam shook his head. "I mean real big money. Vegas kind of money. And it seems we're supposed to hit the Superbowl along with the Titans. Then the betting is going against us."

"Oh, yeah?" Kent said dryly.

"Yeah." Sam hesitated. "There's a rumor going around that some of the guys have been approached."

"Our teammates? You mean to throw the game if we should happen to take the lead?"

"Yeah," Sam replied. "I don't think anyone would throw the game. Business types don't always understand that the playing and winning can mean more than money to most guys. But . . ."

"But what?"

Sam shrugged and wrinkled his face beneath the running water. Then he shook his head, spraying droplets. "There are rumors that some of the Titans' players have been approached with big bucks to kill the quarterback—and the Cougar."

A ripple of unease touched Kent's spine. He dipped his own head beneath the running water, then shook it strenuously. The water felt good. He gazed over at Sam. "They're always out to get us, Sammy—that's half the name of the game."

"This just has a more vicious ring to it," Sam murmured.

"Yeah, well, we haven't reached the Superbowl yet," Kent said dismissively. "If and when we do, well, we'll just have to watch out, right? Come on—we've got a lady waiting on dinner out there."

Dinner that night was one of the nicest occasions of her life, Katie decided halfway through the meal. She was with two of the handsomest men she'd ever met, and they were both on extraordinary behavior, carrying the conversation ball lightly, laughing, filling her in on all sorts of little quips and game plays.

The food was good. They had come to a little out-of-the-way fish place in what seemed to be the middle of an orange grove. It was an all-you-can-eat shrimp night, and she learned that football players could eat enormous amounts of shrimp. Some of the other guys on the team were already there when they had arrived, a few with their families. Katie wondered how the place could stay in business when Sam told her with a wink that the owner was a real Saxon fan, and that he had his all-you-can-eat nights just for the players.

"Wait until we lose a big game," Kent said dryly. "These feasts will probably end quickly then."

"Hey—who said we're going to lose?" Sam retorted.

A teammate stopped by their table then, a young man with enormous, powerful arms. He had a nice farm-fresh face and a huge smile. Katie searched her mind quickly for his name. Patterson! Bobby Patterson, that was it. He was first-string offense, along with Kent, a friendly, pleasant man she had talked to at the party—before Kent had hauled her out.

"Hi, Katie," he greeted her. "Hear you're traveling out with the team tomorrow."

"Am I?" she asked lightly. Raff had promised to fix it, but he was great for making promises that he really expected her to arrange on her own.

Kent was watching her thoughtfully, she sensed. He nodded to her, picking up his beer to take a sip.

"I think you're a lucky charm," Bobby told her, smiling, then turned his attention to Kent. "Heard some talk from the coaches today that they were going to prime you to go in as quarterback—just in case Sam has any problems."

"What?" Kent asked sharply.

Bobby lowered his voice. "I don't think I was supposed to hear it, but I think there's some worry about Sam."

Sam and Kent exchanged quick glances.

"For the game this week?" Kent fired quickly at Bobby.

Bobby shook his head as he leaned over the table. "I don't know what's going on," he said, his voice low. "I mean, there's always talk about killing the quarterback, but it seems the coaches are really worried this time. They need you where you are—but they're gonna train you with Sam here, too."

"Thanks for telling us, Bobby," Kent said.

Bobby rose and patted Sam on the shoulder. Sam watched him walk away with a raised brow. "I'm not that easy to get!" he exclaimed indignantly.

Kent stared at Sam, then he shrugged. "I think we need a team meeting."

The two seemed to exchange something secret in their gazes. Katie was perplexed. She knew Bobby had been right about the "kill the quarterback" talk; it was always rampant before a big game, especially when the quarterback was a Sam Loper with a golden throwing arm and notoriously fast feet.

"Why you?" she asked Kent suddenly. "You're not a quarterback."

He took a long draught of his beer. "No, but I was once." He sat reflectively for a minute, then looked at Sam. "They're really reaching if they're even thinking of using me as a substitute."

"Not really. You came from the draft as a quarterback."

"That," Kent stated flatly, "was years ago." He threw his napkin on the table. "Are you two finished?"

Katie wasn't really—she would have loved coffee, but there was a darkly brooding expression on his face that warned her his mood was a dangerous one. And she didn't feel like tackling an argument tonight. She pushed back her chair and stood.

Both he and Sam were quiet on the drive back to her hotel. And Kent was distracted when he walked her to her door. He didn't touch her when he said good night. All he did was warn her to lock her door.

By the next day his mood had changed completely. Fans had come from miles around to see the Saxons off at the airport, and then they were in a chartered jet, ready to head out for Denver.

Katie found herself between Sam and Kent. She had Mike the bellboy's jersey with her, and she not only got Kent's signature on it, but Kent sent the jersey flying around, and the whole team signed it.

If nothing else, she would have been instrumental in making one bellboy very happy. She'd mail it back to him as soon as they reached Denver.

If nothing else? she wondered starkly. No—she'd turned her own life completely around. The bitterness she had held on to for years was gone. She'd hated Kent Hart from a distance. And now . . . now, like the fool she kept denying herself to be, she was falling under his spell. She might not hate him anymore—she had given up that childhood grudge with remarkable ease—but damn! He was experienced, and she had entered the arena with cool and remote confidence, only to discover that she was playing with fire.

Still, she couldn't deny the softening. She didn't want to fight with him anymore. The past—her love for her father—would never leave her. But the Kent she knew now had little to do with that past.

She glanced up, aware that he was watching her with his intense dark eyes.

"How are you doing?"

"Pardon?" she murmured with a frown, then she said, "Oh," aware that he was referring to the fact that their plane had just risen into the air. "I—I'm fine. Relaxed," she told him, smiling. "I'm not afraid of flying per se, just flying in bad weather."

A hint of demonic mischief touched his eyes. "If you change your mind, you're welcome to my lap."

"Thanks," she murmured, coloring despite herself.

"Could you lay off the sensual innuendos?" Sam complained good-naturedly from her other side. "I must be crazy spending time as a chaperon between the two of you. You're wrecking my libido."

Kent laughed and mentioned the fact that Sam had only to snap his fingers and he could attract a harem.

Sam retorted that the same was true of him.

Katie pretended to read a magazine. She knew Sam's words were fact—and she wasn't fond of "fact" one bit.

Katie had dinner with Kent and Sam again that night. Then, although she sat in on all the very intense practices that took place on the Colorado field, she didn't really see Kent again until Friday night when they ate at a small restaurant near the Saxons' hotel, then walked slowly back to make Kent's curfew.

He was a little on edge that night, she decided; his questions seemed to be taunting ones. He asked her how she was enjoying the team—and if she had come up with anything nasty yet.

"I'm a reporter," Katie resentfully assured him, "and I can get nasty all on my own. You should bear that in mind."

"Oh, I haven't forgotten," he told her.

She gazed at him sharply. He had on an attractive sheepskin jacket against the Denver cold; his collar was raised, making his features appear more severe.

"Are you nervous about the game?" she asked.

He looked at her, then shrugged. "I'm always nervous before a game."

"Afraid if you don't win you'll lose a million a year?" she taunted, regretting her words as soon as they had been spoken.

His stare seemed to cut through her like the cold air around them. "No," he stated simply. He slipped an arm through hers and speeded up his pace. "Come on, let's get back. It's cold enough out here without having to be with you, too."

Katie wrenched her arm free. "No one said you had to be with me."

135

He stopped, planting his hands at his waist, watching her with impatience and annoyance. "Katie—it's night, and Denver may not be the crime capital of the world, but I'm not leaving you on the street alone."

"I've been alone a number of years," she replied dryly.

He smiled but with little humor. "You know I won't leave you," he said flatly. "Want to walk . . . or be carried?"

Katie compressed her lips tightly and started walking. She was able to keep silent for less than a minute. She muttered every name she could think of under her breath and cursed Raff strongly for having sent her out to interview the most egotistical bastard she had ever met.

She heard him laugh behind her, and that was the final straw. Spinning around, she slammed against him, then took a step back. "You want 'nasty,' Mr. Hart? Then if I'm so cold, what are you doing with me? Go warm up. What's your love life been, Mr. Hart? I'm sure the women of America are dying to know. One marriage—was that it? Were you so determined to keep eternally warm that your wife couldn't stand it anymore?"

He went so rigidly tense that she was paralyzed, terrified that his muscled arm was going to shoot out and flatten her. But she had underestimated Kent Hart.

He walked past her. "Why don't you ask my ex-wife about that? We're good friends. Very good friends."

Regretting her outburst, Katie followed slowly behind him. He didn't turn back to her until they had almost reached the hotel.

"I'll give you Paula's number." He seemed perfectly at ease, perfectly in control. His eyes touched into her like fire, though, and despite his pleasant manner, she felt that she had never been more vehemently despised. "But then, perhaps you won't need to bother. You should have everything you want after this weekend, shouldn't you?"

"This weekend?" she repeated vaguely. Was he setting her

up? Was he about to tell her that the last thing he would consider doing now was spend more time with her?

"Miss Hudson, are you chickening out? Dante Hudson's daughter—the woman willing to burst into the showers—giving it all up now?"

"I'm not chickening out on anything," Katie retorted. "If you think I'm afraid of you, you're grossly mistaken."

He laughed dryly, bitterly. "Well, if you're not just a little bit afraid of me, Miss Hudson, you should be. And tossing your chin up in the air won't change a thing."

"Are you threatening me?"

"Warning you."

Katie smiled icily and brushed past him. "Thank you, Mr. Hart, I'm forewarned. Now, if you don't mind—"

His hand was on her arm, stopping her, spinning her around. When she fell hard against his chest, his arms wound tightly around her, pinning her to him. Katie saw the rapid pulse in his throat and looked up to see the living vibrancy of his eyes. She shuddered uncontrollably, not knowing then if she did hate him still or if she had really come to feel far more for him than she was willing to admit. Her heart rattled a furious beat; she was breathless and terribly afraid that she would buckle if he let her go. She was certain that he intended to kiss her; he did not. His lips paused just over hers, hovering there, and his whisper caressed her where his touch did not.

"You've taken on the pros, Kathleen. I really wonder if you're ready for the game."

She didn't fight his hold. She tried to meet his demon's stare without blinking.

"I came from the pros," she told him in a heated whisper. "I know the game very well. And I'll never be afraid of your type."

A chill wind swept around them. Denver was cold now, winter cold. Such a short time ago, she had been lulled by a summer breeze. They stood in the scant shelter of a leafless tree, and for a minute, Katie did feel fright—as if she, like the tree, had been stripped of protection. She thought she had come to know him; she didn't know him at all.

He smiled at her, and she realized then that his hold upon her had changed. His arms were still there, but his hand had moved beneath her jacket . . . beneath her sweater. His fingers were playing lazily and provocatively over the skin of her back. Moving as if they were lovers while they battled like enemies.

"Stop it!" Katie exclaimed defensively, and he instantly released her with a little laugh. She turned around to leave him but was still determined to have the last word. "I hope they stomp all over you tomorrow. I hope they destroy the great Cougar in the first quarter. I hope—"

"I'm so glad you're a pro at the game, Kathleen," he interrupted her coolly. "I won't be afraid to play it anymore."

She threw open the door and hurried into the hotel. Some of the Saxon players were still in the lounge, sitting around a roaring fire. Katie raced past them and rushed up to her own room.

The game tomorrow was the last thing on her mind. All she could think about were the things to come after the game.

Another game . . . a different game. Was that what life—and love—all was to Kent Hart? Nothing more than a game? A challenge to be tried and tested?

"Don't go to the Rockies—don't be with him!" she commanded herself out loud.

But she knew she would go. Nothing on earth could keep her away. Katie knew with a sinking dismay that if someone were to guarantee her that she would be a loser, it was a game she would play anyway. She wanted him with a desperation she had never thought possible. And she had known from his words, from his touch tonight, that she would have what she wanted.

Katie barely slept. She twisted miserably throughout the night. Sometimes too hot, sometimes too cold—and always dreaming, envisioning, imagining his touch . . .

Morning dawned clear and cold. The game was scheduled for one o'clock; by noon the stands were filled to capacity.

Katie had a seat at the fifty-yard line with several of the players' wives. Raff hadn't arranged it, she knew. Kent—or maybe Sam—had done so.

By the end of the first quarter it was obvious that it was going to be a tight game—a "death struggle," as Joan Patterson, Bobby's wife, told her with only a hint of sarcasm in her voice. "This is for the Superbowl," she added with a grimace.

"Umm, the almighty Superbowl," Katie agreed. And she added softly, "Damn, but they're vicious out there."

Joan laughed. "Oh, I suppose it beats feeding Christians to the lions."

"Or a pair of gladiators?" Katie asked dryly.

"Precisely!" Joan laughed.

The game moved into the second quarter with the score tied at seven. Katie found that she was screaming herself hoarse and jumping up and down like everyone else.

"Would we have done this for gladiators?" she asked Joan.

Joan shuddered with wide eyes. "I hope not!"

Halftime came and went. Toward the end of the third quarter, Sam and Kent connected. Kent ran it out for a thirty-five-yard touchdown. The crowd went wild.

He's good at this, Katie thought resentfully. He loves it, and he's good at it, and I resent him for it. Why?

Because my father was good—and he died, she realized dully.

At the beginning of the fourth quarter the opposition moved hard and fierce for a touchdown. The teams were even again. Then the Saxons had the ball. They struggled forward, lost the ball, then regained it. Two minutes remained in the game, and it was beginning to look like it would go into overtime.

Then it happened again—Sam and Kent connected. Katie was on her feet as she watched Kent, racing like a streak down the field, a powerful streak it appeared as men clutched at him but fell. He just kept running until he was over the line. People went wild, screaming, shouting, jumping. Then screaming and shouting all over again.

"Oh, God!" Joan suddenly exclaimed.

"What? *What?*" Katie demanded.

"It's Sam! They must have sacked him really hard after he threw the ball. He isn't up yet."

Someone next to Joan murmured that Sam had to be okay. But he didn't get up. They weren't even helping him limp off the field; they carried him off on a stretcher.

Katie wanted desperately to get to the lockers, but it seemed impossible. People were everywhere, and she couldn't seem to struggle her way through. At last she got onto the field. And at last she neared the Saxons' lockers. Being near wasn't enough. People kept shoving her back.

In the end it was all worthless. Sam had been taken to the hospital, and Kent had gone with him.

CHAPTER EIGHT

News regarding Sam's condition was released immediately. It wasn't that bad by many injury standards of the game. He had three bruised ribs and one cracked one.

By the time the commotion died down and Katie was allowed to see him—only because Sam had asked to see her—he was sitting up in bed, smiling away with Sam Loper's charming and inimitable smile.

Kent was idly leaning against the wall by the window. Somewhere along the line he'd had the opportunity to shower and change. He was wearing jeans, a tailored shirt and vee-necked sweater, and his sheepskin jacket was on a chair in the room. His hands were plunged into his pockets, and he watched Katie enter with casual interest.

She cast him an angry glance. Apparently, while she'd been suffering the agonies of the damned over Sam's condition, he'd been well aware that things hadn't been too bad. He'd taken time for himself, but he hadn't bothered to find her.

"Katie!" Sam exclaimed, wincing only slightly as he moved. "Don't frown like that—you'll get wrinkles. Come here and give me a kiss, chastely on the cheek, before the Cougar there decides to show his claws."

Katie hurried to Sam, took his hands in hers, and kissed him quickly on the mouth. She ignored Kent. Then she leaned back, still looking at him worriedly. "You're really okay? Not just for the press?"

"I'm okay, Katie. It's my first crack, but I've bruised ribs plenty of times before."

Katie gave him a dry smile for his attempt at humor.

"At least it was the last play," he said, then added reproachfully, "You didn't congratulate us yet, Katie. The Saxons are going to the Superbowl."

"I'm sorry, Sam," she said. "Congratulations. I just can't give a damn about the Superbowl. But since it does seem to mean so much to you, I'm sorry you won't be playing."

Sam shot Kent a quick glance. Katie learned that Sam, too, could speak with an edge of steel when he desired. "Oh, I'll be playing in the big game."

"With your ribs like that? You're crazy, Sam! Kent, *tell* him he's crazy."

Kent shrugged. He watched her lazily through half-closed eyes. "I can't tell him anything, Katie. He's over age, and the team doc has said that he should be all right for a quarter or two."

Tears stung her eyes, and she pushed Sam's hands away from her. "You're both insane," she said bitterly.

"Katie . . ." Sam murmured unhappily, "I'm not a fool. I'll be okay."

"That's what my father said," Katie snapped.

Sam glanced at Kent. Katie wasn't watching them, but she sensed their exchange of looks. Kent walked around to her and placed his hands firmly on her shoulders. "You're not being a cheerful visitor, Katie. I think it's time we leave."

Katie tried to shake off his touch; it was no good. She tossed her head around to stare up at Kent. "If you were his friend, you'd talk him out of this."

"I am his friend, and I intend to respect his wishes because of it. Dammit, Katie! It isn't the same game your father played. There are new rules and regulations."

"Oh, great! While Sam is hauled off to the morgue, the refs will be handing out penalties! They'll—oh!" She broke off as Kent's fingers bit into her shoulders.

"Say good-bye to Sam, Katie. Tell him sweetly that you'll see him in New Orleans."

She locked her teeth together and didn't say a word. Kent tightened his grip and lifted her from the side of the hospital bed.

"Bye, Katie." Sam chuckled. "Have a nice trip."

Kent was pulling her out of the room. "Please, Sam, think about it! You're talking about your health, about the rest of your life."

"I'll think about it," Sam promised.

Out in the hall Katie managed to break Kent's grip and face him furiously, her hands clenched at her side. "How can you be like this?" she demanded, only keeping her voice low by forcing herself to remember they were in a hospital. "He's your best friend, and he's been hurt. You should be with him! You should be telling him how foolish it would be to try and play in his condition! But no! You all think you're such muscle men. A few aches and pains go with the territory. I wonder if you even really care! All you seem to be thinking about is getting away for your weekend. Dragging me out like a caveman, thinking of nothing but yourself and fun and games for the weekend—"

"Am I having fun and games?" he interrupted. "Why, Miss Hudson, it sounds to me like you're planning an affair."

For a second she was speechless; then she was furious again. "Don't be ridiculous," she retorted. "I was thinking that the whole thing should be canceled so that you can be with Sam."

"Sam doesn't particularly want me here tonight," Kent said dryly. Katie saw his eyes travel past her shoulder. Then he smiled. The smile was warm—and not for her.

She turned around herself. A tall, pretty, and very sophisticated-looking brunette was walking toward them, her fashionable boots clicking on the tiled floor.

"Hi, Connie," Kent greeted her, and Katie remembered that she had met the woman briefly at the Saxons' party.

"Hi," Connie greeted Kent in return, then her speculative

143

gaze touched on Katie with recognition and speculation. "Katie Hudson, isn't it?" she asked pleasantly. "On the trail of the Cougar still?"

She was very pleasant, warm, and likable—even if she was gorgeous and dressed so well that Katie felt like an urchin in rags. She forced herself to smile in return. "Yes, I'm afraid so," she murmured.

Connie laughed, a delighted and delighting sound. "Well, good luck, honey." She returned her attention to Kent. "How's our wonderboy?"

"Not bad at all," Kent replied, "and anxiously awaiting his nonregistered nurse."

"Wonderful," Connie declared. She lifted herself on her toes and lightly pressed her fingers against Kent's chest as she gave him a little peck on the cheek. "Take care of yourself, Cougar," she murmured huskily. "We can't have two of you down, can we?"

"I'm always careful, Connie," Kent replied softly.

Katie felt as if she were intruding on something more intimate than she cared to understand.

"Bye, Katie," Connie said, waving as she sauntered toward Sam's room.

"Bye," Katie responded.

She watched Connie disappear into the room. Kent cleared his throat. "Can we leave now?"

Katie remained silent for a second, a second apparently too long.

She heard a sigh of exasperation. "Katie, I'm leaving now. Are you coming with me?"

"Yes, yes, I'm coming with you," she said irritably.

"Such enthusiasm! Sure sounds like fun and pleasure to me," he commented dryly. "Yep, sheer fun and pleasure."

He put an arm around her shoulders, but it was hardly an affectionate gesture. He was simply determined to propel her along.

Katie had imagined that Kent's place in the Rockies would be an elegant house, contemporary and full of glass and chrome and conveniences. She began to get the idea that it wasn't long before they reached his place, mainly because it was taking so very long to reach. They had left the city in a Jeep. That should have been another warning point.

Katie watched apprehensively as the terrain became more and more rugged. The road took them through forests, jagged cliffs, and rising hills. They were driving for an hour before it began to grow dark, and then she could only feel their ascension by the climb of the four-wheel-drive vehicle.

Kent was quiet for most of the drive; she'd tried to make conversation when they started out, but his answers had been monosyllables and she had given up. He had that tension about him that he emitted like electricity when he was aggravated with her. Which, of course, aggravated her in return, because he had no right to be angry—she did.

The drive began to wear on her nerves. And for miles now she hadn't been able to see much of anything. She was tired of sitting, and she was thirsty and hungry. He'd been in too much of a hurry to get started when they'd picked up their luggage to stop for anything to eat.

She cleared her throat. "Don't you think we should stop somewhere?"

He didn't take his eyes from the road. "Why?"

"To eat."

"We can eat at the cabin."

She waited a moment, then asked softly, "And when will that be?"

He shrugged. "Okay. It will be awhile. There's a little café up here a bit. Hamburgers and chili and the like. Will that suit you, Miss Hudson?"

She didn't rise to the taunt. "Yes."

It wasn't a "little café"—it was a greasy spoon, a very greasy spoon. But Katie didn't say a word. She ordered a hamburger, fries and a soda. Kent did the same. He ate

145

quickly, then watched her as she tried to finish. There was something about his look that she didn't quite like. He chewed on a piece of ice, then asked her casually, "So, Katie, what do you do when you're not pursuing me?"

She stopped chewing, stilled for a minute, then set her hamburger down and folded her hands together, leaning slightly against the table as she arched a brow. "I thought this was my time to ask the questions."

"We're not there yet," he told her.

"Why are you asking?"

"Point of interest, that's all."

Katie shrugged and picked up her hamburger, but she wasn't hungry anymore. "I don't do much of anything," she replied. "I work."

She could feel his eyes on her. He lightly drummed the table with his fingertips.

"Let's go," he said at last as he put some money on the table. "You're not eating that thing anymore."

Katie rose. He led her out with one hand at the small of her back.

She paused outside, looking around as he opened her door. The air was fresh and clean. It was cold, but it was beautiful. The new moon partially lit the mountains and their snowy peaks, and oddly, a certain peace seemed to settle over her.

Kent prodded her slightly to return to the car. She stepped up into the Jeep.

Kent was quiet again as they started off. Katie yawned, weary of the seemingly never-ending road.

"How much longer?" she asked.

"You know," he responded pleasantly, "you're a pain in the butt to travel with."

"Probably because it's foolish," she retorted. "I'm not even sure that I need to be here. It's more than possible that I have plenty of information on you for a ten-page article."

"Do you really? And just what do you know?"

"That you're an arrogant ass who just happens to have the ability to catch a pigskin ball."

He laughed. "So why are you coming with me?"

"Stupidity."

"Is that it?" he queried softly.

She glanced his way quickly, but she could read nothing from his features. It was too dark in the car. Still, the sound of his voice had been like brushed velvet; she felt as if it had caressed her. Heat shot along her spine, and her fingers were trembling where she clenched them together in her lap.

She didn't respond. The flare of approaching headlights suddenly lit up the car, and she saw that he was smiling sardonically.

He must have felt her gaze. He passed the car, then looked her way. "It's still a ways yet. Why don't you try to sleep?"

She leaned her head against the side of the car and closed her eyes. Katie didn't feel particularly sleepy, but she didn't feel like answering any of his questions either.

To her surprise she did sleep. The next thing she knew, he was shaking her shoulder.

"Are we here?" she asked groggily. Her eyes were still half closed; still, there didn't seem to be a damn thing around them.

No, there was light. A meager little light shining from a shack in the trees. Then she heard a noise—a horrible, obnoxious braying sound.

"Not exactly," Kent answered her as he stepped out of the Jeep. Katie frowned and reached for her door handle. The noise came to her again. Kent came around and opened her door. "What is that?" she demanded. "It sounds like a jackass."

"It is a jackass," Kent replied matter-of-factly. "The only transporation from here on out."

"What?" Katie whispered incredulously.

"Call them mules, if you like!" Kent hollered over his

shoulder as he started walking toward the shack. "Hey, Billy! Bill Maddon. We're here."

Katie gave herself a little shake, trying to rid herself of the last vestiges of sleep, wondering if she had stepped into a nightmare. But, no, this was not a dream. She was standing in almost complete darkness, surrounded by snow and pines—and the braying of a jackass.

"Kent! Kent, boy, it's good to see ya, it is!"

Katie swallowed and glanced at the shack. An old mountaineer was coming out, running on short, spritely legs to grab Kent's hand and pat him on the back. "Heard the game on my radio, boy. Mightly fine playin', son, mighty fine."

"Thanks, Billy," Kent said. He turned back to Katie, and she saw the eternal, irritating speculation in his eyes. What was this, she wondered, a damned test?

"Bill, meet Katie Hudson. Katie, Bill Maddon. He keeps an eye on my place while I'm away."

Katie pulled a hand from her pocket and smiled at the old man with the gray beard and twinkling blue eyes. "You're Dante Hudson's daughter, aren't you, girl?"

"Yes, I am," Katie replied, a little startled.

A grin as wide as a river split the old man's face. "I met your pa, girl. He come up when Kent here had just bought the place. Mighty fine man, he was. Sorry to have heard of his passing."

"Thank you," Katie murmured. Bill Maddon studied her a second longer, then asked Kent, "You two young folks comin' in for coffee?"

"Katie?" Kent asked her

What were her choices? she wondered. Coffee and a mule ride or just a mule ride? She shrugged. She liked Bill Maddon. She liked anyone who had kind words for her father, and she liked his sunny smile and spritely presence. "Coffee sounds good," she said.

It was a one-room shack, sparse and clean, and Bill made a great cup of coffee. He talked while he served them, asking

Kent about Sam, and asking Katie about her life with no hesitation at all. She didn't find him presumptuous.

And in Bill's presence she began to feel more relaxed about Kent. She often sensed his eyes on her, but it was as if the watchful wariness was gone. Had he expected her to throw a temper tantrum over the mules? If so, she was determined to disappoint him. She was going to handle anything he planned to throw her way.

Kent set down his coffee cup and stood, stretching. "Guess we'd better get going, Bill. It was a long day."

Bill nodded. "You two stay warm by the fire. I'll load your stuff on Sarah. How long you going to stay, Kent?"

"Two, three days tops," Kent replied. "The team has to be in New Orleans by Thursday morning."

"Superbowl," Bill said, giving his grizzled head a shake. "If that don't beat all. I'm just as pleased as a hog in the mud, I am."

Katie lowered her head and smiled as Bill went out. Then she looked up, aware that Kent had balanced a foot on the hearth and was watching her.

"You don't mind the mules?" he asked. The firelight was touching his eyes, and she couldn't tell if what they reflected was a demon's glitter or a warm glow.

"Not if they're the only way," she replied politely.

"We could walk, but they have better footing up here."

Katie just smiled.

Five minutes later she was mounting her mule, Clarabelle. Clarabelle was a nasty creature who liked to honk and make noise—and nip at knees. Katie just kept smiling.

"I'll take her lead," Kent told Katie, and she didn't protest. It all looked dark to her. If there was a path, she couldn't see it.

Katie gritted her teeth together and waved good-bye to Bill. Kent held a light before him, and they started moving. Clarabelle seemed to sink more deeply into the snow with every step, but apparently there was a path between the richly smelling pines. Katie closed her eyes as they started up an incline, promising God that she would be nice to Clarabelle even if she were the nastiest creature in the world—as long as she was surefooted.

"You okay?" Kent called back.

"Just wonderful," Katie said.

The powerful torch illuminated Kent's way, but Katie felt shrouded in the shadow, cold and frightened. She wasn't going to let him know it, though.

They had been plodding through the snow for ten or fifteen minutes when Clarabelle came to a jolting stop, crashing into the mule before her.

"We're here," Kent announced quietly.

Sliding from his mule, he held the light before him, but it didn't really matter anymore. Katie could see a big log structure with a warm, golden light welcoming them from within, shining from multipaned windows.

Kent walked around to her; she could hear his footsteps crunching in the snow. His hands went around her waist, and he lifted her to the ground. She slid along his length until her feet touched the snow. Her arms were still braced against his shoulders; his were still about her.

"Like it?" he asked, a crooked grin twisting his lips.

"I don't know yet," she said. Her voice was a whisper, but she could find no more volume for it.

"Go on in. I'll see to the 'girls' "—he inclined his head toward Clarabelle and the other two mules—"and bring in our things."

Katie nodded. She stepped past him and hurried through the snow to the door.

It was rustic. No chrome, no glass, nothing modern. The walls were raw pine and the floors were hardwood, softened by simple braided rugs. The furniture was solid-looking and well stuffed, and Katie instantly liked the cabin. There was nothing pretentious about it; it didn't speak of fame and fortune. It was somehow very much a man's place, yet it welcomed her.

The door opened behind her. Kent came in, stamping the snow from his feet and dusting off his shoulders. "We just beat the new snow," he said casually.

Katie didn't answer him. She walked over to the mantel and looked at the painting above it of a herd of running wild mustangs.

"It's nice," she told him quietly, then she turned around, staring at him as she asked, "Why did you invite me here?"

"Why did you come?" he counterquestioned softly.

She dropped her gaze to the hearth and the fire that burned there. It had been set by Bill Maddon for their arrival, she was certain.

"It isn't much," Kent told her, "but you can't rival the scenery. There's a little brook not far from here. Even in the summer it's as cold as ice, but it's totally secluded and refreshing. And, believe it or not, I've got a great water heater."

Katie laughed. "Are you telling me I need a bath?"

"I just thought you might be interested."

"I am," she admitted.

He picked up her suitcase. "Follow me, Miss Hudson."

She followed him down a long, narrow hall. When he entered a room and flicked on another light, Katie caught her breath with delight. The far wall was all window, and the house lights fell on a panoply of white virgin snow and distant, shadowy pines. The room was enormous, with a huge four-poster bed taking up the left section; a sunken hearth with throw pillows and woolly rugs took up the right.

"It's wonderful!" Katie exclaimed.

Kent set her suitcase down, then went to a door near the foot of the bed. "The tub is in here. I'll leave you to it."

"The room is mine?"

He shrugged. "It's usually mine, but God knows I want to impress the press. It's yours."

The door closed on his words, and Katie smiled slowly; they hadn't carried his usual bitterness.

The tub was a huge wooden one, but the faucets were copper and responded to her touch immediately. Katie was really glad to bathe, but she didn't spend long in the tub; she had the strangest feeling of euphoria, as if a great moment was at hand, a moment she had waited a lifetime for, while never knowing that she waited.

"I am not in love with him," she told the steam that surrounded her. But she was, and both she and Kent knew why they were here. She was hot and then cold as she sat in the tub, languorous and filled with excitement. Something touched her . . . flames of heat that sizzled through her and made her want him, want to be near him, to cast all doubt and inhibition to the night wind and reach out for the magic she could touch.

She didn't dress when she came out; she slipped into a floor-length evergreen robe that belted around her waist. She didn't even put on slippers. The cabin was warm with any number of fires—those in the stone hearths . . . and that in her womb.

Kent was sitting on the overstuffed sofa in the living room. He didn't hear Katie when she emerged from the hall. Her heart took a quick and disastrous lunge as she saw him there; he was tired. His head was leaning back, and his eyes were closed. She saw the tiny lines against the deep tan of his face; his nose, straight except for the crook where it had been broken; his brows, thick but highly arched and defined. She wanted to touch his features, kiss the tiny scars she had inflicted all those years ago.

When she walked around the sofa, his eyes flew open.

"I'm sorry," she murmured. "I startled you. You must be exhausted. I—I keep forgetting you're the Saxon who made the tie-breaking touchdown."

He shrugged and laughed. "To be truthful, I'd forgotten all about the game myself. Sit down and I'll get you a drink."

She shook her head. "I'm already standing. If you'll tell me where things are, I'll make the drinks."

He pointed toward the old country eat-in kitchen. "The cabinet above the sink. Soda and the like should be in the refrigerator. I'll take a scotch on the rocks."

Katie felt as if she were moving in a dreamworld. This was his house, one of his homes, but she felt as if it embraced her, as if she belonged here. It was one thing to accept the fact that she cared for him and wanted him desperately, but it was another thing—a foolish thing—to feel that she belonged. She was spending time with the Cougar. No one pinned down such a cat.

But the sense of euphoria stayed with her as she mixed the drinks. She didn't want to know if she did or didn't love him; she didn't want to know if he cared deeply for her at all. She wanted the magic of a snowy night with Kent Hart—and that was all she cared to know for the moment.

Katie fixed the drinks and walked back out to the living room. She handed Kent his scotch and curled onto the other end of the sofa. He took a sip of his drink, leaned back and smiled, then turned his head to look at her.

"This is nice," he said lightly. "How long do you think it will last?"

"What?" Katie asked.

"The two of us not arguing."

Katie's lashes fell briefly over her eyes, and she tried to suppress a small smile. "I'm too tired to argue," she murmured.

"Too tired?"

"To argue," she repeated, meeting his eyes. They were so dark, encompassing. And, as always, they warmed her with the touch of a fire's glow; they filled her senses, reached to her blood. She didn't feel at all afraid or shy. There was a distance between them on the couch, but it didn't matter. That distance was filled with a delicious tension.

"How did you like Bill?" Kent asked.

"Very much," Katie said.

Kent lowered his lashes for a minute while he sipped his drink. Then he was looking at her again. "Why did you come here, Katie?"

She smiled. "Why did you ask me?"

"Isn't this getting a bit circular?"

"Yes, it is."

"Come here, Katie."

She didn't have to be asked twice; she got to her knees and moved across the sofa, carefully balancing her drink. He set an arm around her, and she wound up with her back resting against his chest, her legs stretched along the length of the sofa. He played with her hair with his free hand as his breath whispered over the top of her head. She felt the supple strength of his body, and she loved it.

"I think I asked you here because—because I wanted you from the very beginning," he said quietly.

Katie closed her eyes, luxuriating in his words. When she opened them, it was to find that he was watching her intently, his features taut but somehow tender. She smiled and told him simply, "I know that I came here because I wanted you."

Why is she so damned beautiful? Kent wondered as he looked into her eyes . . . eyes like a tranquil sea, wide, offering both beguilement and honesty. He touched her cheek with his knuckle . . . silk beneath the roughness of his own flesh. He ran a finger over her lower lip, felt the heated moisture of her breath.

He set down his scotch hastily, took her drink from her fingers, and set it down as well.

Then he wrapped his arms around her and brought his lips to hers.

He wanted to be gentle. Urgency dictated his will. Raw hunger drove his mouth to possess hers completely, exploring her velvety tongue, tasting her sweetness, playing upon her teeth, manipulating her lips to his. God, but she was good, soft and pliant in his arms, returning his urgency with a hot and feminine desire all her own. His hand slipped beneath her robe, and he found nothing there to impede him, nothing but the bare silk of her flesh. He moved his lips from hers with a little groan, caressing her midriff with a feathery touch. "You're naked beneath that robe."

She twisted her head against him, planting light kisses against his neck, teasing his throat with damp flicks of her tongue. "I told you I knew why I came," she said huskily.

"Oh, God!" Kent groaned, and a shudder ripped almost painfully through his body. He embraced her with his arms and stood, unwilling to part with her even for a moment. And those eyes of hers, those beautiful sea eyes, continued to meet his.

He didn't say anything else then; he strode with her down the hall, tense and electric with his desire. He carried her straight to the bed and laid her there, rising over her, falling beside her. He heard her quickened breath as he reached for the tie on her robe. When it gave to his fingers, he brushed the robe from her. His breath caught in his lungs as his heart assumed a frantic beat and his muscles contracted with longing. She was stunning; as perfect and flawless as the fresh snow beyond the window; full breasts to excite his touch; a slim waist his hands could span so easily; long, long legs to entwine with his. All this he had known somewhere inside of him, and yet he felt somewhat in awe. Her eyes, her face, were so beautiful, so trusting, filled with a desire that matched his own. Her hair was like skeins of gold spread across his pillow, ready to entangle him with silken magic . . .

Kent touched her chin with his thumb. He allowed that touch to fall to her throat, then follow a path along the shadowed valley between her breasts to her abdomen. She moaned softly and curled to him. Her fingers, trembling, moved to the buttons on his shirt, but the buttons refused to give. Kent sat up and impatiently pulled at them—three he unbuttoned, two he ripped away. He shifted to pull off his boots and stood to shed his pants, watching Katie smile in the moonlight.

Then he was beside her again, rubbing her body with his, searching for her lips. As he kissed her, he touched her, he knew her. His body hungered for her in a way he'd never known. His palms cupped her breasts, full with them, loving them, tantalizing her and drawing husky whimpers from her. He drew his lips from hers to make love to her breasts, kissing them, laving them with the rough touch of his tongue, taunting them with his teeth until she cried out. He felt her nails lightly raking his back, and he smiled with memory. Who could have known, all those years ago, that a time would come when he was ready to die with desire for the touch of those nails . . .

Hudson's daughter, full-grown, a woman now in every sense of the word, possessing his body and his soul and all that was him . . .

"Kent," she gasped, his name a sweet cry on her lips. She kissed his shoulders urgently, nipping at them, curing each slight bite with another kiss. Her hands, so soft and beautiful against his body, moved over him, sending wave after wave of pleasure ripping through him.

"Katie . . ."

He lifted himself away, watching her lovely body as he feathered his fingers over her thighs, between them. Her palms came to his cheeks, his throat, down his chest.

"Katie . . ." It was a whisper and a groan this time.

She rolled against him again, slipping her arms around him, begging him to come to her. He forced her to her back again and rose over her, parting her thighs with his knee, shuddering just to feel the length of his body against hers again. The feelings within him were almost frightening in their intensity; his body pulsed and screamed with desire and need, but he wanted it to go on and on . . .

Her arms were still entangled around his neck. He saw her eyes in the moonlight . . . wide and as lovely as the sea but no longer tranquil. They mirrored his need with crystal beauty, and he touched her cheek, as fascinated as he was fevered.

"Please," she whispered, and he lowered himself, all too ready to please her. Her resistance stunned him, so much so that he would have drawn away had she let him.

"Kent!" she choked out his name with a sob, her arms clenching more tightly around him, her eyes at last closing with her plea.

"Katie?"

"Please!" She arched to him, breasts pressed high against him, her hips and the damp warmth he had elicited a welcome he could not refuse, no matter what the barriers of her body . . . or his mind. He lifted her buttocks and moved against her, slowly, gently, aware then with an aching delight that his golden goddess was virginal.

She gasped, trembling with the impact of his body. But when he stilled, she wound her legs about him and begged in the softest of whispers for him to love her.

He did, stroking her carefully at first, then venting free rein as she moved fluidly with him, tangling her fingers into his hair, meeting his kisses, learning all about hunger and need and fulfillment. He didn't know how he did it—from the second he had touched her he had been explosive—but in that unique and special tenderness he had for her, he found control and physical patience. Sheer delight grew and spiraled, blazed and blazed again. Not until a strangled cry tore from her lips and he felt the release of her sumptuous body did he find his own, spilling into her a flood of warmth that sent them both shuddering again. They held one another as little waves of afterpleasure gently gave them back their breath and slowed their hearts.

Kent buried his face against her neck and whispered her name, tenderly threading his fingers through her hair. At last he raised himself and rolled to his side, rising on an elbow to stare into her eyes. They were still on his, lazy, sleepy, sensual.

"You should have told me."

She shrugged and smiled, and her body curled to his once more.

"I told you I didn't do much but work," she teased.

"I should have known," he murmured, idly running his fingers over her back, loving the fluid curve of her spine and the firm rise of her buttocks.

"Why?" She kissed the pulse at his throat. "I think you already had reservations about my being Dante's daughter."

"I did," Kent admitted. "But it seems that my reservations were about other men, not myself. But—"

Katie laughed, hugging him. "I wanted you, Kent. I wanted you the night you hauled me away from the party. I wanted you when we were tumbling in the grass. And, as I told you tonight," she added with pride and dignity, "I came here because I wanted you."

He pulled away to kiss her forehead, and when he met her eyes again, he knew he was in love. "Katie—" he began but was startled from speech as his phone started to ring.

She pulled away slightly. "Shouldn't you answer that?"

He shook his head. "The machine will get it."

After three rings the phone was answered automatically. Kent listened to his own voice, then the beep that allowed for a message.

"Kent? It's Sam. Pick up. Kent?"

Katie nudged him. "It's Sam . . . aren't you going to talk to him?"

Kent stared down into her eyes. He shook his head. "I'll call him tomorrow."

"Kent, dammit, It's Sam. Pick up!"

"Kent . . ." Katie murmured.

He slipped both arms around her, luxuriating in the feel of her naked flesh, still slick with the sheen from their lovemaking.

"Sam's just being a pain because he's stuck in a hospital. I'll call him tomorrow. He's jealous. He probably has a good intuition of what's going on."

"Is something going on?" she teased.

"You bet it is." Kent smiled broadly, kissing her lightly, running his tongue over her lips, then pouncing over her again. "Miss Hudson, you should know it takes more than one touchdown to win the game."

"Does it?"

"Mmm . . ."

"Teach me."

"With the greatest pleasure."

Sam kept cursing over the recorder, but neither one of them heard him.

"I want to know all about the game," Katie murmured. "Every last play."

It would be later, much later, that Kent would remember her words. They were destined to haunt him cruelly.

CHAPTER NINE

"Hush," Kent whispered.

Katie felt the light touch of his hands on her shoulders, and the more intimate touch of his body close behind hers. She held perfectly still, gazing in the direction of his pointing finger.

In front of her, frozen into a beautiful picture in the snow, was a large white-tailed deer with full, majestic antlers.

"He's wonderful!" Katie whispered in reply, but even that soft sound of her voice was enough to startle the deer; he fled across the snowy plain, disappearing into the safe shadowland of the pines. "Oh! I'm sorry!" Katie exclaimed.

Kent laughed. "Don't worry, they're always around. That's why I like this place. It's so remote that you see everything, deer, raccoons, rabbits, even mountain lions. They're all timid and run at your approach, but they're always around, too, so you can come upon them again and again."

"Mountain lions are timid?" Katie inquired dubiously.

"Unless they're injured or harassed."

"Something like a cougar?" Katie teased.

He grimaced. "Maybe."

"Like when they attack the press?" Katie asked softly.

Putting his arm about her shoulders, he steered her back toward the cabin. "Come on. The sun is going down, and it will start getting cold. It may snow tonight. I'll tell you about my feud with the press over coffee and brandy."

Katie smiled and followed him. She realized then that she

had been smiling continually for almost twenty-four hours. The muscles around her mouth actually ached from all the smiling she'd done, but it was the most delicious feeling she'd ever known. No, she corrected herself, Kent himself was the most delicious feeling.

"What's that grin for?" he asked as he ushered her into the cabin.

"Nothing," she said with a shake of her head.

He raised a brow but didn't press her. "I'll start the coffee. You can get the brandy."

Katie shed her jacket and did as he told her. "Kent," she said, reaching into the cupboard, "what *did* happen to make you so antagonistic over the press?"

He grimaced as he measured out spoonfuls of coffee. "Exaggeration and innuendo," he told her. He filled the pot with water and set it on the stove, then faced her and leaned against the counter. "Paula had never been fond of the idea of being married to a pro football player." He lifted his hands. "Maybe it was more than that. We'd been college sweethearts and probably married too young. Anyway, we'd been married several years when the trouble really started. A paper did a big write-up on me, accompanied with a picture of one of the cheerleaders. All I was doing was opening a door for her, but along with the reporter's determination to prove that I was leading a wild life, it looked pretty bad. I think Paula might have trusted me, but . . . Well, about a week later I was away from home for a game, and I read a clipping that she was suing me for divorce and didn't intend to allow me anywhere near our daughter. Consequently, she read an article that said I intended to go for child custody. We were divorced before either of us realized that neither one of us ever really wanted to hurt the other."

Katie turned around to fiddle with the brandy bottle. "Then the two of you really are very good friends?" How good? her heart clamored to know.

She felt his hands on her shoulders, massaging them. "The

best," he said cheerfully, but he spun her around so that she was in his arms, and she saw his affectionately taunting grin—along with that glitter to his eyes that warmed her with every touch. "I spend a lot of time with Paula and her husband. He's a great guy."

"She's remarried?" Katie was surprised how relieved she felt.

"For a long, long time."

Katie lowered her head quickly so that he wouldn't see her quick smile. He lifted her chin and kissed her lips lightly. The kiss deepened. She broke from him, breathlessly pressing her face against his sweater.

"No fair," she moaned. "I still need a story."

He brushed a strand of hair from her cheek with a subtle smile. "Quiz away, Miss Hudson."

"Thank you, Mr. Hart. Would you check on the coffee, please?"

"Certainly."

Kent poured out large mugs of coffee, and Katie laced them with brandy.

"Can I sit by you while you quiz me?" he asked her innocently.

Katie pressed her lips together and swept past him without a reply. I should tell him no, she thought. She'd tried to question him that morning in bed, and she hadn't lasted a full minute. They'd laughed and then made love. And in between they'd wound up carrying on serious discussions about football. It had been strange. She had, in her way, despised football ever since her father's injury. But she had been able to listen to Kent. She had even felt okay about it. He had described plays and strategies to her—and she had responded intelligently. She knew he appreciated the depth of her knowledge. She had told him she was worried about the upcoming game, worried about Sam and about him, but he had only laughed, then loved her again. And she hadn't gotten a single question in.

Falling in love . . . it was so nice, so perfect, so warm and wonderful that she couldn't really care.

But now it was her turn, Katie determined. And at least they were dressed now! She should do okay. She should be able to get somewhere. And she had discovered that she was out for far more than a story. She had plenty to write about—this was for her.

Because, like it or not, sensible or not, stupid or not, futile or not, she was falling in love with him.

She sat on the sofa, sipping her strong, fortified coffee. "Okay, Mr. Hart, why the nickname Cougar?"

He sat beside her, drawing her against him, slipping his hand warmly about her midriff.

"Well, at one time I was the fastest thing going in the NFL —*on* my feet, so don't get any other ideas. Actually, the cheetah is the fastest cat, but someone started this thing with 'Cougar,' and it stuck."

"I'll bet you're still the fastest thing in the NFL," Katie murmured dryly, drawing a quick pinch from him.

"Shall we proceed, Miss Hudson . . . or do you want a demonstration?"

Katie laughed as his hand, which had been idly playing along her ribs, cupped her breast. She grasped at his fingers, fighting the breathless feeling his slightest touch could create. She didn't want to succumb to sensation—not yet. She had a few more questions to ask beneath her reporter's guise before she gave in to the need to simply be with him.

"You never remarried?"

"No."

"Why?"

She felt his shrug and a change in him, a restlessness with the question.

"I was bitter for a long time. I didn't think marriage could work for me. I'd been hanged without being guilty once."

"Because of your work."

"Yes."

163

"Why do you think you've been successful so long? How long do you think you'll keep playing?"

"I don't know . . . and I don't know."

Katie hesitated. "Do you feel that you live for the game?"

"No, but my teammates are important to me . . . as is the good of the team."

"Do you ever think about retirement?"

"Yes."

"As in the near future?"

"Yes."

"Oh," Katie murmured, a little surprised—and ridiculously pleased. She quickly drank some of the coffee, gasping a little at its sudden heat and the potency of the brandy.

"What about you, Katie?"

"What do you mean?" she asked a little defensively.

"Have you ever thought there might be something more important than *World Magazine?*"

Katie sighed. "It's a hard world for freelancers."

"But not an impossible one."

"No, but"—she shrugged, pulling away from him to sit up and drink too much coffee once again—"I'm fond of surviving like a respectable citizen. When my dad died"—her voice trailed away for only a minute—"I was up to my ears in debt. Pro quarterbacks weren't as highly paid as they are today, and his illness took everything. I worked day and night to get through college. I had some of the most horrible apartments you'd ever want to see. I'm not sure I have the nerve to take a chance on total poverty again." Katie closed her eyes quickly, sorry she had spoken the way she had. Had she sounded mercenary? She wasn't. She was just determined to support herself. She quickly changed the subject.

"What's your daughter like?" she asked.

"Anne?"

Katie glanced his way and found that he was watching her with amusement and tenderness.

164

"She's a little like you," he finally answered. "Except, as far as I know, she doesn't run around clawing people."

Katie punched him lightly on the shoulder. "Not fair!" she charged. "That was years ago."

"Yes, it was," Kent mused. "Except that I got the feeling you would have happily clawed my eyes out the night we met. Remote, as it was."

"Maybe," Katie admitted with a grin.

He blinked, and the warm tenderness in his eyes changed slightly. His look had a less than subtle effect on her pulse rate.

"Are you finished with your coffee?" he asked.

Katie nodded.

"Have you got any more questions?"

"I—yes, of course, I've got loads of them."

"Want to ask them in the bedroom?"

She started to laugh. There seemed to be no other response to his direct question.

He raised a brow and promised quietly, "I'll make it worth your while."

"When you put it that way," she murmured, "how can I possibly refuse?"

"You can't," he stated flatly.

He reached for her cup, and while he went to set the mugs in the kitchen, she fled down the hall, stripping her clothing as she went. When she reached the bedroom, she plunged onto the four-poster with her heart racing and pulled the covers up to her chin, her flesh already alive with a glow, simply knowing that he was coming to her.

She watched him as he appeared in the bedroom doorway and paused, a wry smile curling his lip. Then he gripped the hem of his sweater and pulled it over his head. There was no moon glow now, just a subtle twilight, but still she trembled as she saw his naked shoulders. Scarred but broad, powerfully muscled and beautiful to her, the sight of them made the tension inside her coil sweetly with anticipation. He walked

165

slowly to the bed, working at his buckle, and in a moment, he was standing naked before her.

Katie closed her eyes, loving the dizzines she felt, the ache to have him, to hold him, to love him. She'd been so terrified of being awkward, so horrified of her own innocence. But Kent had made everything perfect—he'd made her believe she was wonderful. She colored, realizing that no matter what happened in the future, she would never forget her first, tender lover.

Katie, she warned herself, love him but don't ask for his love in return. You deny it to yourself, but you're carrying on a fantasy that it can be a forever kind of love. Don't do that to yourself . . .

"Katie, open your eyes," he commanded, but there was a bit of puzzlement in his words. And as she opened her eyes, she realized that they were damp with tears that had formed absurdly.

He came to rest beside her, kissing her lightly, then leaning on an elbow to watch her. He pulled the covers from her and asked, "You can't be shy now—not of me?"

She shook her head and moved toward him, allowing her fingers to play over the hair on his chest. "I'm not," she whispered.

"Then . . ."

"Nothing, Kent, really." She pressed against him, needing to feel his body with her own. "I want to make love to you, Kent, and . . . I want you to make love to me."

He reached for her chin, lifting it so that her eyes met his. "Katie, I want to know what you feel for me."

"I—"

"I don't want it to be just a weekend in the mountains, Katie."

Emotions raced through, warm like a summer stream, cold with the icy tentacles of fear. He couldn't mean it; she was falling for him, and if she dared believe, she would be dashed against the rocks with the pain . . .

166

"Katie!" He gave her a little shake, then pulled her to him, her face against his heart, her nose tickled by the dark hairs on his chest, her body heated by the force of his. "I want you, Katie, for more than a week or a year. Can you understand that? I did fight it because of your father, because of the past. But from that first time I saw you, wet and bedraggled in the showers, I knew you were a stunning woman. When I touched you, I wanted you. And more. Talk to me, Katie."

She lifted her face to his, and she started to laugh, a little hysterically because there were tears in her laughter. "Oh, Kent! I was so afraid . . . I tried to tell myself that it couldn't be real. I—"

He tangled his fingers into the hair at her nape, tilting her face still further, capturing her lips with heat and passion and promise. He drew away from her. "Keep talking to me, Katie," he whispered, and she smiled with the sheer pleasure of it.

She drew herself over him, palms on his chest, hips to his. She dipped to breathe a kiss on his lips. Her hair fell about him; her eyes shimmered provocatively. "I want you," she whispered, "time and time again." She lowered herself against him, trembling as she grazed his chest with her breasts, then pressed her lips against his throat, his shoulders, and teased his bronzed flesh with the tip of her tongue. "I want you in a way that lives with me night and day . . . I want to kiss you down to your toes and know the taste and scent of you . . ."

"Oh, Lord, go on!" Kent groaned with a shudder. His fingers clutched convulsively into her hair as her body moved along his like an undulating tide. Her kisses were languid and hot, determined to drive him wild. As her husky words had promised, she touched him all over with her lips—boldly, lovingly, with an intimacy he encouraged with hoarse words of soaring pleasure.

He caught her, drew her to him, kissed her passionately, and rolled her to her back. His mouth found her breast, his tongue curled around it, his teeth flicked over the nipple, drawing a delighted cry from her lips. Trembling, she clutched his shoulders and begged him to take her. He forced her to wait, hands and lips eager to know and love her completely. With each new intimacy he sought, she shuddered and murmured out; he refused to allow her inhibitions and exhalted in the response of her body. Her taste was springtime to him; her pleasure something that made him smile. He told her she hadn't failed him at all—she was about to learn that she could find a pinnacle again and again.

He kissed her lips hungrily, shuddering as her long legs teased his body, parting for him. He held her face between his hands and groaned, "Damn! I'd give my eyeteeth not to be heading for New Orleans . . . to spend day after day here with you . . ."

She went rigid suddenly, her eyes troubled as they met his. "Kent . . . I'm so scared."

"Scared?" He shook his head. *Now?*

"The game!" She clutched him strenuously. "Kent, I don't want you out there. I don't want you hurt!"

He was losing her—just when he was about to go mad. "Katie . . . Katie, listen to me. There's nothing to worry about. We plan to take the first half as a running game. As soon as the guards have covered me, I'll switch sides. I'm going in as quarterback for the second half—they'll be expecting to sack me, but we're going to run it then, too. Believe me, the guards are forewarned. We're going to switch places at the last minute before every play."

"I don't want you hurt, Kent," she told him, her voice catching on a little sob. "Please, please, be careful."

"I will be," he promised. And he had never meant it more; the absolute, innocent beauty of her eyes had touched him in a way he couldn't begin to fathom. And then her lips were touching him again, fevered, wonderful. He shuddered, knowing he had to have her soon. And he thought again that she was beautiful, her skin so silken and flawless, her body so curved and slim. And he, beside her, was battle-scarred and rough, but perhaps, he thought, that was the way it should be. "Katie—"

Just as he murmured her name, the phone began to ring. She went rigid once again.

Two rings, then the machine answered. "Kent, damn you, I know you're there. *Pick up the phone!*"

"It's Sam," Katie said.

"I know it's Sam!" Kent snapped with exasperation.

She brought a hand to his cheek. "Talk to him, Kent. I'm not going anywhere. You didn't call him back, you know. Go talk to him—then we can pull the plug out of the wall."

Kent sighed, then decided she was right—he was going to have to pull the damn phone out of the wall. He still had the night, and if he left things as they were, Sam would just hang up and call back.

"Don't move," he warned Katie, "and don't forget where we were!"

"I won't," she promised with a husky laugh.

He rolled over, picking up the bedroom extension. The recorder made a shrill beep, and he turned it off before saying, "Hi, Sam, what's the emergency?"

"Dammit! Why didn't you return my call?" Sam demanded with uncharacteristic impatience.

"I've been busy," Kent replied, smiling at Katie. She returned his smile and sidled against him, running her nails lightly over his arm, brushing the back of his shoulder with kisses.

"Is Katie there?" Sam demanded tensely.

"Yes, of course."

"Well, watch it," Sam said. "Watch yourself . . . and watch what you say to her."

Kent frowned. "What are you talking about?" He heard a long sigh.

"I'm telling you, Kent, I would have never believed it myself. I was completely bowled over. If it hadn't been for your interest, I would have been madly in love with her myself."

"Sam, you're not making any sense." He glanced at Katie's blond head beside him, at her elegant fingers playing along his thigh. He frowned. She glanced up at him, and he forced a smile, pulling away to sit up on the bed, obstensibly to concentrate on Sam's words.

"Listen to me, Kent—Kent, are you listening?"

"Yes, go on."

"Kent, she's after a whole lot more than a story. Has she been asking you about the game?"

"Why?"

"Listen to this: she's been seeing Paul Crane for the last six months. *Paul Crane!* Connie was telling me all about some party Katie had been to with Crane. They were fooling around together, then they left."

Something seemed to pound in Kent's chest, something that hurt like a hammer. "So?"

"Paul Crane! Our opposition for the Superbowl, Kent."

"Maybe it's—nothing."

"Nothing?" Sam laughed hollowly. "I gave the guy a call myself—on the pretext of a 'may the best man win.' He assures me that it really is something. As soon as she gets back to New York, he intends to announce their engagement. Kent, come on! Now, listen to this: I told you about the rumors regarding the betting in Vegas? Well, inside rumor has it that some of those heavy betters have been approaching some of the Titan players. And some of the guys have been accepting pretty high payments to knock us out of the game. Do you understand me, Kent? This game is worth a fortune to Paul Crane. Has she asked you about the game? Hell, Kent, I'm sitting here with the New York papers. There are hints of the damn engagement on the front of the sports section. She's sure as hell going to run back to New York and tell him everything she knows."

So what? Kent wanted to shout. He closed his eyes. He thought of the tears in her eyes when she had told him how she didn't want him hurt. Those beautiful sea blue and green

170

eyes, eyes that beguiled him from the start. He thought of himself telling her their game plan. He thought of her whispering that she wanted to know him time and time again . . .

He remembered the morning. That very morning and how they had lain contentedly together after making love. He had talked to her about very particular plays. Hell, he'd given away more than a stupid first-year rookie. It had just seemed right. She was Dante's daughter—he could talk to her, because she understood the game. Dear God, he'd said so much. He'd talked to her about strengths and weaknesses.

She'd expressed her concern about him so sweetly when all the while, she was planning on returning to New York to announce her engagement to another man.

His mouth went entirely dry. There was no fool like an old fool, he warned himself. But he wanted to shout at Sam. *No!* She was a virgin when she came to me . . .

A sickness pitched its way into his stomach. Paul Crane was known for being hell on his women, for using them. It wouldn't be beneath the man to send out his own fiancée . . .

A woman who was Dante Hudson's daughter. A woman who had wanted to claw Kent's eyes out as a child—and had, as an adult, planned a totally conniving revenge, no matter what the cost to herself?

"Kent, I'm not telling you to bat her in the head or anything," Sam was saying. "Just be careful of what you tell her. Don't give out any of our strategies or tell her any of the plays we're planning on using. Kent?"

"I'm here. I—I'll see you soon, Sam. Thanks for the, uh, call."

He set down the receiver and turned around.

There was something different about him, Katie knew. Something that made her sorry she'd insisted he speak to Sam.

He looked wired, as if he were facing a hefty tackle on the goal line. The lines about his eyes appeared deeper, just as their color seemed darker, tenser. Damn, she thought, Sam

171

probably said something about the game, and the stupid game drove them both.

She longed to ease the strain from his face. Katie reached out to touch his brow, but he caught her hand. For a moment she was certain that his eyes narrowed and glinted. His grip upon her was tight.

But then he lifted her hand to his lips and kissed it. "Where were we?" he asked, smiling. But she didn't like the smile.

"Is Sam all right?" Katie asked worriedly. Maybe that was it.

"Sammy is fine," Kent said quietly, leaning over to kiss her. His fingers grabbed the hair at her nape roughly, but his lips were warm, and his mouth touched hers with fervor and passion. Attuned to him, Katie responded, certain that the edge of roughness had something to do with the interruption in their lovemaking. And yet . . . his hold on her was so fierce that she winced, trying not to cry out or protest.

With that same naked tension and a swift agility, he moved above her, his body taut. His fingers were entwined in her hair as he looked into her eyes as if challenging her in some way.

Kent knew he should let her go . . . now. He should roll away from her with the contempt she deserved—spurn her, hate her, but from a distance. The fury that ripped through him like lightning tempted him to slip his hands around her neck and squeeze. But he couldn't. He hated himself, he hated her, but he had determined that her game would be played out. He'd teach her what it felt like to be used.

He smiled. "Time and time again, Katie?" Damn those eyes of hers, wide and liquid with confusion. When she lifted her hands to his cheek, he found her wrists and held them by her sides, smiling still as he wedged himself deeper between her thighs.

And then he closed his eyes because he felt her embrace despite his sudden entry; he felt her form shudder, heard her little cry. And despite the rage and the wrenching pain of betrayal he felt, Kent wanted her so desperately. A shattering,

172

driving need swept him now, not with violence but with a blinding force. He moved with a furious beat, perhaps believing that the ache in his heart could be released with the fever of his desire.

It was over quickly, a volatile, shuddering explosion. Then he heard her ragged breath—and he knew instantly that his pain hadn't lessened, and his anger grew again because he could not slake her from his system. He rose above her again, moving damp strands of blond hair from her face, watching her eyes, feeling further betrayed by the innocence in them.

"Tell me," he grated, "does Paul enjoy your hair? Does he like to run his fingers through it when he kisses you?"

"Paul?" She seemed confused and dazed, the ultimate actress to the very end.

"Paul Crane."

"What are you talking about?" she asked, impatience and something like apprehension in her voice.

He dropped her hair and rolled to his side, resting on an elbow. "You've never dated the man?"

Katie frowned. The vivid, incredible beauty of a daydream was becoming a nightmare that she didn't comprehend. What was going on? She hadn't imagined the difference in him—it was real—and his rough tension hadn't had anything to do with passion.

She was shaking, thinking—and trying to be honest. "Yes, I've dated him, but I don't—"

"You don't understand?" Kent finished for her, his tone very low, very silky. He ran his fingers over her abdomen, stroking lightly. They caressed the shadow between her breasts, fluttered over the mounds with a loving tenderness that had been absent moments before when she had ached for it.

But now it was wrong. All wrong. And she was too lost, too stunned, still groping for understanding.

"Congratulations," Kent continued with the same husky

tenor in his voice, "I've just heard about your impending marriage."

"What?" Katie whispered in amazement. It didn't make any sense.

"I know that you've been seeing him for the last six months, Katie. But I want to know, was this . . . all this . . . because you love Paul so much or because you still believe I betrayed your father? Or was it just because you still think I stole your time with him?"

She found the strength—and the fury—to push his hand away. In a second she was on her knees, edging away from him, staring at him with the dawning of horror.

"So help me, Kent, I don't know what you're getting at! The extent of any of my previous relationships should have been pretty damn obvious to—"

"Ah, yes," he murmured, "a virgin whore. So much the better."

"Oh, my God! You're insane with your arrogance—" Katie began, her voice as soft as his, her words enunciated clearly as she struggled just to articulate.

"You know," he interrupted calmly, "I thought at first that you were willing to sell anything for a story. But there were higher stakes than an article, weren't there? I never did care much for Paul Crane—even when we were on the same team. He'd sell his own mother for a win; I shouldn't be surprised about you. Of course, you would have thought he'd want to reach the punch first himself, but maybe he didn't think you'd have to go quite so far. But cheer up, he hasn't got any old-fashioned hang-ups that I know of. He'll probably still marry you anyway."

There were things she would think of later, the absurdity of the thought of herself and Paul Crane married, or the idea that Sam—whom she had cared about so much!—had only to make a few statements and she was condemned, but these thoughts escaped Katie at the moment.

With cool reasoning she might have made a mockery of the

174

situation and Kent's behavior, but there could be no reasoning after the things he had said. White hot fury, a roaring blaze of it, washed through her. She screamed and attacked him, sobbing and shouting her hatred for him. She lunged madly, her nails raking for his flesh. He rolled easily from her attack and caught her wrists.

"No, Miss Hudson, I already bear your scars—enough for a lifetime, thank you."

Katie lashed out with a string of expletives, but none of them were quite adequate to describe how she felt about him. Nor could she free herself from his grasp. He listened to her, his features taut and white.

At last she was caught above him, gasping for breath, feeling the heat of his body beneath hers.

He smiled icily at her. "Once more, for old time's sake, Katie?"

When she twisted desperately, he released her. She was still shaking with rage, but now she was seeking the dignity of control.

"I hate you, Kent. I really, truly despise you. I'll never forgive you for this." She managed to stand and find her clothing. "I don't ever want to see you again, as long as I live. I'll dance on your grave when your stupid game pounds you into it."

It was dark. Tears were stinging her eyes, and she couldn't see him anymore.

"What do you think you're doing now?" he demanded harshly.

"Leaving," she said shortly.

He snorted something derisive without rising from the bed. "Don't be a fool. You can't leave a snowbound mountain by yourself."

"Watch me," Katie replied.

"Don't be an idiot! I'll get you back down—without touching you again."

Katie ignored him with single-minded purpose. She was out of the house before he had stumbled from the bed.

And she hurried. Some kind of reason was with her again. She hated him—oh, how she hated him!—but though he was arrogant and stupid, and any number of other things she couldn't begin to think of yet, she knew he would come after her, certain she would perish in the snow if he didn't.

She didn't know if she cared about perishing. All she knew was that she had to get away from him. The snow was ankle-deep on the paths, up to her thighs in the surrounding drifts. It didn't mean a damn thing to her—she just didn't want to be anywhere near him. It might be foolish to attempt a mule ride in the cold of a frozen night, but she was certain she could do it. She would take Clarabelle and ride down to Bill's, then drive the Jeep back to Denver. It was simple, and it was possible to accomplish.

"Katie!"

She looked back. Kent was standing in the doorway, a tall silhouette against the warm flood of light from the cabin. He had his sheepskin jacket on, and he appeared extremely broad-shouldered and muscularly trim as he blew on his hands to keep them warm.

Katie watched him for a second. Then she resolutely turned toward the barn once again.

"Katie! Kathleen Hudson—dammit, woman, just what kind of a fool are you? *What do you think you're doing?*"

She ignored his furious question and didn't look back. What do you think I'm doing, you idiot? she wondered bitterly.

Then she heard his footsteps on the snow. "You're going to get back in here, now, young woman—"

Just who in the hell did he think he was to abuse someone with mental cruelty and then command that same person?

She kept walking, hearing the crunch of her own footsteps, realizing that his were moving more quickly. Was it instinct, she would wonder later, or the result of the fury and pain that touched her heart and soul with lunacy? She began to run.

176

Perhaps it was only a set determination to escape him. If she could reach the mules first, she could take Clarabelle and release the others.

And it felt good to run. The air burst into her lungs like a fresh, cleansing wind. She loved to run, and she was fast. She was Dante Hudson's daughter, and he had been a great runner. Quick to throw the ball, equally quick to charge ahead with it, leaving guards and tackles falling at his feet while he raced for the line . . .

Running faster now, her breath coming in pants, her legs reaching, muscles warming. The cold brought tears to her eyes—or was it the cold? Katie felt like the wounded animals they had discussed earlier . . . a lifetime ago. She would run, glory in it, find victory in escape.

"Kathleen!"

His voice, ragged, incredulous, was close. She made the mistake of looking back and lost a stride. Her heart hammered hard against her chest, and when she tried to look forward again, it was too late. Arms like steel came flying around her, and she was falling into the snow with all the impetus of her speed.

Katie was stunned and breathless as she landed, aware at first only of the snow, cold and biting where it touched her cheeks. She wanted to cry; she refused to. And she felt the greatest bitterness. Something hollow and empty. She'd played it all very badly from the beginning, culminating here.

She could run, yes. But only someone touched by true insanity tried to outrun a man who had broken records with his speed on the field.

"Katie!" He was above her, shaking her, bronzed flesh taut across his features, his mouth grim. He looked tired, she thought, and worn, as if he had just battled the L.A. Raiders instead of a foolish woman who couldn't get close to first down.

Instinctively, she tried to twist away from him. No matter

177

what her action, she could not forget his words or live down the fury.

"Katie!" He grated out her name once again, and she felt a harsh tension in his arms.

"You can't leave, alone in the night!" he told her stiffly. "I'll take you in the morning."

She stared at him blankly.

"Dammit, I won't touch you. I won't even talk to you. But you can't go down the mountain alone at night."

"Would you move then, please?" she requested quietly.

He pushed himself from her and dusted the snow from his pants. Katie stood and stepped over him, walking rigidly toward the cabin. She heard him following behind her, and she heard their footsteps crunching in the snow, echoes in a suddenly very silent night.

CHAPTER TEN

Katie closed the door behind her. Kent opened it, then closed it again. She felt his presence and knowing that he was there made her feel as if she were a stick of dynamite with a very short fuse. It was impossible to be near him.

He moved quietly into the kitchen while she wondered what she should do next. She could lock herself in the bedroom. Yes, she decided, that was probably the smartest thing to do.

"Would you like coffee or a drink?" he asked her tonelessly. "You should have something, or you'll wind up with pneumonia."

"You're not supposed to be talking to me," Katie reminded him sharply, swallowing quickly after her own words. She wanted to be calm and behave rationally, but there was only one thing to do when a relationship—whatever there was of it —was irrevocably broken. The thing to do was leave, and she couldn't. And if she couldn't leave, she was going to feel like fighting and defending herself—proving to him that he was the one who was horribly, stupidly wrong.

Forget it, forget him, she advised herself. But she realized that wouldn't be easy. She had fallen in love with him, and though she hated him for his callous words and accusations, she could not so easily turn off the feelings he had bred in her heart.

"Katie," he said very quietly from the kitchen, and she knew from his rigid stance, from the grim position of his jaw, that he felt the almost unbearable tension himself. "I've prom-

179

ised to leave you alone and see you back to Denver. I couldn't allow you to leave because you could have killed yourself."

"Wouldn't that have been convenient?" she drawled as she fought a new rising fury. "I wouldn't have been able to see Paul and give out any secret game strategies."

"You sound like a child—"

"I do?" Her voice rose incredulously. "You're the child. You and your damned game! Does it ever occur to you that the world is filled with people who don't give a damn about a game?"

He was setting the coffeepot on the stove. If anything, his lips compressed more tightly together, his teeth clenched hard.

"Miss Hudson, Paul Crane cares a great deal about the stupid game. And I care even more, Katie, because I have a real thing against foul play—"

"Foul play! What the hell could be any different? You spend your life talking about 'killing' one another! What could be any different about—"

"I'll tell you what could be different," Kent interrupted icily, striding into the living room before forcing himself to stop a few feet away from her. "Normally, when the game is played, defensive tackles go for the quarterback. Normally. The offensive guards are supposed to guard the quarterback. Sometimes the quarterback gets blitzed anyway. A bunch of guys fall on him, and, yes, sometimes he gets hurt. But in a normal game the ball is the focus of the play. No one tries to 'kill' the quarterback once he's gotten rid of the ball. The way it looks now, it isn't going to matter one bit if Sam's holding that ball or not. Crane isn't going to play for possession of the ball—he's going to play to get Sam out of the game."

Katie watched him in silence for a minute. His hands were on his hips, so tense that the knuckles were white.

She wondered if she had dated a man who could really be so vicious as Kent purported Paul to be. Katie knew that he played rough, but he was a tackle . . . he was supposed to.

"Sam's already hurt, Katie," Kent said more quietly.

"And he shouldn't be playing in the stupid game to begin with!" she retorted in exasperation.

"Don't you understand anything?" he thundered suddenly. "Paul is on the take! He has to made sure his team wins that game!"

"Well, if you know that for sure, then tell someone!" Katie shouted back.

He threw up his arms and looked for a moment as if he intended to choke her—then turned on his heel with a disgusted grunt and returned to the kitchen.

He pulled something from the refrigerator and threw it on the counter with a thud. Then his eyes were on her again. "Go take a bath and put on some dry clothes. Eat something. Then you can go to sleep and pretend that I don't exist."

"Take a bath?" Katie started to laugh. "With you here? Not on your life."

"I won't interrupt you."

"Right," she said bitterly, "just like you won't talk to me."

He looked at her. The expression in his eyes had become a sardonic one. His gaze roamed over her in a long, head-to-toe assessment that was less than flattering.

"Miss Hudson, what makes you think I'm so overwhelmed with desire that I would come running into a bathroom to assault you?" He smiled without humor. "Speak of egos."

What raked along her spine was an emotion so strong it left her feeling weak. She would explode; she felt that terrible urge to cry because it was all so stupid; she wanted to tear him to pieces.

"I think," she managed to say very coolly, "that I have very little reason to trust anything about you, Mr. Hart. I don't know what went on during that phone call, but I've never seen more despicable behavior afterward."

"Oh?" He lifted a brow. "You seemed to be doing all right." He smiled once again, only it wasn't a smile at all. It was serious and controlled. "Your hands were all over me, sweetheart. I couldn't see much sense in disappointing us both."

Katie froze for a minute, then she returned his smile, sweetly. "Kent, I've always abhorred the violent side of football. I had good reason to do so. But when this game does come up, I hope you're 'killed' all the way through."

"Me?" he returned softly. "You know, I have a hard time figuring out why I come out being the bad guy here. I didn't come up to New York to drag you out of your pristine office. You came to me—supposedly hating every minute of it but determined to get your story. Then I get on a plane and you're there. You turn into such a sultry little kitten that you hit your mark right on the line. I invite you here because we both knew by that point that I couldn't keep my hands off you. And everything's great—just great. I'm so totally enamored, I come off like a little kid. I talk to you like I would to Sam—after all, you're Hudson's daughter, you understand everything I'm saying. I admit we have a weak defense. I even tell you how we plan to play the game. Quarter by quarter."

"So what?" Katie hissed.

"So . . ." He gave her a bitter grimace and rounded the counter to face her again. "When I met you in the locker room, Katie, I was led to believe you were closing your eyes to the fact that I was a football player—for the sake of your career. Kathleen Hudson. Surely she would hate the game that cost her father his health and finally his life. And surely, understandably, she would have an anathema for football players. Except that I find out in the middle of very impassioned lovemaking that Miss Kathleen Hudson is about to announce her engagement to another football player—a man she's been seeing for half a year. And not just any football player, somehow, just somehow, this guy turns up being our opposition for the biggest game of the season. Meanwhile, rumor is running rampant that the big betters in Vegas—some real big guys, with questionable underworld associations—have this guy in their pockets. He has to win the game. Has to!

So here we have his lovely fiancée . . . cuddled up to me, listening avidly to every word I have to say. This same woman who disliked me rather personally because I supposedly ignored her father—while she returned my letters. She knows how and when Sam will be vulnerable, all sorts of wonderful information to run back to New York with. What am I supposed to believe? Should I have just lain back and racked my mind for any other helpful details to give you?"

Katie stared at him incredulously—hurt, horrified, and angry. And then, ridiculously, she began to laugh. "You think that I slept with you for football secrets? Oh, my God! The whole pack of you are a bunch of narrow-eyed jocks! I don't give a damn who wins that game."

"Dammit, Kathleen!" The food he'd placed on the counter went flying to the floor, and she was startled at the sheer violence of the action, meeting his eyes with her heart fluttering despite the inner knowledge that he would never really hurt her. "Then why didn't you *TELL ME?*"

"Tell you what?" she cried vehemently.

"About Paul, about the fact you were planning an engagement. That I was in bed worshiping—falling in love with—another man's woman."

She stared at him, mesmerized by his eyes and the tension and pain in his voice. She wanted to go to him, but something inside her prevented it. If he had been falling in love with her, he wouldn't have listened to Sam. Kent would have trusted her enough to talk to her, not mock the very act of love between them and turn it into an act of fury and vengeance.

"I'm not engaged or anything of the like to Paul Crane," Katie said tiredly. "I've dated him, yes. But then"—she hugged her arms about her chest and met his eyes with reproach—"you know just how far my affair with Paul could have gone. An affair with any man, for that matter. I think that has to be the absolute clincher in this whole thing, Kent. You knew there couldn't have been any deep and passionate

183

affair taking place. But Sam Loper calls up, and what Sam says is like the voice of God."

"Then maybe you'd better let the papers—and Paul—know that. The facts coincided nicely, don't you think?"

"I don't have a hell of a lot of say about what someone chooses to print in a paper. And I don't think it matters much, does it?" she asked him coldly. "I'll be out of here tomorrow, running back to New York with all with this world-shaking information for Paul."

"Is that what you're going to do?" he asked in an unexpected whisper.

"It's what you believe, isn't it?" she challenged.

"I'd rather not believe it."

She started to laugh again. "Isn't it a bit late to be asking me for explanations?"

He turned around, and she lost sight of him as he dipped down to retrieve the things that had flown from the counter. When he rose, his back was to her. "It would be nice to know just what you were up to," he said coldly.

"Up to . . ." Katie shook her head, then shivered suddenly. The snow was permeating her clothing; she felt damp and more miserable than she had ever been in her life. Less than an hour ago she had been warmed, touched, by him, glowing as she held tight to a dream. But all that had changed now. As she watched him, it was hard to believe. The man with the broad shoulders and fluid strength was not hers anymore. It was almost impossible to believe that he ever had been—equally impossible to forget how she had loved to love him, and be loved by him in turn. If she could just erase the last hour, the things that he had said . . .

It still wouldn't do any good, Katie thought, a sour taste filling her mouth. He had talked to her now, but he'd offered no apology. He was demanding that she prove her innocence. Innocence! She'd done nothing at all except become a victim of circumstance.

"Okay, Kent," she said at last, "I'm going to tell you the

184

whole horrible truth. I never told you about Paul because it was really none of your business—we haven't been at the confess-all stage for long, you know. Then, too, there just wasn't anything to tell. I did date the man, having no idea that such a thing would brand me as a spy and public-enemy-number-one to the Saxons."

She turned around—not so much because she had finished speaking but because tears were stinging her eyes. After what he had said she would never, never let him see her cry. He would never find her weaknesses.

"What are you doing now?" Kent called out harshly to her.

She spun around, resenting his authoritative tone. "What is this? Dante was my father, Kent. And Dante is gone."

He started walking to her once again; she tensed, fully aware that his temper had eased as little as hers. He didn't look at all like a man ready to offer a humble apology. Yet she feared him, not because of his anger but because of his eyes. They were as dark as the night, full of brooding tension, and she felt then that he was perhaps as torn as she—wondering where the black and white of truth and lies became gray. She didn't want him near her because, for all her fury, she wanted to cradle herself against his chest and burst into tears of confusion and misery.

"Dante is gone," he agreed with her quietly. "But I think we're both walking on thin lines right now. You want to be left alone? Then, please, behave sensibly. I'd just as soon not be responsible for you coming down with a case of pneumonia, so you've got two choices. Take a hot bath and get dressed on your own . . . or I'll see that you do."

Katie stared at him, wishing she dared take a swing at his face. But she didn't dare, and since she knew that he was in the same combustible turmoil as she, she didn't doubt for one minute that he would carry out any soft-spoken threat. Or warning. Whichever it was.

"Do you treat your own daughter like this?" Katie asked him caustically.

"I don't have to," he told her briefly. "Anne has the sense to come in out of the cold."

Katie looked at him slowly, crossing her arms over her chest. "Right," she murmured, "she's probably afraid you'll knock her halfway through a goalpost if she doesn't."

"Someone," he replied coolly, "should have knocked you halfway through a goalpost years ago."

"Yes, that is your opinion, isn't it?"

"Katie, your problem is that you think you can play by your own rules—separate rules—and no one else is supposed to mind."

"Your problem," she replied evenly, "is that you've come to believe that everything is a game."

"Thank you, Miss Hudson. I'll try to mend my ways. Now, are you going to take that bath, or do you need my assistance?"

"I'm going. I just want to remind you of one more thing. What I did or didn't know about the game doesn't mean anything in the long run. None of your meticulous game plans mean a thing. You know as well as I do that when you get on that field, things change. If things always went as planned, Cougar, there wouldn't be any losers, would there?"

Katie left her question hanging in the air. She turned around and walked down the hall, shutting the bedroom door behind her. She turned on the light in the room, and the first sight that greeted her eyes was the bed, tousled and disheveled. She gritted her teeth and closed her eyes, wondering how and why she had ever gotten herself into this position.

Hating a man, loving him—and hating herself because she was foolish enough to love him still, no matter what had been said and done. What was the matter with her? Where was her pride? Hiding behind her hurt, she decided wryly. But it didn't matter if her pride chose to lurk in her soul, as long as she could pretend that it was at the fore.

She closed her eyes against the pictures of the bed, but the memories of whispered moans, entangled limbs, and promises that could never be kept still haunted her.

She let her wet clothing fall to the floor as she filled the tub with water. Then she sank down, glad of the heat, glad that the water dulled the pain that gripped her heart.

Hart, heart . . . heartbreaker Hart. She should be laughing; she had never expected more.

She laid her head against the rim of the tub and closed her eyes. It was over. She still wanted to kill him, to pound the truth into him. She wanted him on his knees, telling her how wrong he was, how very, very sorry—how much he loved her, and how, because he loved her, he'd gotten carried away.

Foolish. He'd never said he loved her. He'd only said he wanted to sleep with her more than once. Big difference, Katie, she told herself bitterly. And he still believed she came here because Paul sent her to figure out the Saxon game plan.

Paul! Damn him. Was he running around telling everyone they were engaged? What a mess . . .

Katie tensed suddenly, wondering if it could be true. Was Paul on the take from big money? She shivered. Katie couldn't believe it; she couldn't believe that anyone—even a rough, burly tackle—would want to seriously injure another player. They got hurt all the time, yes, but seldom as badly as her father had been. And her father's injury had been an accident; he had just been hit once too often in the wrong place.

She shivered again despite the heat of the water. She wanted to wash out Sam Loper's mouth with a dozen different kinds of lye, but she didn't want to see him hurt. Not again, not when his ribs couldn't possibly mend fully before the game.

"What am I doing in the middle of this?" she whispered aloud. And then she decided to put Raff on her list of men to hate with vengeance for getting her involved with the whole thing to begin with.

All she had ever wanted to do was be a writer, she thought in a moment of self-pity. She wanted to write about people.

She loved to talk to them, to find out what made them tick, the quirks behind the genius, the mind behind the athlete . . .

She was finding out all about Kent's mind. It could move in devious and vicious circles when he chose, the tough jock who wasn't about to be used.

But I love him anyway.

She swallowed, steering herself from fantasy once again. Be realistic, she told herself sternly. She would go back to New York and give Raff a sound piece of her mind—then she would deal with Paul and be through with the lot of them.

If only Kent weren't out in the other room, or if only she'd made it down the mountain and was halfway back to Denver herself, it would be so easy. Her pride could be maintained then, and she wouldn't be tempted to hold him, be held by him.

The water was starting to grow cold. Katie opened her eyes —staring toward the bathroom door in horror and disbelief.

There was a snake in the room. Not a little one, like a garden snake. This one was big. A very big snake that looked to be ten feet long at least. It was slithering near the door, its large head reaching upward. Katie didn't know what kind of snake it was—she didn't know anything about snakes at all, except that they didn't belong in bathrooms, especially not a bathroom in the Rockies during the winter.

Its long body twisted. Katie saw its eyes, pitch-black beads in a mottled face. It flicked out its tongue as if it were some ancient sea serpent anticipating its prey—her.

Katie returned the creature's stare, not daring to blink. She swallowed convulsively, aware that she was barely breathing, that her mouth had gone dry. She was absolutely terrified.

She tore her eyes away from the snake's to cast a quick glance down the length of its body again. Fear riddled through her with a sickening, weakening twist. It was so long and thick. Was it a poisonous snake?

It started moving, coming toward her with its strange glide, the body coiling, curling, and uncoiling to slide again. Katie blinked, praying that she was imagining the whole thing. There couldn't be a snake in the bathroom. There couldn't be, there couldn't be . . .

She tried to rack her mind for anything she might have heard. She was in the mountains in the dead of winter—how the hell had a snake this big been able to get into the cabin? Didn't they hibernate or something?

Did it matter? a voice from her numbed and terrified mind asked.

No.

She opened her mouth. "Kent." It came out as a dry croak. She swallowed. The snake was lifting its head to the tub now. It was near her left shoulder, and she felt as if she were becoming paralyzed.

Katie worked her jaw furiously again. "Kent!" It wasn't loud enough yet. She'd always heard that in their dreams many people reached a point of terror and discovered that they couldn't scream. She had never thought it possible. But now she did. There was no fluid in her mouth, and she could barely find air to breathe.

The black eyes locked with hers. She took a breath. Then another.

And then she screamed, long, loud, and shrill.

The bathroom door burst open. The snake's head had crept around until it was exactly at her shoulder. Katie wrenched her gaze from the snake's and leaped from the tub, screaming again as she tripped over the snake's tail.

"Katie!"

She heard Kent's voice; she saw the anxiety in his eyes, caused by the terrified screams that had brought him to her.

She threw herself into his arms, dripping all over him but not caring in the least.

His arms wound around her. "Katie?"

"Kent, my God! What is it? Where did it come from? Oh, God, do something!"

He did. He lifted her against him, closed the bathroom door

189

with his foot, and carried her quickly to the bed, where he wrapped a sheet around her shivering form and held her tightly.

Katie pulled away from him, looking into his eyes. "Kent . . . it's huge. And it's still in there . . . in the bathroom. Oh, my God. How are you going to get it? I've never been so scared in my life. I—"

"Shh," he told her, smoothing back her hair. "It's all right Katie, it's okay—"

"No, no, Kent! It isn't all right! It's still there . . . it was looking at me—watching me!"

He spread his fingers over her nape and urged her head back to his shoulder. His own heart was beating at a furious rate. He was holding her again; he had never thought he would. Nor had he ever thought he'd spend a night like this, knowing the twist of the most bitter pain only to doubt himself with an agony just as fierce. Where did the truth lie? Sam would never have called him if he didn't believe every word he said. But Sam hadn't been with him; Sam hadn't touched her; Sam couldn't have known she was a virgin . . .

I'm in love with her, he thought, feeling the frantic beat of her heart against him, the soft press of her naked breasts, the fevered cling of her fingers. I'm in love with her. And because of it, I'm frightened that I'm a fool—that she can say anything in the world and I'll believe her . . . because I want to. The things she had said to him so bitterly, so scathingly, were the truth. She could not have been Paul Crane's lover. Still, she had been seeing him . . .

And now, right now, while he held her, it didn't seem to matter. He was sorry, so very sorry for the things he had said and done in the midst of pain and fury. He didn't know if he was right or wrong—but he was sorry. Yet he couldn't change what he had done or said. This moment would be fleeting; she wanted no part of him, and she was holding him now only because of her absolute terror.

"We've just got to stay out of there," she said, her eyes wild, on his. "He's big. He can't possibly escape. Oh! But maybe he can! He got in there! How did it get in there? Kent, you can't go after it—it's huge!"

Kent wrapped the sheet about her shoulder, regretfully pulling it more tautly over the engaging softness of her breasts as he pulled away, setting her upon the bed on her own.

"Katie, I don't have to go after it. 'It' is Ed."

She shook her head in vehement misunderstanding, her shocked eyes filled with the certainty that he had either lost his mind or hadn't understood a thing that had happened.

"What are you talking about? There's a snake in there. A monster! It's at least ten feet long, and it has the blackest, most malicious eyes I've ever seen—"

"Katie!" He caught her hands and brought them to her lap. He was shivering with his reaction to her, and every time she waved her arms, he was seeing her breasts, full, rounded—and too enticing for a man who had sworn not to touch a woman. She was fresh and sweet and deliciously scented from the bath; her skin was soft and silky, and her slim, beautiful curves were playing cruelly with his mind and body despite the words and fury that had passed between them.

And as soon as he spoke again, she was going to hate him even more, he thought dryly. "Katie, that snake with the malicious eyes is just Ed."

"Ed?" she repeated, staring at him.

"Ed," he repeated with a sigh. "He's a pet. Not mine—Bill's. I don't know how he got into the bathroom, probably from a drain near the shed and then through the toilet."

"The toilet," Katie repeated blankly.

"They can move from place to place through plumbing systems. Like I said, he might have been out in the shed. It's insulated and warm even in the winter. He loves the shed, so Bill keeps him there."

"Ed is a pet—and he loves the shed?" Katie said, still staring at him as if she didn't believe a word of it.

"He's harmless, Katie, completely harmless. You probably scared him to death."

"I scared *him* to death?"

"Katie, he's an old, old boy. Very old for a boa constrictor. He's almost twenty, but he still likes to explore a bit."

"He's an old boa constrictor—and he likes to explore," Katie repeated again, her voice still dulled with shock.

Kent would have smiled if conditions between them had been a little better. But they weren't, he reminded himself painfully. He rose, a little awkwardly, but Katie didn't notice. "I'll go get him out of—"

"No!" she cried, then she was standing, too, her fingers on his chest, her eyes wide as they stared into his. "No, I—"

"Katie." He had to swallow fiercely. The sheet was hanging off her again. He could feel her naked flesh and smell her evocative scents; her breasts teased his chest mercilessly as she looked into his eyes. He desperately longed to cup her breasts in his hands and feel their firm weight, their softness and peaked nipples. He ached to throw off her sheet and press her supple length to his . . .

"Katie, I'm telling you the truth. Ed won't hurt you—he barely manages against the rats anymore. He's friendly." He caught her hands again, folded them together, and held them away from him. Closing his eyes, Kent fought the power of her blue green eyes and turned quickly, walking to the bathroom.

Suddenly, he heard her laugh behind him.

"A pet. A *pet!* Oh, my God!"

She had obviously realized that she had been scared to death and had hurtled herself into his arms, naked, when there was no need. Kent shrugged. It wasn't his fault the damned snake had gotten into the bathroom.

He opened the bathroom door. Ed was curled around the rim of the tub. "Come on, old boy. The lady isn't fond of you at all."

Ed gave Kent his enigmatic snake's stare. Kent picked the

192

snake up with accustomed ease and curled the reptile over his shoulders. When he stepped back out into the bedroom, Katie scrambled onto the bed.

"He really won't hurt you."

"He's so damn big," she murmured.

"Actually, he's small for his type," Kent said. He left the room with the snake about his shoulders, closing the door behind him.

Katie stared at the door, wondering if she wanted to laugh, scream, rage—or cry herself silly.

CHAPTER ELEVEN

Katie could have—and probably should have—stayed in the bedroom. But she was hungry, wired, and, no matter how ridiculous it seemed, still frightened. Good old Ed might be a pet to Bill, but to Katie he was a snake. Who the hell ever heard of an old mountaineer keeping a boa constrictor? Kent had taken the snake away, but it had spooked Katie. She shook out her clothes strenuously before putting them on, although it was obvious, even to her, that a ten-foot snake could not be hiding in her lingerie.

She paced the room for a long, long time after she had dressed, aware that she should just stay in it. She alternated between righteous anger, total humiliation, and anxiety. Too much had happened in the past few hours, and it was impossible to stay in one place for very long.

At length she left the room, ostensibly to go to the kitchen and get something to eat. A pleasant aroma came to her, the smell of something good cooking.

Kent was at the kitchen table reading an outdated sports magazine. He glanced up as she walked in, regarded her with a enigmatic gaze, then returned his attention to the magazine. Katie opened the refrigerator door.

"The stew's ready any time you like," Kent said without looking at her. Katie paused. He stretched, yawned, glanced at his watch, then stood. "If you don't mind, Miss Hudson, I'll take my bath while you've vacated the bedroom. Then I can be out of your way for the evening."

"Aren't you eating?" she asked brusquely.

"I already have." He started out of the kitchen, then paused. "I've put Ed out in the shed and covered the drain. He won't bother you again."

Katie watched him walk away, her eyes trailing over his back, his long-stepped, easy gait, the slight sway of his powerful shoulders. "Jock!" she muttered beneath her breath. Her lips twisted into a sad smile. She silently added, you are no longer a part of my life—but then, you never really were . . . You weren't meant to be.

She sighed and fixed herself a plate of the stew, irritated with herself for being so annoyed that, among other things, Kent was perfectly capable of cooking and cleaning up after himself. The stew was even good. Very good. She tasted it standing by the stove, then decided that, with the way things had been going, she deserved to have a stiff drink with dinner, something to wear down some of the ragged edges of her nerves.

She sat down to eat her stew, finished it quickly, washed her dish—she didn't intend to leave a mess anywhere—then took her drink to pace around the living room as she had been doing in the bedroom.

Outside, beyond the warm glow of the fire and the coziness of the cabin, the night seemed as black as pitch. Katie held back the drapes and stared out, frowning. It was snowing again, hard. Massive wet flakes hurtled through the dark sky.

She would have killed herself on the highway, she thought with a shiver, if she had even managed to reach the highway. It was, admittedly, a good thing that she hadn't tried going down the mountain. She was accustomed to snow, since New Hampshire had offered plenty of that, but not on a mountain.

"There's another storm?"

Katie started, cracked her head on the pane, and turned around to see that Kent had bathed and was standing beyond the sofa in a sweatshirt and jeans.

"It's snowing," Katie replied stiffly. His appearance should

195

have been her exit cue. It seemed apparent that she was being offered continued residence of the master bedroom, and that he was planning to sleep in one of the guest rooms.

Yes, it was her exit line. She should walk down the hallway with quiet pride and dignity—speak with him only when she was spoken to in the morning, since she would never have to see him again once they reached Denver.

She remained by the window, her drink in one hand, the other hand clutching the drape.

"Did you eat?" he asked.

"Yes." She hesitated, then added a very stiff "Thank you." Distance, she reminded herself. She couldn't run out into the night like a child again—nor was the snake around so that she could forget she was wounded and furious and fly into his arms. "It was very good," she heard herself say, and her voice sounded very remote. "What was it?"

"Venison."

"Venison? You mean one of those beautiful deer?"

"Yes."

Katie felt a little ill. She hadn't been cut out to be a mountain girl, that was for sure.

"Nice night," she murmured dryly. "I get to bathe with a snake, then find out I've eaten Bambi for dinner."

"If you kill an animal," Kent replied softly, "it should only be for food."

She turned around. He had walked back into the kitchen. She heard a chunk of ice falling in a glass. A moment later Kent came back into the room, swirling that ice cube around in a glass of scotch. He approached the window and pulled the drape back further without touching Katie. He frowned, then allowed the drape to fall back in place with a grimace.

"What was that for?" Katie asked as he walked back to the couch.

"What?"

"That frown?"

He shrugged. "The snow just looks pretty severe, that's all."

"Pretty severe? What does that mean?" Katie asked, her dismay growing. "Please don't tell me we could get stuck here."

"It's likely."

"Oh, God!"

Katie strode back to the kitchen and added a little Coke and a lot of rum to her drink. Pausing a moment, she then clutched both bottles beneath her arm and headed through the living room, intending to continue straight down the hallway. Kent's sudden laughter brought her to a halt. She turned and regarded him coolly.

"Going to drink yourself into oblivion, Miss Hudson?"

"Possibly," she replied with a cool smile and slight hike of a brow.

"Rum is a poor substitute for warmth," he said, his features and eyes enigmatic.

She lifted her glass to him. "It will do for the evening."

"Be careful, then, Miss Hudson," he warned her softly. "I seem to recall that you're a woman with a rather low tolerance level."

"As a matter of fact, Mr. Hart, I have no tolerance left at all," she replied, neatly sidestepping his meaning and asserting her own. "And your responsibility is completely at an end. I've been warmly bathed, fed, and watered. I assume I'm completely free to retire for the night?"

"You are." He raised his glass as if toasting her. "But I'm curious, Miss Hudson. What if—just if—the snow continues?"

"It can't," she told him with determination.

"Why? It shouldn't matter so much to you. You were supposed to trail me until the Superbowl—weren't you? Oh, no! I keep forgetting," he added with mock dismay, "there's more in the East than just *World Magazine,* isn't there?"

"Is there?" She saluted him stiffly and started down the hall

197

again. She reached the bedroom door, opened it, and resolutely closed it behind her.

It was going to be a long evening. But she was going to get through it intact, she told herself.

Kent drained his scotch in one long swallow, fully aware that he was drinking more than he should be with the big game only two weeks away. But the alcohol burned nicely through him. He stretched out a hand, clenched it into a fist, unclenched it again, then leaned his head on the back of the sofa and closed his eyes.

Why can't I leave her be? he wondered. Her angry self-defense rang with such a scathing truth! But he had known her for such a short time, and Sam wouldn't have called if there hadn't been some smoke to the fire.

He rubbed his temple and sighed. No fool like an old fool, he reminded himself. And tonight he felt very old and worn. Kent smiled to himself bitterly. Wound an animal, and it will strike. Was he just like an old battle cat, gouged and down, and more than ready to pounce back?

Yes, that was precisely it. She had gotten to him, right beneath the skin. Desire had become caring, and caring . . . somehow it had become love. It had just hurt unbearably to realize that he had trusted love again only to find he was being used.

And he still didn't know just what was or wasn't true. Something about the whole game thing was very wrong; it also seemed as if part of the picture was missing. What? It just wasn't falling completely into place. So Paul Crane was on the take to smash the Saxons into the ground. Crane would be doing his damnedest to do that anyway—every man on the Titans would be playing it that way. It was the name of the game.

There'd be no way in hell to prove any of it. So what did it matter? The Saxons would have to play a very careful game.

Kent closed his eyes, then shook his head. He felt as if he'd been given a child's jigsaw puzzle, only to discover that the piece that completed the whole picture was missing.

He shrugged. It was just a game, right? The Saxons would battle it out their hardest, and they'd either win or lose. So what was he looking for?

The outcome, he thought dryly. The day when he would know whether or not every word he had said to Kathleen Hudson had been repeated to the opposition.

No . . . it went further than that, he thought. Much further. He wasn't as worried about her repeating secrets as he was about her. He didn't wanted her anywhere near Paul Crane. Maybe it was because there was something about being a woman's first lover that entrapped a man's soul; maybe it was just because he had fallen in love with her. But, as mad and furious as he'd been, he didn't want her going back—to either New York or Paul Crane. He wished there were a way to lock her up for the next two weeks—maybe for eternity.

Except, of course, that she was never going to forgive him. His words had been harsh, totally condemning. And if she was innocent, the things he had said and done were totally unforgivable.

Kent rubbed his temple; he was coming down with a hell of a headache. He glanced down the hallway. Damn, but it would be nice if it were still last night, or this morning—any time before Sam's call had turned him into a raving madman and then left him riddled with doubt and guilt. If only he could go to her, lie down beside her, and feel the fluid movements of her fingers tease away his weariness.

The phone rang suddenly, cutting into the pictures in his mind. Kent stayed where he was, since the machine would catch the phone. Then he jumped up and headed for the kitchen extension. He didn't want Katie to hear any recorded messages.

"Hello?"

"Kent?"

"Yes. Paula?" He was startled to hear his ex-wife's voice.

She had known he was coming here with Katie, and Paula never intruded on his private life.

"Oh, Kent! I'm so sorry to be calling you. I wouldn't, you know, unless I was really worried—"

"Paula, it's okay. You can call me any time you need to. Really. What's the matter?"

"Oh, Kent! It's—"

Kent jerked the phone from his ear as static suddenly overwhelmed her words with a loud crackle.

"Kent?"

He heard her voice again.

"I'm here, Paula. We've just got a horrible connection. There's a storm here."

"Oh. I'll try to speak quickly. This all just started yesterday morning—"

"Paula, what started yesterday morning?"

"You know I never say anything at all about what you're doing, even when I know."

"Paula," Kent said quietly and firmly. He frowned quizzically. Paula never stumbled in her speech, and she never prattled.

"I just don't know what's—"

The static came again, wiping out Paula's voice.

"Paula? Paula?"

Kent pulled the receiver from his ear once again, hesitated, then tried again. "Paula?"

The line had gone completely dead. Frustrated, Kent slammed the phone into the receiver. He cautioned himself to patience, then picked up the phone again, assuring himself that he could call her back, but the line was still dead.

He sighed, hung up the phone, and walked back into the living room to pull open the drapes. The snow was coming down with such a force that it looked like one big white sheet. His wires were probably down.

"Damn!" he exploded out loud. Shoving his hands into his

pockets, he began to pace the room restlessly, wondering what had been so serious that Paula had decided to call him.

Maybe, he tried to tell himself, she had heard some more rumors about the upcoming game, and all she had wanted to do was warn him to take care of himself. No, he decided, she'd already told him what she knew about Paul Crane. The name left a bitter taste in his mouth. He forced himself to go forward with his thinking.

Maybe Paula had just had some kind of a really bad argument with Ted and needed some advice or a shoulder to cry on. No to that, too, he decided with a dry groan of irritation. Years ago, Paula had experienced some domestic problems, minor in the full scope of her marriage but major at the time. She'd started to talk to Kent about it but had then withdrawn, saying that it just wasn't fair to Ted to bring Kent in on the situation.

What?

Anne, he thought with a rush of pain. Something was wrong with Anne.

He went to the window and jerked back the curtain again. There wasn't a thing he was going to be able to do about it. Not tonight. It didn't look as if he'd even be able to open the front door.

"Damn!" he muttered again through grated teeth. Restlessly, he strode back to the phone and picked up the receiver to be met by dead silence once again. He slammed the receiver back into the hook and paced furiously back to the living room.

He tried to reason with himself. Paula was worried, but she didn't say that anything had happened. Maybe Anne had discovered boys and was just experiencing the normal emotional crisis that occurred in any thirteen-year-old's life. Not "just," he told himself firmly; whatever was going on was surely very important to his daughter.

But she was all right—Anne had to be all right. He would

make sure that he talked to her as soon as possible and help her through whatever the problem was.

Kent spotted his glass on the end table where he had set it, plucked it irritably into his hand, and strode back to the kitchen. The game was two weeks away. Tonight he needed another drink—a stiff one—if he was going to sleep.

He poured himself the drink, giving himself stern mental warnings as he did so. There wasn't a damn thing he could do with the storm outside. And, as serious as things might be, he'd just have to handle them when he could.

There was a small noise behind him, and he spun around. Katie was standing there, watching him with wide eyes. She'd changed into her forest-green robe, and her hair fell about her shoulders in glossy waves.

"I—I heard the phone," she explained at his questioning look, "and your pacing. Is anything wrong?"

Kent didn't know what stole over him as he watched her standing there—probably a nagging sense of betrayal, an insecurity he had never thought to experience, or maybe guilt. Maybe it was just a combination of his worry about Anne and the tension from all that had happened between them. He needed help, but he didn't know how to reach for it. And so he lashed out instead.

He leaned back against the counter as he looked at her coldly. "Were you expecting a phone call? From your fiancé perhaps? Well, it wasn't for you."

She stared at him a minute, then told him exactly what she thought he should do with himself. When she started down the hallway, he remained silent until she neared the bedroom door.

"Katie!"

She paused, looking back at him.

He straightened, setting down his scotch, sticking his hands into his pockets and clenching them tightly into fists.

"I'm sorry for that. I—uh—yes, something is wrong. It was

202

Paula, my ex-wife, and we were cut off. I'm worried that something might be wrong with my daughter."

Her lashes fell over her eyes; her hand was still on the doorknob. "I hope that everything is all right." She started to push the door open.

"Katie," he said again, wondering how he could feel so awkward.

She looked at him again.

"I am sorry."

"For jumping at me now?" she asked quietly.

"Yes."

"But not for calling me a whore?"

"I—uh—yes. I shouldn't have said that."

She laughed, and the sound carried bitterness. "You're sorry for your language . . . but not the meaning behind it."

He felt very stiff, very rigid. Yes. I'm sorry about everything, about the whole damn mess! he wanted to say. But he couldn't. It was still there. A nagging anxiety and doubt. She was really very, very beautiful. And there had been a time when she had hated him immensely.

Paul Crane, the newspapers, everything; it was just too much of a coincidence.

He stood there mutely, watching her. She waited, but when he didn't speak, she reentered the room.

In the stillness that followed, he clearly heard the click of the lock.

"Oh, the hell with this!" he muttered. "The hell with this whole damn night!"

He stared at his scotch for a minute, then tossed back his head and swallowed it in a gulp. He shook from head to toe as the fiery liquid burned its way down. Then he set the glass down with a sharp click and walked down the hall to the guest bedroom.

He stripped down to his briefs in the darkness and crawled beneath the sheets and blankets. He tossed about, trying to get comfortable on the standard-sized bed. It was just too small—his feet hung off and his arms kept hitting the headboard.

With a long, drawn-out sigh Kent forced himself to settle down. But it felt as if his mind were on fire. He just kept thinking about Katie, the game, about Paula and Anne. What the hell was going on while he was cooped up in this snowbound cage?

The game, injuries, Paul, his daughter. Daughters in general. Katie . . . Dante's daughter.

When he finally slept, his thoughts were in a jumble, so maybe it wasn't so strange that he dreamed of Dante Hudson. They were back on a football field—Kent didn't really know which one, he couldn't even tell the state or the season, but he knew it was a dream, and so it didn't matter. Dante was there. As real as he had ever been in life. A tall man, broad at the shoulders, but very trim, wiry, and as healthy as a thoroughbred horse. He was full of life and laughter.

"Never let them know you're hurting, Cougar. When they've blitzed you into the ground, you just gotta laugh, no matter how much you ache. Keep them all worried about you."

"Sure thing, Dante. But what happens when they drag you off the field?"

"That's when you gotta give them your biggest smile."

Suddenly, there were people all around them. Kent and Dante were in the huddle, and Dante was rattling out the play. Kent ran into position; he hunched down, looking at the linebacker set against him.

"Four!"

The ball went into play. Kent swiftly sidestepped the linebacker and started racing down the field. Dante saw him, and the ball went sailing, flying high in a great arch—falling straight into his arms. Then Kent was running again. He could feel the strength in his muscles, the total joy and exhilaration. He could hear the roar of the crowd, and he felt as if he'd conquered the world.

He made the touchdown, but there was a buzz from the field. When he looked back, the coaches, players, and the team doctor were standing over Dante.

Kent ran to him.

Dante was smiling. "I'm a little winded here, Cougar. Man, did I get a snap in my neck! Help me off the field, will you? Did I ever tell you I was thinking about retiring? Leading the life of Riley, you know, hopping around Europe—I always wanted to have a pretty Spanish señorita, you know?"

There was laughter in his eyes—blue eyes, just like his daughter's. A scream was bubbling up inside him, a scream, high and unbearably shrill . . .

Kent bolted up in the bed, sweating and shaking. The scream had been so damned real!

It came again—a high, piercing sound in the night.

Katie!

He practically tripped over the covers, trying to pitch himself out of the bed. He stubbed his toe instead, hopped about for a second, then wrenched open his door and tore down the hall, but her door was still locked. He threw his shoulder against it, and the wood shattered with an ease that sent him flying into the room. Then he stopped short, feeling more than a little absurd as he faced her.

The light was on, and she was fine. She was sitting up in the bed staring at him—but at least her expression was as sheepish as he felt. She had removed the forest-green robe and was clothed only in a sexy thin gown that was a softer shade. It didn't cover her shoulders; it enhanced the firm curves of her breasts. Not at all fair to his senses. He gave himself a little shake, and—feeling foolish having just broken through the door in his briefs—he planted his hands on his hips.

"What the hell were you screaming about? I thought you were being stabbed, killed. What the hell is the problem?"

"I, uh, nothing," she murmured, a flood of color rising to her cheeks.

"Nothing? You scream like a banshee and tell me *nothing?"*

205

She lowered her chin and her lashes, then met his eyes again quickly. "I'm sorry, it was really nothing."

"Dammit, Kathleen Hudson, you'd better tell me something."

Katie looked at him. He was all bronze and taut, looming over her with his hands on his hips, the muscles of his shoulders and chest straining with tension.

"I, uh . . ."

"You *what?*"

Her lashes fell like chestnut fans, lovely as they shadowed her cheeks. "I thought the snake was in bed with me," she mumbled.

"What?"

Her head snapped back, and she stared at him with her eyes blazing like morning stars. "I thought the damn snake was in the bed with me, that's all."

He was silent, staring at her incredulously. Her scream had probably cost him ten years of his life; his heart was just never going to be the same again.

She started talking again, quickly. "I'm sorry! I was half asleep, and I felt this—this thing against my leg. And all I could think of was the snake, but I guess I'd just set my glass down, not realizing I was half asleep . . ." Her voice trailed off as Kent continued to stare at her.

"You thought you were sleeping with a snake, but it was your stupid glass?"

"Yes."

He threw his hands into the air and began to mutter.

He was definitely angry, Katie thought, gritting her teeth together defensively and trying not to cringe against the bedpost.

But he didn't come anywhere near her. He left the room, emitting another disgusted snort as he saw the door, and then kept muttering as he returned to the guest room.

She wished she could crawl beneath the bed and hide. If

only she hadn't screamed and awakened him! She could have survived the hours until morning . . .

Katie blinked, then stared after him, feeling the physical pain of emptiness. If only she could have left! There was no hope for their relationship and she knew it, but she couldn't stop the feelings. They were so strong, that when she was near him, pride placed a weak second behind love.

"Hey!"

Katie started. Kent was back in the doorway, watching her with dry reproach. His eyes were very dark; it almost appeared as if he were smiling.

"What?" she asked.

"You owe me for that one!"

"Owe you?" she exclaimed, but something warm and thrilling touched her heart, and a weak, delicious dizziness swept through her. No, Katie, she warned herself.

But rationale took care of the warning. She'd be okay once she was away from him, free to pursue her own life and forget the time she'd shared with him. She didn't want to see him again, not after the things he had said, the things he believed . . .

But that could be for later. It was going to take her a long time to forget Kent Hart; she wanted it to be a long, long time before he could forget her.

"I don't owe you anything, Kent," she said quietly. "Nor do you owe me. The sheets are clean, don't you think?"

She couldn't tell what he was thinking as he stood there. His eyes were too dark, his mouth too tight. But did it matter what he thought? She wanted him, and she didn't want to think beyond that right now.

One last time . . .

She smiled at him slowly and saw his eyes narrow, his brows lift in surprise.

Katie reached over to the bedside table and turned off the light. Then she slid her legs to the side of the bed and got to her feet, walking to him.

Darkness curled around them and caressed them; she could see only his silhouette, then a moon fire reflection in his eyes as he watched her come to him.

She stopped a foot away from him and caught his eyes with her own as she lifted her hands to her shoulders, sliding away the straps of her nightgown and allowing the silky material to fall to the floor in a languid cascade. For a moment her heart quickened: what if he repelled her?

She heard the sharp intake of his breath, then she felt his hands, hard as they gripped her arms and pulled her to his chest. She felt the heat of his gaze as he stared down into her eyes.

"I thought," he muttered hoarsely, "you said you didn't owe me."

Katie tossed her head back, lifting her chin, not at all sure if she was seeking love or vengeance.

"I don't owe you a damn thing, Kent Hart. I never did."

"Then, why . . ." His hands moved to her face, his thumbs raking over her cheeks. His eyes continued to stare into hers, and she felt the tremendous heat of him, the tension that crackled all around them. "Then why am I holding you?" he asked.

She smiled, then slipped her arms around his neck, pressing the length of her body to his, savoring the rush to her system as her naked breasts touched his chest. She pressed her hips to him and shivered, knowing the power of his arousal.

"Because," she said with a cool touch of regal disdain, "you're wrong, Cougar. Dead wrong. You lost something tonight, something very special. And when I'm gone, you're going to know just how special it was."

"You think so?" he demanded with a throaty dare.

"Yes." Katie whispered, narrowing her eyes.

For a moment they stood there, caught in the static tension. Then Kent cried out fiercely, enveloped her in his arms, and pressed fevered lips to the pulse at the base of her throat. Held by him, she found his eyes on hers once more, dark as the night, alive with an inner fire.

"God help me, Katie, I can't care why." he muttered.

She didn't know he had moved, but he had. His weight followed hers down to the bed, and she felt his heat between her thighs, the intoxicating ripple of muscle to her touch.

She smiled and shimmied from beneath him. She slid her body over his and kissed him, deeply, languorously. And when she was done, she made love to his body with her own, caressing him with her entire length, burning a trail of hot, passionate kisses down his length. There were tears in her eyes as she loved him with an aching vehemence—loved him intimately, taking all of him.

He twisted with a sharp groan, calling out her name, raking his fingers into her hair to bring her to him, then beneath him. He took the lead with a fierce and passionate strength; her body shivered in the sweetest ecstasy at his entry, and then it was she crying out his name, arching, striving, soaring . . . undulating as her soul found solace from pain in the sweeping beauty of sensation.

She bit lightly into his shoulder as the storm cascaded around her; the tears stung her eyes through it all. It would be hard for him to forget her. Oh, yes! That she promised herself. But as long as she lived, she would never forget him. Inside of her she knew that there just wasn't another man like him. If she searched a lifetime, she would never find another . . .

CHAPTER TWELVE

Morning came to Katie softly at first, slowly. She was warm beneath the covers, warm with her body curled next to Kent's. She felt the light first, permeating the room, awakening her. She opened her eyes, then closed them again, filled with a sense of pain so acute, it made her shudder.

Morning had, as always, come. She would have to turn her back on this man who could not trust her and return to New York. If it was possible.

She stirred, pushing back the covers to rise slightly in the bed and look toward the window. The sun was shining almost fiercely. There would be nothing to prevent her from leaving. Her eyes fell on the bedside clock. It was a few minutes after ten. They had slept late, but she felt unrested.

Katie lowered herself to the bed again and risked a glance at Kent. He was still sleeping. She smiled a little with both bitterness and pain; this morning he looked rested and very young. His hair lay over his forehead, and a curve graced his lips as if his dreams were sweet. Even the grooves and lines about his eyes and mouth seemed to have eased; he might have been a young man of twenty. Except, she thought, for his shoulders and chest. Broad, fully filled, powerfully muscled, they were marred here and there by scars. His chest was thickly covered with short dark hairs. It was a mature chest, no matter what the image of youth his face portrayed this morning.

Katie closed her eyes and lay down for a moment longer.

She opened her eyes once again to look at him; she had determined not to touch him. She'd had her time last night and wanted to believe that he would miss her, but she had to find the strength to pit herself against him. She didn't know if there had ever been a chance for a real relationship to begin with; now, it was impossible. Nothing could be right when it was based on pain and distrust and anger. And she knew that if she didn't leave him, she would never have her own self-respect again and therefore could never command his.

But as long as he slept . . .

She smiled at the barely perceptible crook in his otherwise long and straight nose. My love, she thought, you have been beat to hell. As well as three scars that had faded on his shoulders, there were scars about his knees, too, surgical scars. Still, she thought he had the most beautiful body she could ever imagine. For all his physical attraction though, she could never have fallen in love with a body. She had fallen in love with him.

Careful to not awaken him, Katie crawled from the bed and quickly searched her suitcase for her clothes. She started to dress, then was distracted by sounds outside. Voices? Who could be coming to the cabin?

Kent was not sleeping soundly, yet neither had he fully wakened. The light touched his consciousness, but he didn't want to acknowledge it. It was a nice place where he drifted, a misted dawn. He frowned in his state of half sleep as he heard voices. Was he dreaming again? he wondered idly. He thought he heard Anne. It was a dream, surely it was a dream, because he had been so worried about her last night. Just as he had recalled Dante from his memory, now he was recalling his daughter. She was talking and laughing, just as she had on her last visit here. There had been high, white drifts of snow then, too. She had been bundled in boots and a parka, and she had loved the snow. Like the child she was, she had played in it. He smiled vaguely in his sleep, then frowned as her shouts took form and substance—very real for a dream. It wasn't just

Anne's voice he was hearing; it was Bill's, too, calling to Anne.

"You wait up there just a minute, young lady. That's your father's house, and you let him know you're out here."

"Bill! He's *my* father. His house is my house, and I don't have to knock at his door!"

Kent could see his daughter, tossing her head with a certain hauteur. Anne was a proud young lady, sometimes a little too assured for her own good.

A sharp slam sounded, and Kent's eyes flew open. He sure as hell wasn't dreaming—the outside door had just opened and closed with a tremendous force.

"Dad!"

Kent bolted up, and he was sitting, astonished, on the bed. He saw Katie standing beside the bed, looking as confused as he felt. She was halfway dressed—her jeans and boots were on, and she wore a bra. Apparently, she had been searching her luggage for a sweater. She was staring at him with bewilderment, reproach—and ardent dismay. And it was all happening too quickly for either of them to do a thing about it.

"Dad!"

Fleeting thoughts crossed his mind. Paula had called last night, worried crazy because of Anne. What the hell had happened? How in God's name had his daughter gotten to Denver?

"Dad!"

Anne was standing in the doorway then, in a parka and boots, just as he had imagined her. She was staring at Katie.

"Dad!" she gasped as she looked at Kent, her eyes horrified and angry.

"Young lady!" he snapped in return, feeling a little absurd from the position by which he was forced to greet her. "What the hell do you think you're doing? Your mother is frantic!"

"My mother is frantic?" Anne gasped out. "Oh, hell!" Kent saw the tears rise to her eyes and knew she was uncomfortable with her own outburst and profanity. But she was also upset, and before he could speak again, she was speaking—and staring venomously at Katie, who returned her gaze with unwavering eyes.

"I thought—" Anne choked out, "I thought you were hurt! I thought you needed me. I thought you had decided not to come to see me before the big game because you were hurt and you thought that I would worry."

"Anne—" Kent began, startled. Good God! What had been going on in her heart and mind? It had never occurred to him that he would hurt her by his absence.

What had she done? Run away and flown all the way out to Denver, alone? Where had she gotten the money? How the hell had she accomplished the feat? No wonder Paula was half crazy. Suddenly, Kent was really furious, not just because he was lying naked in a bed with Katie half dressed beside him as he was being attacked by his child but also because he knew Paula had to be beside herself with worry. How could Anne have done such a thing to her mother?

"Don't!" Anne screamed to him, and he saw that tears were racing down her cheeks. "I loved you—I had to see you. I didn't know some—whore was with you instead of me!"

His face whitened, and Kent felt every muscle in his body tense. He could feel Katie's startled, horrified reaction to Anne's words. And the pain that had been brought to her suddenly filled him with a new sense of shame and absolute fury.

"You obnoxious little brat!" he yelled. "You apologize this minute, or, so help me God, young lady, you won't be sitting for a week! Then you can call your mother. I'm your father, Anne, and don't you ever forget it; you show me a lack of respect like this again—"

Anne's small face was pinched, her lips pursed, her complexion white. Katie was dead still, and every bit as pale.

"No!" Anne screamed, shaking her head. With a sob she repeated, "No!" Then she turned to run from the room.

Kent swore loudly and jumped from the bed, grabbing his clothes.

"What do you think you're doing?" Katie asked.

He stared at her with surprise. She had found a sweater and pulled it over her head. She was fully dressed and ready to leave the room.

"What am I doing?" he snapped furiously. "I'm going after her. I'm going to tan her hide for what she said to me, for what she did to her mother, and for what she said about you."

Katie smiled at him bitterly. "Why? It's no worse than what you called me."

"Katie," he began, starting to walk to her.

She raised a hand against him, shaking her head. "I'm going after her, Kent. You can punish her and settle the other matter between the two of you later, but don't punish her on account of me. That is one area where I do have the expertise. She might have been wrong, but I know what it's like to be the daughter of a 'hero.' It's damned hard. She's your daughter, Kent. She loves you with all her heart, and it's real love, the kind that's hard to come by. If I were you, I'd settle the matter calmly. I'm not a part of your life—she is." Katie stared at him to make sure he understood, then turned around and left him quickly.

Kent stared after her and groaned. Should he chase her— chase them both?

He pulled on his jeans, then sat down on the foot of the bed, pressing his temples strenuously between his hands and wondering how it was possible to have such a pounding headache when he had only been awake for a matter of minutes.

Katie hurried down the hallway. In the living room she met Bill. The old mountaineer was standing there, his hat in his hands. His face was bleak with discomfort and misery.

"Miz Hudson, I'm sorry, m'am, I really am. I just didn't know what to do. She showed up at my place last night before the storm started. I couldn't get through on the phone. I figured her ma and pa had to be just about fevered by now, wonderin' where she was. I tried to hold back as late as I could—"

"Mike, you did the right thing," Katie interrupted. "It's not your fault. Which way did she go?"

"Out—either to the barn or the shed in back."

"Thanks," Katie said briefly.

Outside the cabin the cold morning air pierced her lungs. She hugged her arms about her chest and plowed through the new-fallen snow, deciding to try the barn first.

She didn't know why her heart felt so heavy—why she was so determined to set things straight. She'd never seen Anne Hart before, and she sure as hell didn't owe Kent anything.

But there was an aching sense of déjà vu about the whole thing. She had been there before, jealous, hurt, lost, and so in love with a parent she didn't get to see often enough.

Quite simply, Katie knew, she saw herself in Anne. And she understood as no one else would ever be able to do.

Katie's breath was fogging before her, and she was shivering when she reached the barn. But there was no one there except Clarabelle and the other mules, who eyed her starkly. Katie left the barn, shivering anew as she fought her way through the snow drifts to get around the back of the house to the shed.

The door to the shed was about an inch ajar. Katie pulled it open, allowing the sunlight to filter in. She saw a light switch and turned it on, then drew the door closed. The shed then offered some warmth as she quickly scanned it.

There were shelves with the usual tools one might expect to find; paint brushes, fuses, wires, hammers, nails, and wrenches. To the far left were several cords of firewood.

And to the far right, huddled in a corner with her knees drawn up and her arms wrapped around them, was Anne. An Anne who stared at her belligerently with eyes and tense features remarkably like her father's—except that Anne was a very pretty child with a very feminine softness that could have only come from her mother.

Katie hesitated, pausing to clench her teeth together as she discovered something else about Anne and her defensive position. The child had Ed, Bill's boa constrictor, wrapped over her shoulders. Obviously, Anne didn't have any of her hang-ups about snakes.

Still, Katie determined, she wasn't going to let Anne know she was afraid. Hadn't Kent assured her that the creature was a pet—completely safe? And surely, Anne and the beast had met before. If Ed wasn't safe, Kent would never allow the snake near his daughter.

Katie was wondering where to start when the little girl gave her the opening she needed.

"What are you doing here?" Anne snapped out waspishly. "I would have thought you'd be crying on my father's shoulder."

Katie lifted a brow. "I try not to make a habit of crying on people's shoulders. Besides, I don't see any reason to cry."

"I'm not going to apologize," Anne told her. "He can't make me. He can beat me, but he can't make me say I'm sorry. And if you come near me, I'll sic Ed on you. He's mean and vicious, and he'll strangle you if I tell him to."

"No, he won't," Katie said. "We both know that. And I don't care if you apologize or not. You should, of course, because you can't run around calling people horrible names. Nor do you have the right to charge into your father's life like that."

"And who do you think you are?" Anne sneered at her, but Katie saw that the little girl was frightened, and more than anything she wished that she could hug her and assure her that she was no threat. But she couldn't, and she knew it well.

"Why did you come here?" Anne demanded with a sniff. "Are you trying to coddle up to me and convince my father that you're great with kids? Don't bother—I hate you. What are you going to try to do? Sweet-talk me and hug me?"

Katie leaned against the wall and crossed her arms over her chest. "Certainly not. Your behavior was obnoxious—you were acting like a little brat. You do deserve a sound thrashing, but I have nothing to do with any of this."

"You don't?" The suspicious question came out before Anne had a chance to think. "You're not trying to get my father to marry you? He won't, you know."

Katie smiled grimly. "No, your father won't marry me. But I told you, I'm not important here. You're important, and so is your father—and your mother. Anne, I know what it's like to love someone and worry about them terribly. But what you did was wrong. Your mother is probably sick with fear that something has happened to you."

Anne stroked the snake. "Mom shouldn't be worried. I left her a note. She told me where Dad was, and I'm not an infant, you know. I've been here before." She looked at Katie, renewed hostility in her eyes. "I've been here lots of times, and I'll be here again. My father says that any home of his will always be a home of mine."

"Anne, it was wrong, and you know it. Even in your own home, you don't burst in on other people's privacy."

"I told you—I'm not an infant. I know exactly what you and my father were doing."

"Well, then," Katie said coolly, "you'll understand that your father is an adult, a mature, responsible man who has every right to a private life. That certainly doesn't take anything away from you, Anne."

"How do you know?" Anne charged. Then she lowered her lashes, hugging the snake. "I thought he was hurt; I thought they hurt him in that last game. I thought he was afraid to see me, and I wanted him to know that I loved him no matter what."

Katie heard the anguish in Anne's softly belligerent voice. She didn't approach the child, but she knelt down to be on eye level with her. "I understand that."

Anne's eyes met hers cynically. "No you don't. And don't try to butter me up. I hate you."

Katie shrugged. "Anne, I told you. It doesn't matter if you hate me. What matters is you and your dad. And if you're at all interested, I'll tell you how I know what you're feeling and why it's important that you do apologize—to him, not me."

Anne tried to give her a look of vast boredom. It failed, and she shrugged, curious in spite of herself.

"I can't run past you—you'd probably beat me if I did. And I can't stop you from talking."

Katie laughed. "I doubt if you've ever been beaten in your life. I know I wasn't."

Anne raised a brow in another gesture remarkably like her father's—so much so that Katie winced.

She decided to plunge in. "Anne, have you ever noticed those scars on your dad's cheek? They're very pale."

"Sure," Ann said with a shrug. "He's got lots of scars," she said proudly, and Katie almost laughed. "He's a football player."

"Well," Katie said, sitting on the dirt floor and dusting off her hands as she drew up her knees like Anne. "He didn't get those scars from playing football. I gave them to him when I was young."

"You gave them to him?" Anne gasped with surprise.

Katie did smile then. She had certainly caught Anne's attention. "Yes. You see, I was the daughter of a football player, too. You probably met my dad when you were a little, little girl. He and your father were good friends. Best friends. Anyway," Katie shrugged, "my parents were divorced, too, but my case was a little worse because my mom died right after the divorce, and I lived with a very nice aunt. But she was older and not very exciting, and I think I lived just for those times when my father would come to see me and give me all his attention. Well, one day he showed up with your father, and I was so jealous I could barely stand it. So, I—I scratched him. My father was furious, and I don't think he ever really forgave me. You see, I knew that I was wrong, but I just couldn't apologize." She paused, silent for a minute, then said regretfully, "I'd hate to see you make the same mistake, Anne."

Anne stared at her for several seconds. Katie could see all kinds of mixed emotions reflected in the little girl's eyes. Then Anne said, "I—I'm really not completely like you. My mother is alive, and she"—Anne caught her lower lip, then continued —"she's a nice lady, and my stepdad is great, too."

Katie felt as if her heart had caught in her throat. "I'm glad, Anne. And I know they all love you very much. You are really a lucky girl."

"Why didn't he want to see me?" Anne asked suddenly, her voice hurt again. Katie knew she was talking about Kent.

"I think that maybe he didn't know you wanted to see him. I know your father would never hurt you on purpose."

Anne unwrapped the snake from her neck and shoulders and set the heavy thing on the floor. As Ed started slithering around, Katie braced herself, determined not to shy away when she had reached this point with Kent's daughter.

And Anne wasn't trying to frighten or hurt her, Katie realized. She had just decided to set the snake down. She was silent and pensive, then she looked at Katie.

"I guess you're not as bad as you could be. I mean, at least you haven't tried to gush all over me to make Dad think you're sweet and wonderful or anything."

Katie laughed. "Anne, I don't think anything would convince your father that I'm sweet and wonderful."

The girl became earnest suddenly. "It's really all right with me if you see him again. I mean, I guess that he has to see somebody."

What flattery, Katie thought, and then she swallowed, trying to pull her feet closer in. Poor old Ed was slinking toward her, raising his head with the beady black eyes to give her a thorough scrutiny.

"He scares you, doesn't he?" Anne asked suddenly, and for a minute Katie wondered if Anne meant the snake or Kent.

"What?"

"Ed. You're frightened of him, aren't you?"

Katie knew she had been truly forgiven when Anne reached for the snake again, dragging the heavy body back across the dirt floor. "Don't be frightened of Ed," she proclaimed reassuringly. "He really won't hurt you. I—I lied about that."

Katie laughed. "I'm just not used to snakes."

"Touch him," Anne suggested.

Katie recoiled at the thought, then reached out to touch the snake. He felt cold but not slimy at all. She smiled weakly, then settled back against the wall. "Thanks, Anne," she said softly, "I won't be terrified of him anymore."

Anne grinned broadly. "He's really neat."

They were both quiet for a minute, then Anne shifted and said softly, "I guess I should go in and tell Dad I'm sorry for the way I burst in on him. And for scaring Mom. And—and for the things I said."

Katie smiled. "I guess that would be a good idea."

They both stood. Anne looked almost as if she wanted to touch Katie; she didn't. Instead she said, "It's really all right with me if you want to sleep with my father."

Katie felt the blood drain from her face, and she lowered her eyes. The words had been said with no rancor, with no desire to hurt.

"I'd like it if you came with me," Anne said. "Maybe he won't be so mad at me."

Katie lifted her eyes to Anne's and shook her head. "I've got to go, Anne. And you have to face your father by yourself. I'm very glad that I got to meet you. But I . . . I won't be seeing your father again."

Anne frowned. "But why—"

"Why is my business, and his," Katie said flatly. But she smiled again, then offered Anne her hand. Anne hesitated, then took it.

"Go on now," Katie said. "I told you what's important is you and your dad. I meant it. Go fix things."

Anne started out of the shed uncertainly, turning back to Katie.

"You're not going to stay in the shed, are you?"

Katie shook her head. "No, I'm coming."

She followed Anne back around the trail in the snow. Every once in a while, Anne turned around to be sure that Katie was following.

She stopped once and said, "You really scratched my father and gave him those scars?"

Katie nodded. "I'm not particularly proud of it," she murmured.

"Where on earth did you get the nerve?" Anne demanded, and Katie had to laugh. "I mean, he's awfully big. He could chew you up in one gulp if he decided to—even now."

He has chewed me up, Katie thought.. But she kept that reflection to herself and replied, "I guess because my father was there—and I knew he'd never let your father kill me."

Anne shook her head, lost in her own reflection.

"Anne," Katie persisted quietly, and Anne started walking again.

They reached the house and went in. Bill was sitting on the sofa. "Where's Dad?" Anne asked, having to clear her throat first.

Bill inclined his head toward the bedroom. "He's on the phone. Seems they fixed the wires. He's telling your mom that you're here, and that you're okay."

"Anne?"

The question came from Kent. Katie, standing just inside the doorway, saw him step into the hall from the bedroom. He was fully dressed; his features were strained and haggard, his voice gruff; and his hands were on his hips. But his voice spoke of his pain and his love for his daughter.

"Oh, Dad!" Anne cried out, "I'm sorry, I'm so sorry!" And

then she was running down the hallway, catapulting into his arms.

Katie saw Kent's eyes close. She saw his arms wrap tightly around his daughter with love.

"We've got some talking to do, young lady," he told her then, sternly but with understanding. He set her down and indicated the bedroom. "But first I've got your mother on the line. Go talk to her so that she can hear your voice and know you're okay."

Anne went into the bedroom.

For one minute Kent's eyes rose and met Katie's. They were very dark, thoughtful, and reflective. But she didn't know what he was thinking or feeling. She couldn't begin to tell. She returned his stare without moving or smiling. And she thought that it was going to be the hardest thing she had ever done in her life to walk out.

Kent spoke very quietly. She couldn't tell if there was warmth in his voice or anger. "I'll deal with you shortly," he told her, and then he followed his daughter into the bedroom.

Katie was left with a picture of him in her mind—the striking dark power of his eyes, his anger, his warmth.

She turned her gaze to Bill. "Can you please get me down to your place in the Jeep?" she asked.

Billshuffled in his seat uneasily.

"Well, I—I think that Kent wants a word with you first, Katie Hudson."

Katie tried a very winning smile. "Bill, today should be special between Kent and Anne. I can talk to him later. Please, can you get me out of here?"

"What about your things—"

"I just need my purse and my coat. Kent can send the rest of my stuff. Please, Bill, it's very important."

The old man sighed, definitely unhappy about the entire situation.

"Please?" Katie asked softly.

"All right, but put your coat on, girl, and button up. The storm's gone, but it's colder than a witch's tit out there!"

Katie bowed her head, amused by his expression. Then she realized that she wasn't going to laugh after all; she couldn't, not when she felt so much like crying.

Bill helped her into her jacket. They left the cabin, closing the door quietly behind them.

Katie left the mountain, promising herself that she wouldn't look back.

CHAPTER THIRTEEN

The flight from Denver to Philadelphia had been long, yet in many ways, not long enough. Kent had never felt closer to his daughter or more introspective about himself. It was strange; he had always thought that he knew her well, but now he realized he had only known what she had wanted him to see. He had thought that he had been good—decent and responsible. He had only seen what he chose to.

Anne knew that she was going to be punished; she had stolen the money from her stepfather to buy the plane ticket, which she ordered over the phone, by pretending to be her mother.

But Kent was almost sorry he was going to have to take action against her; she was so repentant and so sweet and so in need to be held by him that he felt as if his heart was breaking.

And though he didn't quite know how or why, he knew the bond that resulted from the chaos was due to Katie.

Anne fell asleep halfway through the return trip, and Kent was left to ponder another complex problem of his heart—Katie Hudson.

She had gone; left him as she had promised to do. She had vowed that he would miss her. He did. He missed her in a way that hurt, a way that not even the sweet love of his own flesh and blood, cuddled trustingly beside him, could cure.

What was the truth? he wondered bitterly. Did it even matter? He wanted her no matter what had happened before this weekend, but she was gone, determined that she didn't want to see him again.

And then there was the game. Almighty heaven. Just what was going on? He sighed, closing his eyes as he leaned back in his seat. In a little over twenty-four hours he would have to report back to work. The team would move to New Orleans to start practicing on the playing field.

What would Katie be doing? And why couldn't he stop himself from caring so vehemently?

Well, he thought sheepishly, she'd duped him, for one thing, disappearing when he'd meant to challenge her, competently taking herself away. He scowled, knowing he'd try to make sure she made it back to New York all right as soon as possible.

If only he could stop thinking about her—just for a little while!

They reached Philadelphia by early evening. Paula was crying as she held and greeted Anne at first. Then, having ascertained that her daughter really was okay, she became angry, telling Anne the same thing that Kent had, another stunt like that and she wouldn't be able to sit for a week. But Paula's anger couldn't last because Anne was in such a state of tears herself, asking her mother if she could go and try to set things straight with her stepfather.

Paula's and Kent's eyes met over their daughter's head, and they both smiled a little, pleased that, now that Anne had made her peace with them, she was so eager to do so with Ted.

When Anne had hurried up the stairs to confront her stepfather, Paula brought Kent coffee in the parlor.

"Are you sure you don't want something to eat?" Paula asked.

He shook his head. "We had plenty on the plane."

Paula took her coffee and curled up on the other end of the sofa, watching him with a dry smile. "It was probably my fault, Kent. I had no idea what she was thinking. And she'd just seen you—"

225

"It wasn't your fault, Paula, really. And everything is fine."

Paula gazed at her coffee. "So where is Miss Hudson?"

"In New York—I hope," Kent said with a scowl.

Paula frowned. "What happened? Did Anne—"

"Anne caught me in bed, yes. And I reacted badly, yes."

"And what about Miss Hudson?"

Kent got up, stuck his hands in his pockets, and started pacing around the small confines of the room.

He paused at last, looking blindly out the prettily decorated window. "Anne called her a whore."

"Oh, God, no!" Paula gasped. "What did she do?"

"Who, Anne?"

"No, Miss Hudson."

Kent fell back into his seat at the end of the sofa and lifted his hands in a helpless gesture. "I don't know, exactly. She went out to talk to Anne, and Anne came back full of repentance."

"And then?"

"Anne and I made it up."

"And Miss Hudson?"

"Katie . . . disappeared."

"Disappeared? Kent, on a mountain—"

"Not alone. She got Bill to take her down."

"Because of Anne?"

"No," Kent said quietly with a wince, "because of me."

"I don't understand."

"Neither do I, Paula, not really. Not yet. And I—I can't really talk about it, yet."

"Okay," Paula said. She stood up. "Are you staying?"

"Uh—yes, overnight, I guess. If you don't mind."

"Of course I don't mind, and you know I don't. I'm glad that you can stay. I think it will be good for Anne to have the three of us here tonight. United ogres, you might say."

Kent smiled, but his smile didn't reach his eyes. "Paula, can I use the phone?"

"Sure. Go on into Ted's den if you want some privacy."

Kent did so. Paula went to the foot of the stairs. She could hear the low murmur of her daughter's voice and that of her husband. She smiled; they were working it out. Ted was such a good man, she thought, and he loved Anne with a devotion that almost equaled that of her natural father.

Paula brought the coffee cups into the kitchen and refilled them. When she came back into the parlor, she paused. She could hear Kent softly swearing away in the den.

He came out, fists clenching and unclenching at his sides, the skin of his face stretched with anger.

Paula didn't say anything; if he wanted to talk about it, he would.

"Dammit!" he exploded.

"What?" she asked softly. She hadn't been good at all handling the man as a wife; as a friend she was damned efficient.

He looked at her, his eyes very dark and flashing, a little distracted. "She's got a damned answering machine on. I hate those damned machines!"

Paula didn't think it prudent to remind him that he had an answering machine himself.

"I'm sure she's all right," Paula said reassuringly. "Did you try the magazine offices?"

"Yes, but they're closed for the day." He sat again, more frustrated than Paula had seen him in years. He looked at her suddenly. "Does Ted have any of the New York papers from Saturday handy?"

"Yes, I think so. In his den. He won't mind. Go ahead and look through them."

Kent got up and headed to the den again. He paused. "Thanks, Paula."

"For what?" she asked.

Kent just smiled and went into the den.

Later that night, when Anne had gone up to bed and Kent and Ted had taken a ride out to buy milk and bread, Paula slipped into the den. She found the Saturday paper on top of Ted's desk, opened to one of the sports pages.

She read the article, then thoughtfully closed the paper. When the men returned, she didn't say a word. Eventually, she and Ted went up to bed. But hours later, she awakened. Frowning, she put on her robe and went downstairs.

Kent was still wide awake, sipping a beer and staring broodingly into the fire.

"Kent!"

He looked at her distractedly. "I'm sorry, Paula, did I awaken you?"

She shook her head. "No. But, Kent, you've got to get some sleep. The Superbowl is less than two weeks away now; you're not a young kid. You've got to take care of yourself, or they'll tear you up out there."

He laughed suddenly. "Thanks for the vote of confidence."

"It's a vote for reason," Paula said sharply.

"I just can't sleep . . ." He looked up at her again, then rose, putting a friendly arm around her shoulder. "Okay, I'll go up to bed, and I'll make myself sleep."

He paused at the foot of the staircase. "I may go to New York tomorrow afternoon. Think it would upset Annie? I could drive back tomorrow night, then fly home Tuesday morning and make it in plenty of time to get to New Orleans with the team."

"It sounds okay to me."

He smiled at her and brushed her cheek with his knuckle. Paula smiled softly in return, for one brief moment allowing herself to remember what it had been like to be married to this man.

"You're a great lady, Paula, the best," he told her tenderly.

"You're a little wonderful yourself, Cougar," she said lightly. "Kent . . ."

"Yes?"

"You know, I'm always going to love you a little."

"I'm always going to love you, Paula."

They both smiled. When Kent started up the stairs, Paula hung back a minute, then gave herself a mental shake.

She loved Ted with all her heart; they had been made for one another. She started up the stairs. To her husband's surprise and delight, she woke him in a very erotic way. Later, exhausted and very much at peace with herself, Paula fell asleep.

Kent still lay awake brooding, wishing that morning would come so he could put through his calls to New York once again.

Julie started when Katie literally slammed the door when she arrived at the offices of *World Magazine* on Tuesday morning. She eyed her friend curiously.

"Hi. What are you doing here?"

"I plan on telling Raff what to do with his story," Katie said bluntly. "And his job," she added more softly, "if my career here hinges on this one article." She smiled bleakly at Julie, then hurried past the reception desk and the rows of little cubicles that led to her own.

Julie paused for a minute, grimaced, then rose to follow Katie back to her desk. She leaned against the door frame, a delicate brow rising as she watched Katie set down her purse and hang up her coat.

"I've a score of messages for you."

"You have?"

"Paul Crane called a dozen times yesterday. He had assumed you were only on a weekend trip. And . . ."

Katie's eyes were like windswept seas. "And?"

"Kent Hart has been trying to get you all morning."

Katie sat in her swivel chair and turned around to face her desk, showing Julie the back of her head.

"I don't want to talk to him. Tell him I haven't come in. Better yet, I flew to Paris. Tell him anything."

Julie raised both brows, pondering her friend's reaction. When Katie's phone rang, she remembered that there was no one on the reception desk and moved to pick up the line. She answered, then put her hand over the receiver and told Katie,

"It's Paul. Where would you like me to tell him you went? South Africa?"

Katie looked up at her friend. "Fine. *No!*" she contradicted herself almost immediately, her eyes hardening. "Get a number, please, and tell him I'll call him as soon as I 'come in.' "

Julie shrugged and did as she was asked, scribbling the number on Katie's blotter. She hung up the phone.

"Katie, I know about these things. If you do stay at *World,* you're going to need a private secretary."

Katie closed her eyes and leaned back in her chair. "I'm sorry, Julie."

"Might help if you told me about it," Julie advised softly, the warmth of her friendship in her voice.

Katie sighed. "I—I can't. Not here at any rate. These little cubicles definitely have ears."

Julie laughed. "Well, I have a break coming, and you don't even have to be here. Let me get someone to cover the desk, and we'll go out for decent coffee and a talk."

"It's a long story," Katie warned.

Julie laughed. "I can't wait. And don't worry about the time—Raff wouldn't dare fire me. I'm the only person who can stand him."

Julie was about to walk out when the phone started ringing again. She paused to catch it quickly. *"World.* May I help you?" She looked at Katie again, placing her hand over the receiver. "It's Kent Hart. What did you want me to tell him?"

"That I'm not here."

"I'm sorry, Mr. Hart," Julie began, "Miss Hudson—" Julie broke off, pulling the phone from her ear with a grimace. "He says he doesn't want to speak with you, either, Katie. He just wants to know that you're alive and in one piece."

"Then tell him that I am," Katie said dryly.

Julie smiled and spoke to the telephone again. "She's alive and uninjured, Mr. Hart . . . Yes, I'm sure, I'm looking right at her. As to being all in one piece—"

"Julie!"

Julie smiled serenely. "Excuse me, Mr. Hart. Another line is ringing. It was nice talking to you." She hung up the phone.

"You're supposed to be my friend!" Katie exclaimed. "Good Lord, I don't need enemies."

Julie laughed. "Meet me out front in five minutes. I've got to hear this story."

Fifteen minutes later they were seated in a back corner of an attractive coffee shop on Park Avenue. Katie skimmed over a number of details, but she managed to tell Julie the gist of the weekend—emphasizing Kent's sudden fury after talking to Sam and his certainty that Paul Crane was on the take.

"He might well be," Julie told her.

"But where did he get off to tell any of the papers that he was about to become engaged? I should be able to sue someone!"

Julie shrugged. "Paul Crane isn't the point here. You are—and so is Kent. Katie, you told me that you went back to him after all this happened."

"Yes. That was a disaster, too, because that's when his daughter showed up."

"But that seems to have worked out well," Julie said, smiling tolerantly. "It sounds to me like you're really in love with the man."

"How can I be after what he said?"

Julie laughed. "It isn't a matter of 'can.' You are. And I don't blame you for being angry. It was pretty vile, but . . ."

"But what?" Katie demanded miserably.

Julie hesitated, her beautifully manicured fingers running along the rim of her cup. "Look at it from his point: Paul is throwing threats all over the place, you're in bed with Kent, and the papers are saying you're about to be engaged to another man, a man who will be in direct opposition to him—and Sam Loper—in the Superbowl. It does look suspicious, Katie. And if he's in love with you, it must have hurt like hell!"

"He's not in love with me," Katie said dully.

Julie lifted a brow. "It sounds to me as if he might have been trying to make it up to you." She laughed. "And he did come running to save you from the snake. Twice actually. Except that the second time, the snake was only a rum bottle."

"Not a rum bottle, just a glass."

"What difference does it make? Katie, just what do you want? Do you really hate him? Do you really not want to see him again? If you love him, swallow a little pride. Go out and prove to him that he was wrong!"

Something felt very tight in Katie's throat. "I just don't know, Julie." She flushed, but Julie was a dear, dear friend. "Julie," she said softly, "I'd never been . . . with a man . . . like that before. And even after that, he called me a—"

"Yes, yes," Julie interrupted shrewdly. "He had some horrible and certainly not very pleasant things to say. But if I know you, you've probably called him a number of not-so-pleasant things, too. It's you, Katie, you've got to think."

"I think I'm still furious . . . and I—I think I'm still in love anyway."

Julie burst into laughter. "Then just what do you want?"

Katie pondered the question for a minute. "I want to tell both Raff and Paul Crane to go rot in hell. Then I want Kent to do just that. And then . . ."

"Then?" Julie inquired.

And Katie smiled bitterly. "I want Kent to come to me with an abject apology. I want him on his knees, absolutely begging for my forgiveness."

Julie laughed. "That's a tall order. And speaking of order, why don't you get started? We'll head back, and Raff can be the first to bear the brunt of your vengeance. I'm going to love this!"

"Good. I hope you've got another job lined up for me," Katie said dryly.

"Don't worry, you can always move in with me. And if

worse comes to worst, I can play the violin. New Yorkers are great for supporting street acts."

"Wonderful," Katie murmured, but she was determined.

Raff was furious when they returned to the office—it was true that he couldn't seem to move a step without Julie at the helm. He was further infuriated to see Katie.

"What the hell are you doing back here?" he demanded bluntly. "You're supposed to be following Kent Hart!"

Katie clenched her hands. "Shall we discuss it in public or private, Raff?"

There must have been a go-for-the-jugular gleam in her eye, because Raff gave her question a moment's pause, his eyes narrowing. "Hold my calls, Julie."

"Yes, sir!" Julie saluted. Raff ignored her.

"Katie—my office, please."

She stopped by her office and picked up her notes. When she reached his, she didn't sit. She dropped her notes on his desk.

"I'm off the story, Raff. And if it means my job, I'll clean out my desk."

He stared at her silently. He was watching her for a weakness, Katie decided, searching for vulnerability.

But apparently, he didn't find any. He leaned forward; his lashes fell briefly over his assertive eyes, then he smiled. "All right, Katie. You can go get started on some of the investigative stuff for the summer sporting issue."

She felt numb. "You mean I'm not fired?"

"No." Raff turned his attention to the calendar on his desk.

Katie felt stunned; she just couldn't believe him. He looked up at her again, expectantly, then smiled again.

"You're not fired. Go back to work."

She didn't say anything else. She realized then that Raff played out his bluffs; when they didn't work, he acquiesced. She turned around quickly, not about to lose her job now for idleness.

When she reached her cubicle again, she saw the number

for Paul Crane that Julie scribbled on her blotter. She pressed her lips together, ready to do battle again. Katie quickly tapped out the number with the eraser end of a pencil.

When Paul came on the line she lit into him furiously—making him fully aware how she felt about what he had done.

"Whoa, whoa! Honey!" he proclaimed, ignoring her anger. "Hey, I know what an honorable kid you are, sweet. That's why I assumed it was marriage you wanted. How can you be so upset that I intended to give it to you?"

She sighed. "Paul, I told you—"

"Ah, come on, honey!" he said, undaunted. "Everybody loves a winner!"

Her heart took a sudden jolt. "A winner, Paul?"

"Wait till we win the Superbowl, honey. You'll love being with me. Just like being with a god!"

"How can you be so positive you're going to win, Paul?"

"Inside info, Kate." He laughed huskily. Katie hesitated, not liking the sound of his voice. Kent had believed Paul could really be on the take—but didn't there have to be more than that? Something nagged at her. Paul, whether he was on the take or not, would naturally be trying to do in the Saxons.

"Katie, honey, I've just got to see you, and we leave for New Orleans tomorrow afternoon. Please, let me come up and take you ɔ dinner tonight?"

She hesitated again. She'd fully intended to tell him to take the fast route to hell. She didn't really know what she expected to find out, but somehow, she believed there just might be something.

"Paul, let's get this straight. I'm not engaged to you. I don't even think I like you."

He laughed, obviously not believing her. What the hell was the matter with men anyway? Katie wondered.

"Can I take you to dinner?"

"No. I'm already going to dinner with Julie," Katie invented quickly. She didn't want to be alone with him. "But you can meet us if you like."

"When and where?"

Katie thought quickly. Then she gave him the name of a restaurant on Fifth Avenue and a time and quickly hung up.

"What am I after?" she whispered aloud, then she shook her head because she just didn't know. Raff would call it a journalist's hunch, but it didn't have anything at all to do with her career.

She swallowed. She was supposed to be working. She didn't want to work. Everything about her was tense; she felt as if her stomach were slightly sick, there was such a pain in it.

She stood up again, convinced that she was crazy. Then she walked back into Raff's office, forgetting to knock, pausing with a little horror as he stared at her, a brow lifted at her invasion.

Katie swallowed, then nervously started toward his desk. Her notes were still on the corner where she had dropped them.

"I—I've been thinking."

"Yes?"

"I think I can finish the story."

He threw his pencil on his desk and leaned back, lacing his fingers behind his head.

"Oh?"

"Yes."

He smiled, leaned forward, and handed her the notes. "Then, please, by all means, do."

Katie accepted the sheaf of papers but still stood there, watching him.

He emitted an exasperated sigh. "For heaven's sake, Katie, what else? I have to work, too, you know. We can't all go traipsing off to the pro games!"

"I need a favor."

"What?"

"I can't explain all this yet, Raff, but I need Julie. Do you think she could leave a little early with me?"

He threw his pencil down on the desk, then threw up his

arms. "Go—take her—get out of here! You're driving me crazy. Just be sure that you get her back here on time in the morning . . . and tell her to be damned sure she gets the desk covered by someone competent. Understand?"

"Yes, completely," Katie murmured, moving quickly for the door. But she heard Raff's quick rejoinder before she could close it in her wake.

He snorted with absolute impatience. "Women!" he exclaimed disgustedly.

Katie smiled. All of a sudden, she didn't feel that she was dealing so terribly with men.

CHAPTER FOURTEEN

"I don't understand why we're doing what we're doing," Julie murmured as she and Katie hurried along the street to reach the restaurant.

"Hey, what's the complaint? We're away from the office, and dinner will be on *World Magazine,*" Katie replied, rushing to catch the walk sign at the traffic light.

"Wait a minute, wait a minute." Julie paused, catching Katie's arm. "You told me what you said to Paul. So not only am I amazed that we're meeting him, I'm amazed the guy is taking a two-hour drive to see you!"

"Julie!" It was rush hour and people were walking all around them in a flurry of coats and winter paraphernalia. The sky was quickly darkening. Katie and Julie blocked a crowd that simply weaved around them.

Katie opened her mouth to try and give an explanation, then snapped it shut and started walking again.

"Kathleen Hudson, you explain this to me now! And explain why we had to go home first and dress up for a man you hate!"

Katie paused again. She grinned sheepishly. "I don't know what we're doing. Not exactly."

"Oh, great! This is getting better and better! You don't know what you're doing, but I get to do it with you! You hate the guy, but we're meeting him for dinner. He's already got a crush on you so lethal that he's announcing a nonexistent engagement to the newspapers, so you go to meet him looking like a million. Brilliant, Katie. I think you're suffering from mountain fever."

Katie cast her a dry, totally unappreciative glance. "I'm hoping he'll be so taken with you he won't be pressuring me."

"What a friend!" Julie moaned. "The guy might be a possessive crook—so she hands him over to me!"

"No, it's not that. Julie, listen. There are some nice things to be said about Paul, right? He's courteous, good-looking, bright, a decent conversationalist."

"I'll go that far," Julie agreed suspiciously.

"And," Katie continued, "there are some not-so-nice things to be said about him—other than that he might be a cheat and a crook. Mainly, that the man is a braggart. Julie, he's convinced that they're going to win that game! Okay, suppose he is on the take. That's still no guarantee. There has to be something else going on. I don't know what, but if we can get him talking, he just might let something slip. After all, he think's we're a pair of women—"

"We are a pair of women," Julie interrupted.

"Who," Katie continued firmly, "really don't know much about the world of sports."

"Oh, come on, Katie. He knows who your father was."

"And he also knows I'm not crazy about football anymore. And unless Sam Loper told him, he has no idea that I was anywhere near Kent or any of the other Saxons recently."

Julie shrugged and kept walking. "I just hope it's a decent restaurant!"

"You called for the reservations."

"You gave me the name!"

The restaurant Katie had named off the top of her head turned out to be rather nice. It was in the basement of a huge bank building; the decor was Old English, and the clientele seemed to be what Raff would call "upwardly mobile." The dining room was situated in a little enclave, while a long oak bar, a small bandstand, and a shiny parquet dance floor were set away so that the music would be muted for the diners.

Katie and Julie were early; they decided to sit and order drinks and have the maître d' bring Paul to the table when he arrived.

Julie gave her friend a critical glance as the waiter hurried off to fill their drink orders. "I don't think you should have worn that dress."

Katie stared down at herself consciously, then looked back at Julie. "I wore this because it covers everything."

Julie surveyed the clinging silk gown Katie wore and sighed. It did have a high neckline and long sleeves, but it hugged Katie's curves like a glove. "It covers everything—and absolutely enhances everything," she told Katie.

"Well, it's too late to change now," Katie murmured. "Oh, there's Paul."

It was easy to see Paul; he towered over other people. He was an attractive man, muscular, but he dressed to appear sleek. His hair was blond, his eyes a friendly hazel. As she watched him then, Katie wondered what it was about him that she had never been able to really like. She decided she didn't know—the chemistry just wasn't there. She forced herself to smile as he came to the table and slid beside her.

"Hi, gorgeous. Have I missed you!" Before she could stop him, he had leaned over to kiss her. It was a quick kiss, and then he was smiling at Julie. "Hi, Julie. You look great. What a treat . . . not just one beautiful woman, but two."

Julie smiled a bit awkwardly. "How are things going, Paul?"

"Great. We've been training away like madmen. Did you order drinks?"

"Yes, ours," Katie murmured, suddenly sure that she'd made a tremendous mistake. What was she going to prove by this little outing? She couldn't come right out and ask him if he was taking payments from a gambling concern. She was probably doing the one thing she didn't want to do: leading Paul to believe there was something between them.

She lowered her lashes uneasily, then noticed as she did so

239

that his wallet had slipped from his back pocket and was on the seat. Not at all sure of what she was doing, but going on a sudden instinct, she cleared her throat and gave him a quick smile. "Paul, there's our waiter by the bar. Why don't you just run up and give him your order, so that we all get our drinks at the same time. You know how these places can be around cocktail hour. You might never get your drink."

Paul shrugged. "I guess I can do that. Excuse me."

Katie waited until he had cleared the dining room and was headed through a throng of dancers to the bar. She quickly retrieved the wallet and began to leaf through it under cover of the table.

"What are you doing?" Julie gasped with alarm.

"I don't know!" Katie whispered back. "I'm looking."

"For what? A signed and sealed confession?"

"Of course not—and shut up, will you? Keep an eye on him and let me know as soon as he starts heading back."

"Oh, this is wonderful," Julie muttered. "Just wonderful. The guy is close to three hundred pounds, and you want to get him mad at me, too. Wonderful—"

Julie muttered away at her; Katie kept delving into the wallet, halfway convinced she was nuts herself. There wasn't anything to find. Just his driver's license, credit cards, team affiliation, and a few pictures. She checked the billfold— money. What else, stupid? she asked herself. There was only one pocket left. It held business cards, one for *World Magazine,* others for an accountant, a lawyer, a barber. Impatient and feeling a little like a fool, she started to stuff the cards back into the wallet. She dropped them onto the seat.

"He's heading back!" Julie exclaimed.

"Okay, okay!" She picked up the cards quickly and tried to put them all in order. It was then that she noticed something peculiar, a name and phone number hastily written on the back of one of the cards. The name was Humpty-Dumpty— the nickname of one of the Saxons guards.

Katie shoved the card into the wallet, let the wallet sit on the seat, and folded her hands above the table, a sweet smile of pure guilt lighting up her features as Paul returned.

"Did you give him your order?" she asked.

"Yeah."

He slid beside her again. Something in her stomach seemed to recoil as his thigh brushed against hers intimately. What did she do now? She still didn't know quite what she had discovered—if anything. There wasn't anything illegal or immoral about carrying around a name and phone number. But it wasn't *just* a number. It was a number that belonged to a Saxon guard, a man assigned to protect Sam Loper.

All of a sudden Katie couldn't breathe. The answer was swirling around in her mind, not quite there, but she knew it had to be obvious once she thought it out.

She couldn't seem to talk, but bless Julie! Her friend was carrying the conversational ball well.

Paul suddenly cleared his throat. "This is kind of personal, Julie, so I hope you won't mind." He looked at Katie. "Look, honey, I know you're furious about all that newspaper stuff on the engagement. I'm sorry. You say you don't want to marry me. I guess I have to accept that—for now." He smiled broadly, the type of smile that indicated an intimacy that didn't exist. "But I plan on talking you into it in the future. You'll see."

"Paul," Katie began, uncomfortably but firmly, "I don't want to marry you now—"

"But we're here tonight, right? I'll make it up to you." He gave Julie a confident laugh. "She'll marry me, wait and see."

Katie decided to give up for the night. Nothing too bad could happen with Julie as a chaperon, she assured herself. And at the moment, it just seemed so much easier to let the evening go on amicably. She had too many things on her mind to try for a showdown.

"Have you taken a look at the menu yet?" he asked them. "That duck sounds great."

"Duck. Just great," Katie murmured.

Kent arrived at the *World* offices at five. He had decided it would be just the right time not to intrude on Katie's work and still not to miss her before she left for the day.

The woman at the receptionist's desk was young and became totally flustered when she saw him.

"You're—him," she said, enormous brown eyes looking into his before he could even ask for Katie.

He grinned. "My name is Kent Hart. I'm looking for Miss Kathleen Hudson. Could you ring her for me, please?"

"Oh, I'd love to! My God, you really *are* tall, aren't you?"

"I suppose so," Kent murmured dryly. "Could you call Miss Hudson for me?"

She was scrambling around for a sheet of paper, not taking her eyes off him. "Would you—could I have your autograph, please? You're just my absolute favorite, Mr. Hart. I don't even know that much about football, but I watch almost all your games. You're wonderful."

"Thank you," Kent said, quickly scratching out his name.

"You look even better up close!" the young woman exclaimed. "Are you going to do commercials when you retire?"

Kent sighed, trying to get a firm grasp on his patience. "I don't think so. Look, I'm in a bit of a hurry. Would you mind calling Miss Hudson for me?"

"Oh!" The young woman sat back, looking truly upset. "I'd do anything in the world for you if I could." She giggled. "World! How funny! But I can't call Katie—er—Miss Hudson. She left early."

"She left? Do you know where she went?"

"Somewhere to dinner with Julie—our real receptionist. I'm just filling in."

That was lucky for the sake of *World Magazine,* Kent thought wryly. He frowned with his frustration. "You have no idea where?"

"No . . . no, I don't. I'm sorry."

"Well, thanks anyway." He almost left in total frustration,

but at the door he paused, returning to give her a warm smile. "Does this—Julie, was it?—yes, does Julie keep a calendar or a notebook or anything?"

"Gee, Mr. Hart, I'm really not sure."

Kent sat on the corner of the desk and offered her another warm smile. "Mind if I take a look?"

She shook her head, enthralled. Kent reached over and opened the top drawer. He found a calendar, but all the notes scratched out for the day referred to meetings for a man named Raff. He put the calendar back in the drawer, still smiling at the girl.

"Oh!" she exclaimed suddenly.

"What?"

"Here, on the blotter. It's right here! Three for drinks and dinner at five o'clock at—"

"Three?" Kent said sharply, taking a quick look at the scrawled name and number. "Who else was going?"

"Gee, Mr. Hart, I don't know."

He smiled at her. "Thanks. Thanks a lot."

Kent hurried out to the street and hailed a taxi. With any luck he'd reach the restaurant while Katie was still there.

The duck had been fine; the drinks had been fine. Julie looked exhausted, having spent the entire evening trying to keep the conversation light.

Katie wanted to go home. She started to say so just as Paul grasped her wrist. "One dance, Katie. Julie won't mind. They're playing something nice and slow."

"No, Paul, really—"

"Hey, come on! I'm a poor working guy about to be shipped to New Orleans!"

"Paul—"

It was too late; he was up on his feet and dragging Katie to hers. It was impossible to fight the grasp of a tackle.

"Dammit, Paul!" Katie exploded as he led her through the

dining room to the dance floor. "This is the kind of thing that puts an end to things in the first place! I do not like being—"

Her words were cut off as she found her face crushed to his chest.

"Ah, come on, Katie. Women like their men tough. All this lib stuff is a fantasy."

"It's no fantasy!" Katie exclaimed. "I do not want to dance, and I don't like rude men!"

It was incredible really . . . She wasn't dancing, but she was being led around the floor. She couldn't break his hold and couldn't even see because her face was pressed so hard to his jacket.

How had she ever gotten involved with him? she wondered bleakly. He had been so nice at first.

She was so busy fighting that she didn't realize another tall man had entered the restaurant just as she was heading for the dance floor.

But Kent saw her—and the table from which she had departed. He walked over to it and to the lovely, sophisticated blond sitting there. He slid into the vacated booth and watched her as she turned to watch him—apparently with no surprise.

"You're Kent Hart," she murmured, assessing him curiously.

"And you're Julie."

"Yes." She glanced nervously at the dance floor and moistened her lips. Then she gazed back at him. "Are we going to have trouble here tonight?"

He shook his head. "I guess not, not if she wants to be with him."

The sound of his voice was very, very bitter. "Oh, no!" Julie cried in dismay, remembering Katie's story. Oh, this really was wonderful! Kent Hart must be assuming that Katie *had* seduced him, only to betray him.

Kent raised a dark brow to her; Julie decided that she would never want to be on his bad side.

"I—uh—it's not what you think," she began, but then she realized suddenly that she had lost his attention. His hand, a big hand with long fingers, was curled over the table's edge so tightly, she thought the wood would split. And then Julie saw why.

Out on the dance floor it was evident that Katie was fighting a back hold that was more like a derriere hold.

"Excuse me," Kent said briefly.

"Oh, hell!" Julie moaned. She watched as Kent strode quickly toward the crowd of whirling dancers and tapped Paul on the shoulder. Julie realized vaguely that she was standing and rushing out to the dance floor herself—although heaven knew why.

"Paul," Katie was gasping, "I swear I'll scream loud enough to stop the band if you don't—"

"What the hell?" Paul interrupted, and Katie saw that he was turning around because someone was tapping his shoulder. "Hart!" he exclaimed. "What the hell are you doing here?"

"Oh!" Katie gasped, stunned—then horrified. Kent was standing there, very civil and handsome in a three-piece suit, but wearing a thunderous expression that was gaunt and tense and anything but civil. He looked as if he wanted to kill Paul.

"I don't think the lady wants to dance with you, Crane," he began stonily, but then his eyes caught hers and they were like burning coals. Though it might appear that he was defending her, Katie had the sickening sensation that it was only so that he might kill her himself.

"What?" Paul demanded incredulously. Then he was mad. "Damn you, Hart, get out of my life! What I do with my woman is my concern."

"Only if she's your woman—which I doubt," Kent replied tensely.

Paul glowered at him for a minute. "Want to take this outside, Hart?" His voice was low and threatening.

"I sure as hell do."

Katie and Julie were left with a milling crowd as the two men walked off the dance floor to the street door.

Katie looked at Julie desperately. She started to talk and couldn't. She turned and followed after the men in a rush. Julie followed on her heels.

"Oh, this is stupid!" Katie cried to Julie on the restaurant steps. Kent and Paul were circling one another like a pair of boxers in the ring. Katie caught her breath in a crazy rush of fear. Tears sprang to her eyes. "Oh, Julie, he's going to get hurt! Paul has about fifty pounds on him, and he's almost ten years younger."

Julie was silent for a minute, then she murmured rather lightly, "Oh, I don't know. The Cougar is tough. Tall and wiry and lean. I think I'll put my money on him."

"Julie!" Katie wailed. She shuddered as Kent took the first punch, but then he returned it with a resounding speed that sent Paul flying into a pair of garbage cans. Instantly, he was back on his feet.

Suddenly, it seemed to Katie, there were people all over the street, cheering the fighters on. And she realized that they were both willing to get torn to shreds to get at the other. The fight was a very tense one, something they seemed to have wanted for a long time. Punch for punch, they were both back at it again.

"Where are the police when you need them?" Katie muttered. Then she pursed her lips together and turned around.

"What are you doing?" Julie asked.

"I'm getting my purse, and I'm leaving. As soon as I'm gone, see that someone reminds them both that the Superbowl is in less than two weeks. That should break them up."

Julie smiled. She would have offered to go with Katie, but she had a hunch she should stick around. She waited until she saw Katie enter the cab. Then she nervously risked life and limb to get near the fighters.

"Hey, you two are supposed to be doing something like that on the field in two weeks!"

Both of them were staggering; both of them paused. Paul made the mistake of staring too long at Julie.

Kent smiled grimly and landed one last punch.

Paul fell to the pavement with a little groan. The crowd cheered and began to break up. Julie stepped toward Kent, handing him the jacket she'd found on the stairs.

"You look like hell," she told him, smiling. He might look like hell, but she liked his looks. He wiped a trickle of blood from his jaw, and Julie noticed it was a strong jaw, determined and well defined.

"Where's Katie?" he asked.

Someone had helped Paul. He was back on his feet, putting his own jacket back on.

"I'll be seeing you soon, Hart—real soon. And on that football field, there won't be anything but rubbish left of you."

Kent ignored him. Paul straightened his shoulders, gave Julie an evil glare, and started back into the restaurant. Julie decided he would figure out that Katie had already left.

She gave her attention to Kent. "Katie left."

"Left?" He was incredulous and obviously growing angry. There was a definite pulse ticking madly in his throat. Julie thought it looked sexy.

"Yes, she left," Julie said, watching his dark eyes.

He didn't get mad; he didn't rave at her. He lifted a brow again, then sighed. "You said this wasn't what it seemed. What was it, then?"

Julie lifted her hands a little bit helplessly. "I can't really explain. Katie was after something. You could . . . trust me." When he kept staring at her, she sighed with exasperation. "You could trust her, you know. I think she's in love with you."

He laughed hollowly. "In love with me? Then why did she leave?"

"Well," Julie murmured uneasily, lowering her eyes, "you really haven't been all that charming to her, you know. And she certainly doesn't know . . ."

"Know what?"

"What you feel for her."

He planted his hands on his hips, aggravated. Then he threw them up into the air. "I came after her, didn't I?"

"Yes," Julie admitted, restraining a laugh. "You did come after her."

He looked bewildered then—tense, perplexed, and a little bit lost. "Just what does she want out of me?"

Julie smiled. "I can tell you if you really want to know."

"Oh?" He crossed his arms over his chest. He had a really nice smile, and he was smiling at her then. "Well, tell me."

Julie's smile became a very broad grin. "She wants you down on your knees, absolutely begging her forgiveness!"

"She *what?*"

"She wants you down on your knees, begging her forgiveness—" Julie broke off when Kent started laughing.

"Little witch, isn't she?" he inquired pleasantly.

"Well, she is stubborn," Julie agreed. She hesitated a minute. "I can give you a few suggestions to go with that if you'd like."

"Oh, please, do go ahead," he said, watching her with that good-natured smile in place, his arms still laced across his chest.

Oh, I like him, Julie thought. I like him very much. "Hmm," she murmured out loud. "If you have forgiven her, that is. She is innocent, by the way."

"Go on."

"Well, then, I think—as long as you're going to be on your knees anyway—you should ask her to marry you. And it wouldn't be a bad idea if you promised to retire from the game soon. Not that she'd mind the traveling, or that she's the jealous type—never mind, I take that back. Any normal woman would get jealous over you. But seriously, she's naturally frightened by the game. Besides, she loves you, and you've been out there a long time. Why take added risks?"

Kent dusted off his jacket the best he could. "Shall we get a cab? I'd like to see that you get home. Then you can call Katie, then call me to let me know she got home all right. I don't think I'm going to try and call myself."

"No?"

He shook his head. "No. I've got to get back to Philadelphia tonight, and I have to report back to work tomorrow." He paused for a minute. "What do you think she'll do? Is she going to head for New Orleans?"

"I have a funny feeling she won't miss this game for the world."

Kent slipped a friendly arm around Julie's shoulder, and they started down the street looking for a cab.

"Kent?"

"Yes?"

"You should be worried about this game."

"I am. But we've got to play it out. There's no way to prove anything."

"I guess," Julie murmured.

"It would be nice to win," Kent said softly. He smiled down at Julie, who was surprised to see that his dark eyes could sizzle with laughter every bit as compellingly as they could with anger.

Julie merely nodded in acquiescence, content for the moment just to listen.

"It would be nice to go out in a blaze of glory, don't you think?" he asked.

CHAPTER FIFTEEN

Katie sat at her desk, paper in her typewriter, ostensibly turning her notes into a smooth, cohesive story. It wasn't going well. She had been given a reprieve over the holidays when Raff assigned her an interview with the mayor, but her deadline on Kent's story was nearing and she only had a rough draft of the first half done.

Katie turned from her typewriter and began to doodle on her blotter. She glanced at her calendar and began to circle the day. It was Thursday, and the nation was gearing up. The Superbowl was only days away, and the players had all been down in New Orleans for more than a week, testing out the turf for the big day. And she hadn't heard from any of them, not even at Christmas or New Year's, days she had spent with Julie.

He wasn't going to call her, she thought bleakly. He had come to New York, somehow discovered where she was, and found her dancing with Paul. Surely, it had been like the closing of a lid on a coffin.

It shouldn't hurt so badly, she told herself. When she left him in Denver, she knew that it was over, that it had to be over.

But it did hurt terribly. Every night was a new agony; after a lifetime of sleeping alone, it had suddenly become the most painful thing in the world to do.

Katie started to chew on the eraser at the end of her pencil, realized it tasted horrible, and forced herself to stop. She set the pencil down, then picked it up again. Idly, she began to draw on her blotter. She realized that she was drawing a possible lineup of players for the Superbowl. Then she started to write down names: Sam Loper, Kent Hart, Paul Crane, and Harry Kolan, also known as Humpty Dumpty. Why had Paul had Harry's name and number in his wallet? Did it mean anything—or nothing?

Her phone rang. Katie glanced at the blinking lights and saw that there was an outside call but that the interoffice line was also lit up, so Julie apparently wanted to talk to her before she picked up the outside line.

She hesitated before touching the phone. Even Julie had been completely won over by Kent Hart. She'd called Katie the night of the fight and told her what a nice night she'd had with Kent. He'd insisted on taking her home, but they'd wound up stopping for drinks first. He'd been an absolute gentleman, and, oh, Julie was sorry, he hadn't really said a thing at all about Katie.

That had been the hardest night. The one in which it had been absolutely impossible to sleep. Julie, she knew, would never hurt her on purpose. She really had no right to be jealous. And yet the fact that her best friend had apparently had a lovely time enjoying drinks with Kent had made her ache impossibly, eating herself alive with jealousy.

Katie picked up the phone. "What's up?"

"An unusual call—at least I think so," Julie murmured.

Katie's heartbeat quickened. "Is it—"

"No, it's not Kent. But it's a woman who says she used to be his wife."

"Oh," Katie replied, depressed but startled . . . and very curious.

"I thought you'd like to be forewarned."

"Yes, thanks," Katie murmured. She pressed the other button. "Hello, this is Kathleen Hudson. May I help you?"

There was the slightest hesitance. "Miss Hudson, this is Paula Blank. I'm Kent's ex-wife. I hope I'm not interrupting you. None of this is my business . . . I just—well, I just thought that it might be important to call."

A strange, uneasy feeling settled over Katie. "You're not interrupting me. It's a pleasure to meet you, over the phone, that is," Katie murmured. Was it? What was going on here? Ex-wives were supposed to be nasty people, determined to mess up their ex-spouses lives. She didn't sound at all nasty. "What can I do for you, Mrs. Blank?"

"Well, you can start by calling me Paula, please. I'm hoping that we can be friends."

"Paula," Katie murmured. Why should it matter that they be friends—or even acquaintances? Was there a reason? "Paula," she repeated, "what can I do for you?"

"Well, I understand that you're doing an article on Kent. I thought perhaps we could have lunch. I could probably give you some information on him."

"Oh, uh, well, thank you," Katie said, stumbling over her words a bit, and she heard a pleasant, husky laughter in return.

"Don't thank me—not yet. To be perfectly honest, I want to find out a few things myself."

"Oh?"

The woman's pleasant, husky chuckle came to Katie again, a bit rueful. "Yes. You see, Miss Hudson, Kent has remained an old and dear friend. And quite frankly, I'd like to know just what you did to him."

"What I did to him?" Katie gasped.

"Oh, I am sorry! Bad wording, wasn't it? Please forgive me . . . and let me start over. I'm worried about him. He didn't sleep at all when he was here—"

"When he was there?" Katie interrupted, swallowing.

"Oh, not with me, Miss Hudson, I assure you. I was with my husband. My current husband. Oh, God, this is starting to sound like a soap opera, isn't it? I'm doing this horribly."

"No, no," Katie murmured. "None of this is *my* business."

"But it is. I'm in the city, Miss Hudson. Could you—would you be willing to meet me for lunch?"

Katie didn't hesitate a second. She didn't know if she was longing for any association with Kent or if it was pure curiosity driving her or both, but she said, "Of course I'll meet you. On one condition."

"What's that?"

"If you'll call me Katie, please."

"Certainly, Katie. Where shall we meet?"

"Which station are you at?"

Paula told her. Katie mentioned a Chinese restaurant on a nearby corner where the seating was private. She was reaching for her purse and coat before she had set the phone down.

Katie's breath caught in her throat when the waiter led her back to the small, round table where Paula was already waiting. For some reason she had wanted Kent's ex-wife to have aged into a pleasantly plump and matronly lady. But Paula was anything but plump. She was slim, her hair was soft and swingy, and she had deep, laughing hazel eyes that were very open and honest. She was wearing a very fashionable red business suit with a wide-brimmed hat that created a more than arresting picture. The woman was lovely.

"Katie!" Paula rose to greet her, extending a slim, manicured hand in a strong, warm handshake.

Katie smiled and sat and quickly ordered a drink. She felt comfortable, and completely uncomfortable.

While they waited for Katie's drink to arrive, Paula chatted about the weather and the subway system. But once Katie's drink had arrived and they were left alone, Paula lowered her voice and got directly to the point.

"I appreciate your coming very much, and again, I know that none of this is my business." She grinned. "But you've won my daughter's heart, Katie, which isn't an easy feat. Oh, I—um—heard a little of what happened, and I want to apologize. Anne's behavior was just horrible."

Katie lowered her eyes to sip her drink quickly, aware that

a heated flush was rising in her cheeks. It seemed terribly embarrassing to know that this lovely and elegant woman— who had been married to Kent—knew some of the circumstances of what must look like a rather cheap affair.

"I've done it again!" Paula moaned. "Oh, Katie, I didn't mean to make you uncomfortable—"

"It's all right, really. And I—I wasn't upset at all by Anne." Katie grinned. "I've been there myself, you see."

Paula watched her a minute, then turned her attention to her own drink, a pink concoction with a little umbrella sticking out of it. "I knew your father," she murmured. "He was a wonderful, wonderful man. During the divorce, he managed to be Kent's friend as well as mine. I think your father was the one who made a friendship possible between us afterward. Which was, for Anne's sake, wonderful."

Katie smiled. It only hurt a little to think about her father. And it felt very good to hear Paula's words. They brought something back to her—all the greatness that had been the man, not the football player.

"Thank you for telling me that," Katie said.

Paula gazed at her again, flashing a quick smile. Katie realized she was also being assessed, but she couldn't resent Paula for it. No more than she could condemn her own curiosity about this woman who had once held Kent's heart.

The waiter was hovering near the table. "Let's order," Paula suggested, "so that we can be left alone." She grinned.

They ordered, then discussed some of the new buildings in New York City until their food arrived. They'd both decided on shrimp with lobster sauce—it didn't matter what they ate, and they both knew it.

"Katie, I don't really know how to say this, and I don't really know what I want you to do. But you're angry with Kent . . . and I know Kent—you probably have every right to be! I only wish you'd find it in your heart to forgive him. Or at least pretend to." Paula hesitated a minute, pushing a shrimp around on her plate. "Quite frankly, I'm worried sick.

There are all kinds of rumors floating around about the game. They're going to be going after Kent like wild animals. I know he's a grown man who has chosen to play the game, but . . ." She stared into Katie's eyes suddenly. "Katie, he isn't a kid anymore. If he goes into that game on Sunday without concentrating or being in form, they'll massacre him."

Katie shivered. Cold fingers squeezed her heart, both because she couldn't bear the thought of Kent being injured, as her father had been, and because Paula, too, had heard something about the proposed viciousness of the game.

Katie dropped her eyes from Paula's, hesitating before she spoke. "I'm not so sure he wants to talk to me, Paula. He came up here one night to see me, and I—I was in a position that must have proved to him that I was guilty of something he had accused me of that I really wasn't guilty of at all." She listened to herself and had to laugh. "I realize that I just made next to no sense at all."

Paula smiled a little secretively and lowered her head. "I understood you!" She chuckled. "You're talking about Paul Crane, I assume."

"Ah, yes."

"Would you mind me asking you—well, I'm sure you would mind, but I've gone this far, I might as well plunge ahead. Why were you out with him?"

Katie shrugged. "There are all these rumors about the game, about Paul being on the take and the heavy betting. But it doesn't make sense, because Paul would be trying to get at Sam and Kent no matter what. I don't know what I was thinking. I just thought that I might be able to find something out that made sense out of the whole thing. Kent and Paul got into a fight—"

"Yes, I know." Paula grinned. "I got to run around with an ice bag once he got back to Philly."

Katie grimaced. "I left the scene. I'm not sure if I thought one of them would turn around and kill me or if I just couldn't take it if Kent lit into me for being the traitor he had assumed I was in the first place." She took a deep breath, then looked at Paula. "Maybe I was hoping that if—if he really cared, if he was ready to trust me, he would follow me home or call. Something," she finished weakly. "Paula, a self-respecting person just wouldn't go near Kent again without an apology."

Paula grimaced and nodded slowly. "I don't know the particulars, Katie, but I trust you—and I believe you." She hesitated. "Has it occurred to you that he might be . . . hurt? A little too insecure to take a chance?"

Katie laughed hollowly. "Kent hurt? He's the Cougar, Paula, not me. We both know he leads the life of a living idol. He can have any woman he wants."

Paula lowered her lashes, smiling a little secretively again—and a little regretfully, too, Katie thought. "Don't judge Kent that way. I made that mistake once myself. Even living idols fall in love, and love gives the most rugged man an Achilles' heel."

Katie shrugged, then said quietly, "I'm not at all sure he's in love with me. And I—I don't know if I could call him. He's in training now anyway."

"Are you going to the game?"

Katie shrugged again, grimacing. "Yes. I've been trying to tell myself that I shouldn't go, but the weaker side of me keeps winning the argument. Are you going?"

"Yes, we'll all be there. Ted, my husband, Anne, and myself. You can't keep a young girl away when her father's playing in the Superbowl, you know."

"Yes, I know," Katie said softly.

"And like I said," Paula added, "I'm worried sick."

Katie picked up a shrimp to chew. It tasted like rubber, even though she knew the food was usually very good. It wasn't the shrimp—it was her. She was feeling Paula's concern, and the lineup and the names were rushing through her mind once again. Sam—already injured, Kent . . . and Paul. Paul Crane, who was carrying around the name and number of a Saxon guard, a man who would be protecting Sam in the game—

"Oh, my God!" Katie gasped suddenly.

"What?" Paula demanded, startled.

"I think I've got it. Paul isn't the only one on the take!"

"What do you mean?"

Katie looked at Paula. "The other night I went through Paul's wallet—not a nice thing to do, I'll admit, but I thought I might find something . . . and I did. I just didn't realize what it meant until now. I think that one of the Saxons is on the take, too. A guard. Paula, don't you see? That makes everything fit. Whether he was on the take or not, Paul couldn't really change the game himself. But if there was a Saxon—a guard—helping him, a man who could let him through to Sam, he could guarantee the game! He'd know he'd get a chance to blitz Sam!"

Paula watched her, then nodded slowly. "It does make sense," she said slowly. "The problem is, there isn't any way to prove any of this."

"Paula, you've got to call Kent. You've got to warn him—"

"Katie, they'll think I'm crazy! I'm just a 'woman.' And 'women' aren't supposed to understand the great fraternity of football. But you're different because you're Hudson's daughter. You know the team. You've got to call."

Something very painful constricted Katie's throat. "I really don't think I can call Kent. And I don't know what good it would do. He already thinks I'm guilty as hell, and it's going to be almost impossible to convince him that a member of his own team is playing against him. He might think I'm making the whole thing up to put myself in the clear."

"I don't think so, Katie. I really don't think so. He said that everything that had happened was his own fault."

"I don't know," Katie murmured miserably.

"Katie, please! When they finish with Sam, they'll go for Kent! Sam is already hurt—" She stopped abruptly. "Sam! That's it! Katie, at least call Sam."

"Sam's the one who turned everything into a fiasco!" Katie exclaimed irritably.

Paula shook her head vehemently. "Sam's not a bad guy, Katie. If he hurt you, it wasn't on purpose. At least call Sam if you can't talk to Kent. Please."

Katie hesitated a long while. "All right," she said at last. "I'll call Sam."

"One more thing, Katie," Paula murmured.

"What's that?"

"I know this isn't fair, but, please, think about Kent."

"If he wanted me—"

Paula shook her head. "I'm just asking you to think about it all, Katie. And trust me—I know him well. He *is* in love with you."

Katie wasn't so sure, but she promised Paula she would think about the situation. When they parted in front of the restaurant, Katie was also promising to try and reach Sam Loper as soon as she could. Paula gave her an affectionate hug. As they parted, Katie walked away from her former lover's ex-wife with an incredible feeling of warmth, a feeling that helped her finish the rough draft of the article that afternoon.

She also tried to reach Sam. It wasn't difficult to find out where the Saxons were staying in New Orleans; it was almost impossible to get the hotel's receptionist to promise to give Sam a message. Katie left her work number and her home number; by six he still hadn't called the office. Katie decided to go home.

She straightened up her apartment, ate a salad, and took a long bath. She washed her hair and did her nails and watched the time creep by. At midnight she gave up with a sigh. Sam Loper wasn't going to call her back. In the morning she'd call New Orleans and stress that her message was urgent.

She tossed around a long time that night. She grew warm when she allowed herself to wonder if Kent could really be in love with her; tingling, electrical sensations haunted her body. Then she tried to convince herself that it couldn't be true, because if she allowed herself to believe it and it wasn't, she wouldn't be able to bear the pain. And he hadn't tried to contact her. He'd seen her dancing with Paul Crane. Yes, he'd gotten into a fight with Paul, but she also thought that the fight really had little to do with her; the two of them had been more than ready to jump at each other's throats over nothing —or everything, as the case might be.

Katie plumped her pillow and covered her eyes with her arm. Was it possible that the game was really rigged? Could a Saxon have willingly sold out for the right price? How could any man be willing to see a teammate torn apart?

The right price. Good men could be tempted for the right price. And it wasn't as if Harry Kolan was going to have to hurt Sam himself. All he was going to have to do was slip or fall—and leave an opening for Paul Crane to get through to Sam. Quarterbacks got rushed and blitzed all the time. It would look like typical game procedure. And if Sam went out of the game . . .

Well, the news media were proclaiming him the hottest quarterback in almost a decade. They were comparing him to the great Dante Hudson. The Saxons were a good team on their own; with Sam and a legendary wide receiver like Kent, they were great. But it was also true that take away Sam, and they'd be fighting tooth and nail. A. J. Timmons was their second quarterback, and he was good, too. But take him away, and Kent—if he was still walking!—would be thrown in. And if you took away Kent . . .

Katie didn't even really give a damn about the game, about who won and who lost. She did care about Sam, and more than anything, she cared about Kent.

She felt like screaming, because it all came back to her now, her father's last game, the knowledge that he'd never play again because of the injury to his spinal cord. And then, a few years down the line, the doctors telling her that he had cancer associated with the deadened nerves.

Katie got up and made herself a cup of tea. She wished then

that she took sleeping pills. But since she didn't, she decided a few aspirin might help her drift off.

Before she got back into bed, she looked at the phone and shook an aggravated fist at it.

"Damn you, Sam Loper! You troublemaker! You'd better call me back!"

When she finally fell asleep, it felt as if morning came almost instantly—much too soon. When the phone first started shrilling, she was hoping she had left her answering machine on and nastily wishing that whoever could interrupt her so rudely when she had finally fallen asleep would fall into an icy lake somewhere.

Then she thought that it just might be Sam, and she scrambled quickly to her knees to catch the phone.

"Hello?"

"Katie?"

"Yes?" It sounded like Sam.

"Well, hi, doll. I've missed seeing you around."

It *was* Sam. Suddenly, Katie was furious with him again. "Cut it, Sam—right now. You know damned well that you haven't seen me around because you personally had me hanged before I knew there was a trial going on."

"Ah, come on, Katie! I—I talked to Paul Crane, and Kent is my friend. Then there's the game, you know. Katie—"

"I don't want to hear it, Sam. I—"

"You want me to try and straighten things out between you and Kent? But Katie, Crane said that you had been dating him, and Connie was at the party, and—"

"Stop it, Sam! I do *not* want you to set things straight between Kent and me, and I don't need to offer you any explanations about anything. I called you about the game."

"The game?" Sam said quizzically. "Oh, I can get you tickets, if that's what you need—"

"Sam!" She was almost screaming. "I don't *need* tickets . . . the magazine arranged for my ticket a long time ago. Sam, please, listen to me. Pay attention."

260

"I'm listening, Katie," he said quietly.

"Okay, Sam, follow my reasoning. Everyone is saying that players have been approached with some hefty gambling cash to make sure that the Saxons don't win the game, right?"

"Right," Sam agreed slowly.

"And you are all convinced that Paul is the one on the take, right?"

He hesitated a minute. "You know that, Katie—"

"Sam, I asked you to listen to me. Paul's against you no matter what. So how could he really throw the game?"

"Well," Sam said patiently, "usually when they say, 'kill the quarterback,' they don't mean it literally. Most guys are out there getting tough, but—"

"Sam, that still wouldn't guarantee a win. But if someone on your team were ready to throw the game, it would."

Sam was silent a long, long time. "What are you getting at, Katie?" he asked at last.

"Sam, I went out with Paul last week, which I'm sure you know—and you have the nerve to call women gossips!"

"Katie—"

"Sorry, that's beside the point. Anyway, I went through his wallet—"

"You went through his what?"

"His wallet, Sam, his wallet."

"You didn't!"

Katie sighed. "Believe it or not, Sam, I'm on your side. I was trying to see what I could find out. And—"

"How did you get his wallet, Katie?" Sam asked her with a peculiar note to his voice. Then she thought she understood the suspicious ring to the question, and she felt as if steam were rising inside her all over again.

"It was on the chair, Sam. That's how! And it's none of your damned business, you little snitch!"

"Katie! That's not fair at all—"

"And I don't want to discuss it either! Sam, I'm begging you. Will you let me get to the point?"

"Sorry, Katie, go on."

"Paul was carrying around Harry Kolan's name and phone number."

"So what?"

"So what? Harry Kolan is supposed to be guarding you!"

"I still don't see what you're getting at, Katie. Lots of guys have friends on different teams. Hell, before the Saxons existed, Kent—and your father, too, by the way—were playing with Paul for the Titans—"

"Sam! You stupid jock!" Katie raged. "I think it means that Harry is in on this, too."

"Katie." There was a rough edge to Sam's voice; she knew she'd made him angry, but he deserved it. He deserved more, she thought. "I am not a 'stupid jock,' " he told her flatly.

"And I'm not exactly a Mata Hari in the bedroom," Katie retorted.

There was a short silence on the line, then Sam sighed. "I'm sorry."

"So am I."

"I just can't believe that Harry would be on the take, that he would purposely allow his own team to lose. Hell, Katie, the big thing to half these guys isn't even the money—they want Superbowl rings, they want the win itself. Don't you understand?"

"I do understand. But you see, it makes sense. One of the Saxons being willing to throw the game would be a much better guarantee than the Titans *claiming* that they could kill them!"

Sam was silent again. Katie called to him softly.

"I'm here, Katie. Suppose—just suppose, I'm not saying that I believe it yet—that Harry has been accepting bribes. How am I going to prove it? What the hell could I do?"

"I—I don't know," Katie replied. "But something, Sam. Surely you can do something!"

"I don't know. I can confront him, and come out being the

bad guy myself. Or I could go to the coaches, and Harry could deny it. I don't have any proof, Katie."

"I know, but . . ."

"But what?"

"Sam, you should stay out of the game."

She could almost see his smile. "Not on your life, sweets. It's the Superbowl."

"You and your stupid games!" She was mad at Sam, furious; she still felt ridiculously like crying. Nothing she could say or do would change any of their minds.

He accepted her comment with a tolerant silence, then asked, "Are you coming down, Katie?"

"I—uh—I don't know. I haven't decided yet."

"Can you get here today?"

"Probably. Why?"

"Because we've got some time this afternoon. I'd like to get together with you and Kent—"

"If I'd wanted to talk to Kent," Katie said softly, "I'd have called him."

Sam paused just a moment. When he spoke again, Katie knew he was purposely baiting her. He was trying with a velvet reproach to touch all the feminine strings around her heart.

"Katie, if this is real, and if you really care, don't you think you should do anything in your power to help?"

"That's not fair, Sam."

"Please, Katie? Maybe, between the three of us, we could come up with something. Katie, I can't believe that—no matter what's happened—you'd want to see either Kent or me injured. Hurt and bleeding on the field . . ."

"Damn you, Sam!" she cried.

"Will you be here, Katie?"

"Yes."

"Good," he said quickly. "Listen, don't worry about your bookings. I'll get you a room here."

"Sam, why are you doing this?"

He paused. "Maybe because I want you to forgive me. And maybe because I think I was really, really wrong. Call me back with your flight info, and I'll get you at the airport later. Okay?"

"All right," Katie replied quietly.

She said good-bye, then hung up the phone. She turned on the television to keep her company while she started going through her clothing to see what she did and didn't want to take. She wanted to make damn sure that when she met Kent Hart again, she looked her absolute best—as stunning and sexy as possible!

The television caught her attention, and she smiled. The big news was the Superbowl, and all she kept hearing were the names of the two men now haunting her life.

Sam Loper and . . . Kent Hart, the Cougar.

The game rested on the two of them, and so, Katie admitted, did the rest of her life.

CHAPTER SIXTEEN

Sam was waiting for Katie at the airport that afternoon. He wore a pinstripe, wonderfully tailored three-piece suit, and he looked more like an up-and-coming businessman than an all-star quarterback. Although he had promised to come, Katie was surprised to see him; football fans were flocking in from across the nation, and he might have been swamped by the hordes. But he didn't appear to be worried—he appeared impatient.

"Katie," was all that he said when he saw her. He gave her a quick hug, took her by the elbow, and started hurrying toward the baggage claim. Katie decided then that he must have had an in with the airlines, because within ten minutes, they had her bags and were driving away from the airport.

Katie cast a glance at his handsome countenance and smiled. "I was surprised to see you, you know. Weren't you worried about being recognized?"

Sam grinned. "Not really. Most of the time people don't recognize me unless I'm wearing dirt and a helmet."

Katie smiled again and leaned back against the seat. She tried to appear completely relaxed, but her heart was pounding. She had thought Kent might have come to the airport with Sam. She was afraid to ask if he even intended to see her, but she had to ask.

"Where's Kent?"

"On the field," Sam replied briefly. He gave Katie a quick glance. "They're trying not to work me so hard because of the ribs, you know." He grinned. "But Kent's nice and healthy, so they're willing to make him do a lot of sweating."

"Oh," Katie murmured.

"He'll be with us soon."

"What have you told him?"

"Everything."

"And?"

"We're all in the same position, Katie. There's no proof."

She gazed out the window. She loved the streets of New Orleans with all their old-world flavor. But today she couldn't appreciate a thing she saw.

Sam took her to the hotel and stayed with her while she checked in. The process went surprisingly quickly, and this time Katie was certain that Sam had managed to cut a lot of red tape for her. There was a long line at the counter; a man came out from behind it to give her her key and wish her a pleasant stay in New Orleans.

Sam went up with her. The room was a suite with a huge bedroom and an even larger sitting room. Sam seemed edgy; he kept pacing around the room.

Katie was definitely feeling a little edgy herself. Sam's pacing wasn't helping her at all. "What is the matter with you?" Katie demanded.

He stopped, startled. "I'm just . . . worried."

"Why?"

"Because I think Kent intended to confront Harry and find out what he might have to say."

"Oh, God!" Katie murmured. A few minutes later she discovered she was pacing the room along with Sam.

Kent waited until the majority of the team had showered and left the locker room after a grueling practice. Luck was with him, and he was able to corner Harry Kolan alone near his locker.

"Kolan, I want to talk to you."

266

"Yeah?" Harry dried his face with a towel and gave Kent a broad grin. "What's up, Cougar?"

Kent crossed his arms over his chest and leaned against a locker, watching Kolan's round face for reaction. Kolan was a big guy, tall and heavy, a solid rock in front of the quarterback—supposedly.

"I've heard a rumor about something, Kolan, that makes me a little sick. Gut sick, in the stomach, you know? I've heard that you might be making some big bucks on this game —to lose it."

It was there. It was just a second, but it was there, a startled look in Harry's eyes that hinted of fear and guilt. But then he started smiling again.

"Ah, come on, Cougar! Money against my own team? Where did you hear such a thing?"

"It's true, isn't it, Harry?"

"Hell, no!" His eyes narrowed, almost disappearing in the heavy lines of his face. "And you listen to me, Hart, you come to me with an accusation like that again, and I'll bash your brains into a sidewalk, you hear?" He eased up then, chuckling. "You heard it from the girl, right? That Hudson woman who's so chummy with Paul Crane? And you believe her. You're whipped, Cougar. You're whipped over that blond. Not that she isn't something hot, man, but it sounds to me like you're losing your jockstrap over her. You know what I mean?"

Kent's hands were clenched into tight fists; he didn't dare move. "I'm not losing anything but my temper, Kolan."

"You're losing your temper? You come to me with an accusation like that? All over some . . ."

He had a few uncomplimentary things to say about Kate. A few too many.

"You're a liar and the worst kind of cheat in the world, Kolan."

Kent was never sure who took the first swing. All he knew later was that he pounded the hell out of Kolan, and Kolan pounded the hell out of him. Kent managed to hold his own, though, until one of the assistant coaches came running in, threatening to bench them both.

They separated and eyed one another warily. When the coach demanded to know what the hell was going on, they both shrugged and agreed stiffly that it was pregame jitters.

But when they left the locker room, Kent had a chance to get in one last verbal volley.

"So help me, God, Kolan, if Sam gets flattened in that game, I'll have your ass in a wringer."

Kolan cast him a fleeting, furious stare.

Kent was still dabbing at the blood on his forehead when he reached Katie's room. He felt weary through and through—from the practice and the fight . . . and because he was going to see her again, and he still didn't know what to say to her. He wanted to see her so badly he felt shaky. But she'd called Sam, not him. It didn't seem that she was so crazy about the prospect of seeing him.

Sam answered the door. He took one look at Kent and murmured, "Oh, hell!"

Katie was standing behind Sam. Beautiful, fresh, lovely—almost touchable—in a tailored mauve suit and ruffled off-white silk blouse.

"Dammit, Kent, you've been fighting again."

"Fighting again!" He strode into the room, forcing her to move back with his angry steps. "Yes, I've been fighting again—and it's your damn fault again!"

"I never asked you to get into a fight!" she yelled back.

"Hey, Kent, Katie—" Sam began.

They both looked at him and yelled with spontaneous harmony, "Stay out of it, Sam!"

He lifted his hands. "I'm going. Kent, you said something to Harry, I take it. What happened?"

"He denied it, what else? And he suggested I was listening

268

to a blond—among other not-so-nice things—woman who was twisting me around by certain parts of my anatomy."

"Oh!" Katie gasped furiously. When Sam laughed, she gave him a vehement look.

"I'm sorry, I'm sorry!" he protested, then he walked to the door. "My turn to try something, Kent."

"What?"

"Don't worry about it. I don't plan on getting into a fight. I'm going to go a diplomatic route."

He was gone suddenly, and Kent and Katie were left to stare at one another. But she just couldn't keep eye contact with him, and she strode to the window to look out at the city. "Do you believe me, Kent?"

When he didn't answer right away, she felt ill. Waves of shivering heat seemed to be washing through her. She wanted him to believe in her so badly! She wanted to rip him up; she wanted him to beg an apology. And more than anything else, she suddenly knew that she wanted the future to wait; she didn't want any words between them at all. She wanted to turn to him and hold him, dim the lights, and pretend that he was in love with her and nothing else mattered so that she could make love with him again.

"Yes," he said at last, and she did turn to him. His hands were on his hips, pushing his jacket back. He seemed tall and trim and very unique—both oddly relaxed and tense. In the bronze column of his neck she saw the beat of his pulse. His forehead was bruised, still oozing a trickle of blood. He wasn't frowning, but neither was he smiling; there was an air of expectancy about him that was electrical. He walked toward her then, slowly. She had the strangest sense that she should move, and yet she couldn't. He stopped in front of her and lifted her chin, bringing her eyes to meet the fathomless darkness of his own.

"You're very sure about this, Katie, aren't you?" he asked quietly.

"I—yes," she said, her voice wavering.

"You wouldn't use me, would you, Katie?"

"I—oh, stop it!" she cried suddenly. "I don't want you hurt, you idiot. Can't you understand that, believe that?"

"Yes," he murmured, and she found that she was imprisoned by his eyes. This wasn't what she had wanted at all, more doubt, more uncertainty, but she knew from the dark and heated midnight fire in his eyes that he had no intention of giving her a chance to plague him with reproach.

No, she thought fleetingly, but then his lips touched hers, briefly, stirringly. His tongue brushed over them and then between them, and then he took a full, forceful possession of her mouth.

She moaned something, passion or protest, Katie wasn't sure. She had come to know Kent too well; heady excitement coursed through her as he pulled her body to him. His fingers wound into her hair; his lips left hers to tenderly ravage the soft flesh along her cheek and throat.

"Kent," she murmured weakly, bracing herself with her hands on his shoulders, nails digging into the material of his jacket, "we haven't solved anything."

"We've solved everything!" he told her harshly, and God help her, for the moment she believed him.

Katie was suddenly dizzy and a bit lost, but either too helpless or too heedless to fight his strength of purpose as he strode across the room with her, kicking open the bedroom door. The light was dim in the bedroom, providing an aura of sweet illusion, allowing Katie to forget everything except her love for him. She could only stare at the planes and angles of his beloved rugged features as he eased her down and laid down beside her, his fingers working the buttons of her blouse, his eyes following the work of his fingers. The material fell away, and she closed her eyes, shivering with delight as his lips, heated and moist and hungry, touched her flesh. His hand slipped beneath her skirt, hiking it up. His fingers moved over her thighs until she was twisting to him, whispering his name, almost sobbing with frustration as she tugged at his clothing.

He rose over her, pulling off his jacket. Katie didn't meet his eyes; she raked her fingers over his chest, finding the buttons of his shirt, undoing each one with trembling fingers. And when his chest was bare, she pressed her face to it, kissing him and feeling the luxury of that intimate touch explode in her mind. He left her, and she felt cold. She heard his shoes fall to the floor, then heard him curse as he tripped in his effort to rid himself of trousers and briefs. Suddenly, he was beside her again, making love to her while removing her shoes and stockings, her jacket, blouse, and skirt. And then, with slow, sensual movements, he removed her panties and bra.

When they were naked together, she rolled over him, her kisses finding his shoulders, giving loving attention to the thin, white scar lines that marred their tanned breadth. She felt his fingers moving over her back, stroking her spine, cupping her buttocks, pulling her ever closer to him. He kissed her again, rolling her to her back, playing the palm of his hand over her breasts and abdomen until he parted her thighs and caressed her intimately, knowingly. His kisses left her mouth to cover her breasts; her fingers tore madly into his hair, and she was whispering incoherently, needing him, wanting him.

"Touch me," he commanded huskily, and she did so, finding sheer pleasure in the strength of his need for her.

She cried out for him, but his hands were already on her hips, raising them, ready to join them. Sweet and shimmering, his initial rhythm was slow, then took flight. She stretched with the ache of desire, gasped as his hands found her breasts, as he touched her neck with his lips, caught her earlobe between his teeth.

She felt that he had loved her forever. And then all that was building inside her soared to a crest. And she clung to him, loving the moments that followed, intimate and good. Then they both drifted, fulfilled, two lovers on a bed once again, both aware they had been there even when it felt as if they had soared on clouds.

"Kent," she murmured.

"Shh, Katie, just let me hold you."

And so she lay quietly, perhaps because she wanted so badly to hold on to the peace she felt . . . because while she held him, she had him, and words just might change that.

The words would have to come . . .

But ironically, they both drifted into sleep. And when Katie awoke, Kent was dressed, slipping into his jacket.

"You can't leave now!" she told him. "Kent—"

"Katie, I'm sorry. There's a curfew, and if I'm lucky, I'll make it."

"No!" she cried furiously. "Kent, this isn't fair. It isn't right—"

"Katie," he said, sitting on the bed, pulling her against him, "I've got to go. This will all be over soon. We'll talk after the game . . . I promise."

"I'm not even sure I'm going to the damn game! Damn you, Kent, you can't keep doing this to me—"

"Katie, you've walked out on me—twice, if I recall."

"Kent, don't play in that game! I don't want to see you beaten or crippled for life."

"Katie," he said quietly, "I have to play. Don't you see? The only way we could possibly beat this whole thing is to win."

"You don't believe me, do you? You bastard!" she exclaimed. "You still don't believe that a guy on your own team—"

He kissed her quickly, then firmly placed her away from him. "Katie, I *do* believe you. But I still have to play."

He walked to the door. She could barely see him because a sudden rush of tears was blinding her.

"I won't be there, Kent."

He looked around, and his eyes caught hers. "Please, Katie." Then he was gone.

Sunday dawned bright and clear. Beautiful weather for a game. The stands were filled to capacity, Katie thought. She was there—she had always known she would be.

Her seat was right on the fifty-yard line. Joan Patterson was on her right, and Julie—who had somehow convinced Raff to send her down—was on Katie's left. Paula, Anne, and Ted were behind her. Sometimes she would turn and catch Paula's eyes. They would exchange mute signals of worry—and try to smile.

The excitement was high in the stadium; cheers were never-ending for both teams. The amount of electricity and tension racing among the spectators was almost frightening.

Katie barely heard the singing of the national anthem; she was waiting for the kickoff. The Saxons won the coin toss and elected to receive the ball.

The offense was on the field.

The first quarter went well. Unbelievably well. The Saxons inched along the field, it seemed, but kept making first downs. Sam took off on a run and made the first touchdown himself. Then the Saxon defense intercepted a ball, and the Saxons made a field goal. The score was ten to nothing as they neared the end of the quarter. The Saxons got the ball again, and Sam and Kent connected for a twenty-five-yard run and a touchdown; the kick gave them the extra point, and the score stood at seventeen to nothing at the end of the quarter.

It wasn't until the second quarter that things began to happen. Katie stood in horror, screaming but unheard against the roar of the crowd when Sam Loper was viciously blitzed by three Titan players—including Paul Crane.

Sam was carried off the field; the Saxon fans were going wild. He managed to pull his helmet off and grimace and wave to the crowd. Then he was gone.

Timmons came in as quarterback. He was a good player; he just wasn't as fast as Sam. Still, he kept the second quarter at an even keel. He connected with another wide receiver named

Ted Johnson once for a fifty-yard drive, then managed to find Kent standing over the goal line. With a good kick the Saxons' score was twenty-four. But the opposition had scored twice, so they were facing twenty-four to fourteen at halftime.

Katie wanted to scream all during the show, her tension was so great. Afterward, she couldn't even recall if it was a good one or a bad one. She wanted the game to end. So far, Kent was emerging uninjured, but he'd already been beneath three pileups. How much more could he take? she wondered frantically.

In the third quarter came another blow. Katie could have sworn she actually saw Harry Kolan step aside—and then the Titan defense blitzed Timmons. Timmons was down, and time was called.

"No!" Katie gasped, but the announcer said that Timmons had a dislocated shoulder. He was out of the game.

With ten seconds left in the third quarter, Kent was put into the game as quarterback. He ran the ball himself and gained ten yards and a first down.

Katie closed her eyes. She didn't think she could bear to watch the fourth quarter of the game.

"Fourteen, eighteen, twenty-five, ten!"

The ball was in Kent's hands; he had to throw—they were prepared for a run. He found Ted Johnson on the field and threw the ball. Johnson leaped high to receive it; he caught it but was dragged down. The next pass was intercepted, and the Saxons lost the ball. The opposition scored, made the kick, and it was twenty-four to twenty-one.

Coach Griffith told Kent to run the ball. Kent relayed the message in the huddle, then caught Harry Kolan by the shoulder pads when they broke.

"So help me, Kolan—"

"I'll be there!" Kolan snapped.

The Saxons took their positions. Kent called off a spate of

274

numbers. He was dripping with sweat, bone-tired and aching all over. He had to keep the ball once he got it.

It was in his hands. Paul Crane was rushing him. Kent zigzagged in back of Harry Kolan and saw his opening. He started to run.

The Titans were behind him all the way; arms grasped at him, men fell at his feet. He strained with all his being, heaving, hurting—desperate to make it, to cross the magic line. A few more feet, a few more feet . . .

Sweat dripped through his eyebrows and stung his eyes. He was almost there . . . He was there!

But someone was on his tail. Paul Crane caught him right at the line. Kent pitched his shoulders forward with a death grip on the ball. He would make the touchdown, but he was going down himself. He hit the field hard and tried to roll.

He saw Crane's eyes, then saw the man hurtle into him, carefully, but with all his strength. His shoulder slammed full force against Kent's knee.

A scream of agony tore from him as the pain in his knee penetrated his body. Crane jumped away from him, then the field was alive with running doctors and coaches.

Kent closed his eyes. He was out of it. The Saxons were out of it. But he'd tried. He'd tried his damnedest. One day, he vowed, one day he was going to tear both Kolan and Crane apart.

They brought him into the locker room. Sam was there, his ribs freshly bandaged. He was sitting up on a table. "Ah, hell, Cougar, they got you, too? I'm going to have to go back out," he said desperately.

"No way, Sam."

The doctor forced Kent to lie down. His pants leg was cut away, and he was told that his ligaments were torn. "Good thing the season is over," the doctor said glumly.

"I'm going back out," Sam insisted.

"Can he, do you think?" Coach Griffith asked the doctor hopefully.

The doctor shook his head. "I don't know. You want to step outside and discuss it?"

They did, leaving Sam and Kent alone. "I've got to, Kent . . . It's our only chance."

Kent looked at Sam, then shook his head sadly. "One more time, Sammy, and they'll kill you. Don't do it—you've got a lifetime of games ahead of you."

Sam started to stand. Kent sat up quickly, wincing at the sharp pain in his leg. "Sam?"

"Yeah, what is it, buddy?" Sam leaned over him.

Kent smiled sadly. "I'm sorry, kid, but I love you like a brother." He brought his right fist flying across Sam's jaw. The quarterback crumbled to the floor.

The coach stuck his head back in. "Sam?"

"Sam's decided not to go out after all, coach," Kent said. He lay back wearily, smiling ruefully as he closed his eyes.

Katie didn't care what she had to do to reach Kent. Julie was right behind her as she made a fleet journey through the stands, apologizing but willing to knock over anyone to get where she had to be.

Outside the locker she ran into a policeman. "Hold it, young lady!"

"I'm—I'm his sister!" Katie cried, Julie still behind her.

"And who is she?"

"His sister, too. We've got a big family," Julie said.

The policeman obviously didn't believe her; he was about to have Katie hauled off, but Coach Griffith saw her then, smiled, and told the policeman to let them through.

Katie saw Kent and Sam on the stretchers. Tears came to her eyes instantly and rolled down her cheeks. She rushed to Kent and gripped his hand. He tried to grin at her.

"We lost it, Katie."

"Oh, Kent, who cares? Oh, my God! What happened to Sam?"

"I happened to Sam. I had to hit him. Katie—Katie, I'm trying to talk to you!"

But Katie had run over to see Sam. She felt the tears rising in a fresh wave, and suddenly she was furious. "Oh, the hell with the two of you. You're both fools!"

"Katie!" Somehow he got hold of her wrist. "Katie—dammit! I know I'm supposed to be on my knees begging, but I just can't get to my knees right now. Katie—"

"Oh, God!" A long, groggy moan interrupted Kent's words. Sam staggered to a sitting position. "What the hell happened to me?"

"Kent hit you," Katie told him.

"Cougar! *You* did this to me? Why? We've lost the game for sure now."

"Oh, what's in a game?" Julie inquired sweetly from a corner.

"Would you both, please, *please,* shut up? My Romeo act is already screwed to death!" Kent exclaimed. "Katie!"

"What?"

"Katie, I'm begging you to forgive me for ever doubting or not trusting you. I'm begging you to be my wife!"

Katie looked at Kent, then at Sam, then at Julie. "He's crazy, you know—"

"Julie, help! I know I'm supposed to be on my knees—"

"They've both been hit in the head one time too many!" Katie didn't know what to think, and she couldn't believe what she was hearing. She was going to break into a real storm of tears any moment. "I'm going to get out of here," she murmured, edging nervously away from both Kent and Sam.

"Oh, no, you're not!" Kent snapped. She saw his eyes and all the determination in them. "Sam, get her!"

Sam gave Katie an apologetic grin. "Please, Katie, don't fight. I have a hell of a headache to go with everything else."

"Sam!" she protested.

But, apologetic as he might be, Kent had asked Sam to bring her back, and he was going to do just that. Sam braced himself, leaped from the stretcher, caught her shoulders, and firmly propelled her back to Kent's side. Kent clasped her hand with all his strength, and she knew she could never escape. Nor, staring into his face, marked with black beneath his eyes, smudged with dirt, did she want to.

She loved him and everything about him: his nose with the little crook; his mouth, sometimes grim—but, oh, when he smiled, and his eyes, dark as coal and filled with love and tenderness.

"Miss Hudson, I love you. I really love you. Please, tell an aching and injured man that you will love him, too, until the end of his days. That you'll stand by his side through thick and thin and make love to him very gently and carefully just as soon as they let him out of the hospital. Tell him that as soon as we can get the legal papers, you'll become his wife."

Katie stared at him, stunned—and so deliriously happy she couldn't speak.

"I think that was just fine," Julie commented. "I mean, you can always get down on your knees later, you know."

"Katie, for God's sake, answer the man!" Sam ordered.

"I—oh, you're an idiot!" Katie exclaimed as she bent down to kiss him, long and languorously, not at all caring that Julie and Sam were standing by, laughing witnesses.

There was a commotion in the room. Dazed, Katie rose to turn around. Anne was in the room, racing for her father.

"Dad!"

"Hey, kitten!"

"Oh, are you all right?"

"I will be."

"Dad—they just won the game. The Saxons lost!"

"It doesn't matter, Annie . . . It was just a game."

Anne smiled at Katie. "Does this mean that you're slee— I mean, seeing Dad again?"

Katie smiled. "I'm going to marry him."

"Oh," Anne murmured. She looked at them both. "Do you think you'll have children?"

"Probably," Katie said cheerfully. She slipped an arm around Anne's shoulder. "But we'll work it out, I promise you."

"I don't know about that," Anne admitted unhappily, "but —we'll try."

Katie caught Paula's eyes over her daughter's head. They both smiled. "Come on, Annie," Paula said. "I think they're coming now to take your dad and Sam to the hospital." She waved at Sam. "Next year, Sam, Kent!"

"Next year!" Sam agreed. He was rubbing his jaw. "I think you're crazy, Kent."

Katie laughed. "But, Sam, there *will* be a next year!"

He grimaced, and she was glad. He knew that she was right. Kent tugged at her hand.

"Katie, would you mind if I gave it one last shot? One more year, just to see if we could have made it?"

She bent down to him, loving him so much that it almost hurt. "I want what you want."

"Just one more year."

"One more year. It doesn't matter at all," she murmured, "because I intend to have you for life."

He smiled. Julie and Sam were still watching them. The team, beaten and disheartened, started trailing in as the medics were coming for Kent and Sam.

Katie just didn't care.

She kissed him again for all she was worth.

"Eighteen, twenty-four, seven . . ."

Sam Loper was calling off the numbers. There was no screaming or shouting in the stadium; everything had gone silent with tension and expectation.

It was the final quarter, and the final seconds of the game were ticking away. The Saxons had made it to the Superbowl for the second season in a row; it was a Washington team they faced this year, and the game had been a rough one. Good football, played hard.

Kent felt a sizzling along his spine; it was right, everything was just right. He was playing with top-notch guys, not like last year . . .

Sam's "diplomatic" way of handling things had been to go to the NFL with advice regarding the rumors. Nothing could change the outcome of the last game, but after the game, things had happened—quietly but severely. Paul Crane and Harry Kolan would never again play professional ball.

But that was last year. This was now. And Kent continued to feel that sizzle. It was time. The Sarasota Saxons were about to come into their own.

The score was even; if it remained so, the game would go into overtime until it was won. There could be no tie for the Superbowl.

"Come on, Sammy, come on, Sammy," Kent whispered. God, how he wanted that ball! He was hunched down at the scrimmage line, staring at a hefty cornerback named Lou Sutton. Sutton started to smile; it was a narrow-eyed smile that warned, "One move, boy, and I'll be on your tail."

The temperature was cool, but Lou was sweating away. Kent could see the drops and grime on his face; he knew it was a mirror image of his own. The game was wearing on him badly. He ached in a thousand places.

"Fourteen," Sam called.

Kent returned the grim smile being given him. He felt a new surge of energy. They were thirty feet from the goal.

Thirty feet, Kent thought, that's not so far, Sammy. We can do it, Sammy, we can do it.

"Eight!"

The ball was in Sam Loper's hand. He was doing an impossible backstep. Kent lifted a brow to the brawny Lou Sutton, neatly sidestepped him—and ran.

Come on, Sam, give it to me . . . I'm in the clear . . . Come on . . .

Sam saw him. The ball went up, up in the air. It sailed as smoothly and sweetly as a missile, right into Kent's hands.

His legs moved, his chest heaved. The adrenaline was with him. Longer, longer, his legs stretched out. Excitement and the sweet expectation of victory swept through him. It was going to be the last professional play of his life, and damned, if he wasn't going to go out in a blaze of glory!

Kent could feel the air sweeping by him, the strain and pulse of his muscles, the ground beneath his feet.

Lou Sutton made a grab for his legs and missed, inertia sending Sutton crashing heavily to the ground.

Kent kept running, elated, the roar of the crowd spurring him on. One after another, the tackles and backs after him fell by the wayside.

The magic line stretched before him. He knew he could reach it, knew he could sail over it . . .

He did. He raised the football high in the air. It was a sweet moment. Sam was rushing to him, leading the rest of the Saxons. The raucous crowd had risen, and horns were blaring.

"Cougar, Cougar, Cougar . . ."

It was nice, nice to hear Sam's shouted cries, nice to feel the thunder of his teammates' arms pounding him.

But he wasn't seeing any of them. He was searching the crowd.

Then he saw her. She was being jostled and delayed as she made her way to the field, but she was a bit of a fighter, he knew, and she was going to get to him.

He caught her eyes above the milling heads and faces, sea blue and sea green, shining with pride and love. She really hadn't given a damn about the game—she would be happy because he was happy.

She finally reached him. The noise of horns and shouting was still a cacophony around them.

Kent swept her into his arms. More than any touchdown, she was the magic line in his life. They had passed an elusive goal together. In her arms he was all that he would ever need to be.

Kent jerked off his helmet to kiss her. A long kiss, full of promise. She drew away, grimacing at the salty sweat and dirt that smudged her cheeks. Then she smiled. His hands were tangled into the wealth of her blond hair, his eyes were locked with hers.

"We made it, babe."

"I know. Congratulations, Cougar."

"Want to go to the locker room with me?"

"I'd love to."

He grinned. They were being shoved off the field. There was a score of microphones sticking in his face, and questions were shouted to him. Kent kept an arm firmly around Katie. He admitted that he was retiring from pro ball. He even told them he had accepted a broadcasting position with one of the networks in New York. Did that decision have anything to do with his wife? Yes, of course. There were rumors floating around that he and his wife—the late Dante Hudson's daughter—would be working together on certain sports projects.

Were they true? Yes, Kent told them, but he refused to give them any specifics.

"Hey—there's Sam Loper. Go hound him for a while, will you?" Kent teased the reporters, but they did as he asked and joined the throng around Sam.

Kent and Katie paused on the field for a minute. Kent gave it one last, sweeping glance.

"Are you sorry?" Katie asked softly.

He looked down into her eyes, eyes so like Dante's, so uniquely her own. Those sea-changing eyes that had captured his heart and his senses.

"I would never want you to be sorry, Kent," she continued quietly. "I don't want you to quit because of me."

He smiled and hugged her closer, oblivious to all the spectators still crowding the stands.

"I'm quitting because of both of us. Because I want to . . . and because I want us to be together. It's time."

She smiled contentedly and leaned her head against him. They started walking off the field. Kent knew he wouldn't look back.

"I was just thinking, though . . ." he murmured.

"Thinking what?"

"Well, Dante Hudson brought me into pro ball, and Dante Hudson's daughter brought me out."

"Kent!"

He laughed, pausing to kiss her very thoroughly, then laughed again as she squirmed beneath the public eye.

"I haven't got a single regret, Mrs. Hart. I'd rather hug you than an old pigskin ball any day!"

"I don't think that was much of a compliment," Katie observed, then added, "You never had to make a choice, Kent. I'd be with you no matter what."

"I know that, Katie. And I appreciate it."

He smiled suddenly. A warm rush of sweet excitement swept through him. They'd been together a year; thoughts of her could still make his senses swim at the most inopportune times.

"Let's get going. Annie and Paula and Ted will be waiting. I want to see them and . . ."

"And what?"

"I seem to have this streak of adrenaline still racing through me. I want to be alone with my wife and see where it leads."

Katie laughed and touched his cheek, mindless of the grime. "I'll count on a touchdown, Cougar."

"Count on several!" he warned her. "After all, it takes a lot more than one play to win the game."

"Got ya, Cougar."

The sun was setting as they continued off the field, arm in arm. Somehow, it seemed right to Kent that it should do so.

He smiled. They would say he had gone out in a blaze of glory. But to him, all the glory lay ahead, because of one lovely and loving woman . . .

Hudson's daughter.